DANCES WITH ALIENS

D1518246

Drayton Alan

DRAYTON
ALAN

ISBN: 9798453839698
Imprint: Independently published

DEDICATION

To my wife, who is my strength, my love.

ACKNOWLEDGMENTS

Thank you to my friends for their help and support.

Chapter 1 The Rescue

Intense pain racked Thomas' neck and shoulders. It took every ounce of his resolve, and a hefty dose of fear, not to pull his head off in public. The pads supporting the giant head had rubbed his shoulders raw, and his clumsy, oversized paws proved useless to help soothe them. He'd been a dog for days now. Not a dog that stands on all fours and goes woof, but a singing, dancing, two-legged dog of the theme park variety. Earth's most famous and popular theme park, Mercury World, now swarmed with families of wrinkled gray-skinned aliens.

Thomas sat in a feeble bit of shade on a hard plastic faux-wood bench situated under a heat stroked oak tree and surrounded by meticulously groomed flower beds and whimsical topiaries. The location featured a carefully engineered view of the lake, at an intersection of three brightly colored brick paths connecting different parts of the park. Ducks swam near the lake's edge, intent on catching the silvery minnows darting below the surface.

Hot, hungry, and exhausted, Thomas ached for comfort. Covered in foam and fur, the relentless Florida sun had made his giant head an oven. While this costume might have been his salvation, it now seemed a cruel prison. He'd been living by his wits, in a state of constant vigilance, ever since these "people" arrived. He struggled to understand the miracle of his survival.

"Miracle?" he mumbled.

That word implied a blessing of some sort. The cruelty of his current situation suggested survival had been a curse. Traumatized and tired, Thomas numbly contemplated his situation. Why had the aliens ignored him when they disintegrated everyone else? How could intelligent beings, with the ability to travel space and conquer Earth, not recognize a man in a dog suit?

A sudden jab in the ribs interrupted his speculation. He jumped up from the bench and let out a dog-like whine. He cursed the suit's tiny plastic lenses, and its restricted vision. Spinning around, he found his tiny assailant. On the bench, next to where he'd been sitting, sat three neatly dressed alien children. Each looked up at him, smiling expectantly.

Oh lord, no way. Not again. It's too hot. I'm too tired, he thought.

He walked away, pretending he hadn't seen them. No one would care. What would they do, fire him?

Pleased with himself he headed up the path that led away from the bench and the kids.

His pleasure was short lived, as another group of about twenty aliens, adult aliens with children, turned the corner ahead on the path coming toward him.

"Crap! No avoiding it now. Time for another Jupiter-D-Dog dance."

With his remaining strength, he danced. He danced to forget the agonizing pain of his burning neck and the smothering heat. He danced to wipe away the horrors of this nightmare.

As always, he began his performance with the big friendly wave and a happy tippy toed dance for the kiddies. It made his heart pound, shoulders throb, and legs ache. He worked his routine hard.

The sizable group of alien children and adults he guessed might be parents encircled him, captivated by his one man show. After doing his best, Thomas did his big finishing *Ta-Da* move–legs spread, tilt at the waist, arms out. Breathing hard and dizzy, it was all he could do to remain standing. He sipped water from the suit's built-in insulated water pouch.

The alien audience smiled and cheered, making strange hand gestures, their equivalent of applause, perhaps. He stood, suspended in this fleeting moment of triumph. He could ignore the pain, suffocating heat, and his oppressive ever-present anxiety. In that singular moment it was only about his craft, and he bathed in the honest appreciation of a grateful audience.

After the moment passed and he returned to reality, he once again saw his audience as the evil spawn of murdering aliens they were.

Those ivory grins of pointy teeth set against a wrinkled gray skin made his flesh crawl. He dare not allow himself to forget these children will grow up to become the future butchers of other worlds. How many days had it been now? Four, perhaps five days ago? Had all of Earth's billions really been zapped into oblivion?

The group of children ran to him in appreciation. All of them trying to hug him, laughing and talking excitedly in their strange language. The frantic jumble of hugs, smiles, and laughter made Thomas uncomfortable. He wanted to run. These beings, even the children, frightened him and they smelled like sweaty fish!

"Could you guys tell your kids not to wipe their noses on me?" He said under his breath. Wishing he had the courage to say it aloud.

An adult standing nearby clapped its hands and made an announcement in a serious tone. The harsh alien language grated on Thomas' ears like metal on cement.

That's when he remembered this was the stupid alien thanking ceremony they did every time he'd performed for a large group. It was like a weird reception line and he was the bride.

Instantly, the children became quiet, the smiles and laughter vanished. They queued up in front of him, taking turns saying something in a somber tone. They each bowed and walked to stand with one of the adults. Thomas hadn't a clue what they were saying, but it seemed sad. Everyone else watched and listened respectfully to each child. Bewildered, Thomas could only pat their backs, hoping this wouldn't take long.

All he could think of was getting away as soon as possible.

He looked around at the alien women who had formed a circle around him. They each had a serious expression on their face. As if they'd just devoured the neighbor's pet. They dressed in simple tunics, in dreary shades of gray or brown, except for one woman. She differed from the rest. Her manner exuded confidence and control. She wore a beautiful shimmering purple and silver material, far more elaborate than the others. She must be their leader.

The woman in purple gave him a polite smile that made Thomas uneasy. He must have been staring at her. So, he looked down and pretended to pay attention to the child speaking to him. Finally, the weird alien ritual was over. Every child had taken their turn.

Seeing his chance to get away, Thomas bolted. He didn't get three steps when one kid let out a howling scream! He missed one! You'd think the kid was hurt, the way it was screaming and fussing. Sounded like a wounded dog.

Thomas walked back and picked up the screaming kid.

"Fine, just shut up and tell me whatever and get it over," Thomas said under his breath.

That didn't work, so he tried dancing and rocking the child, trying to make it shut up.

That's when he finally noticed the reaction of the alien women. They stood in shocked disbelief.

Oh crap, what did I do? He wondered.

One woman, possibly the child's mother, looked stricken with panic and ready to scream as well. The other children had stopped playing, frightened by whatever he'd done. His heart pounded. This might have been a huge, even fatal mistake. The woman dressed in purple gave him a severe look.

In a panic, Thomas put the child down and did another of his goofy dances. This one ended in a silly pratfall to get a laugh. The fall hurt his blistered shoulders and back, making him whimper.

Oh lord, why did I do that?

That move always got a great reaction from Earth kids. Perhaps they'd all think it was part of the routine? For a moment, it seemed like a big hit with the alien kiddos, too. But what about the adults?

He dared a glance at the woman in purple. She was more puzzled than concerned now. The obnoxious kid's mom wasted no time scooping up the screaming little monster. The woman in purple walked toward him. He hadn't gotten up after the fall and he sat on the sidewalk. Thomas awaited his doom, too exhausted to be properly terrified.

Instead of being upset, she said something in a pleasant tone and placed two alien food bars on the ground next to him. After that, the other women followed suit. Each placing food for him. Then they all moved on. A few children secretly waved and smiled at him as they followed their mothers toward the lakeshore.

That was close, he thought.

The food bars were now familiar. In the days since the invasion, the aliens had given him a few every time he'd danced. Strange symbols covered their brightly colored wrappers. The bars were his primary source of nourishment. Should he feel guilty about taking food from the aliens? Is it wrong to entertain a race of murdering invaders? He could worry later about the ethical implications. That presumed he would have a later.

Thomas stood up and spun in a circle to be certain no one watched. Then, without stopping, he reached down and scooped up the food. There was a more secluded, shady area not far away. It was near the lake and he could sit up against a big tree.

Once he was situated. He slipped his hands out through hidden slits above his paws, reached into his pouch, and withdrew a food bar. He cautiously unwrapped it. Then, carefully, hiding his human hands, he slid the food through an inconspicuous neck flap and into his mouth. At once, he returned his hands inside the paws and chewed quickly, swallowing hard. The bars tasted weird, perhaps a little fishy, like sushi flavored granola. Not awful if you're hungry enough. At least it tasted better than it smelled. He sipped again from his water tube. The water remained refreshingly cold from his recent filling at a nearby drinking fountain. It was the suits' only luxury.

Thomas sat on the ground, back against a tree, appreciating the last bits of the food and fading refreshment of the cool water. He could see the children playing at the lakeshore in the distance. Sadness surged as he watched the kids through the plastic lenses of his head. Seeing them laugh and play reminded him of everything he'd lost, family, friends, a future. Long suppressed grief welled up and threatened to break his fragile composure.

In the days since the invasion, he'd noticed two main varieties of aliens. There were the common ones, like the children he'd just entertained. They had gray, wrinkled skin. Both the soldiers and the families were all this type. The second group of aliens was different. They looked like patched together robot people of different alien types, everything from blue and furry to orange and slimy. All sewn together, often with strange devices attached to them. These robo-aliens always ignored him. He'd tried to get their attention, but they acted like he didn't exist.

It was only the gray aliens that would stop to enjoy his dances. These gray ones, although the same rough outline of a human, but very different. Just one look at their wrinkled skin, yellowish eyes, pointy teeth, and strange facial bone structure, and you knew they were not from Earth. If he tried hard enough, he might convince himself they were TV characters with some oddly realistic makeup. It reminded him of the very human-looking aliens on the original *Galaxy Track* TV show from the 1960s.

Out of habit, he corrected himself. The park's Code of Conduct, rule eight, stated that cast members must never refer to the name or fictional characters of any franchise not licensed by Waldo Mercury Inc. or any of its subsidiaries. He had been a loyal employee for two years now. Odd that obeying park rules still seemed important.

Thomas was at a loss for what to do. If he stays here, eating these vile food bars and living off handouts they will eventually find him. Death could come tomorrow, or even today. But where else could he go?

The character Thomas portrayed, Jupiter-D-Dog, would have no problem with living off handouts and dancing for kids. He'd probably love the taste of these disgusting alien fish bars. Dogs love stinky things.

Jupiter-D was one of the principal characters in Waldo Mercury's classic animated short cartoons. Mercury's cartoons had been on television for decades. He is one of the world's most adored animators, and Mercury-D-Moose, Jupiter-D's owner, is his most famous and beloved character. His entire corporation was represented by the antlered hat.

Thomas wondered what Waldo Mercury would have thought of the aliens in his park. He'd probably have enjoyed it… except for the part where they murdered humanity. It saddened Thomas that Waldo, like everyone else, was most likely killed. Was everyone else gone? How could he know for sure?

It was strange how, despite the changes, many things had remained the same since that awful day. The park was never without power or stopped working. The rides ran, the lights stayed on, and the repetitive music from the attractions played without a missing a note. It suggested a degree of unseen planning and organization frightening to contemplate.

His stomach full, Thomas slipped off into a blissful sleep.

Minutes later he woke feeling numb and oddly comfortable. Mindlessly, he watched the children still playing in the water. Moms napping by the shore. A child climbed over the low fence to access the cooler deep water of the lake. The cool water would feel nice, he thought. Something about the ripples on the lake unsettled him, and a vague feeling of wrongness nibbled at him. Ripples, but no breeze?

The alien adults idly sat or slept on the grass, none of them seeing or watching. Thomas felt irritated. He was finally comfortable. Besides, why should he do anything? His sleepy mind refused to focus. Half-dreaming, he remembered sitting in this same spot a few weeks ago, eating his lunch. It had an excellent view of the feeding area. He'd come here frequently to watch the wranglers feed the alligators.

The park's rangers would explain to the crowds how much money Waldo Mercury had spent to preserve the alligator's habitat. Waldo had spent millions on an elaborate, foolproof barrier fence, and special collars for each of the gators. He employed an entire team of rangers and wranglers to track the animals and patrol the pond. To avoid incidents, they made sure the gators were fed daily. He was irritated that the alligators weren't being fed. Was he expected to find food for them? They'd been without food for days, and they'd be hungry soon.

The pond erupted in a bloodcurdling scream! It jolted his drowsy mind awake. Childhood terror sounds the same on every world.

Before he was aware of it, Thomas was up and running straight toward the water. He didn't think twice. There was an alien child, out past the short barrier, and it was being pulled under. Its hands were splashing as it disappeared beneath the water.

Thomas ran headlong into the water, struggled over the barrier, and grabbed the screaming child before it disappeared into the murky depths. The big gator had misjudged its bite and only snagged its teeth in the alien's shirt. Thankfully, these gators were poor hunters, hand fed all their lives.

"No, you don't! No kids are to be eaten in my park!" Thomas yelled at the gator.

But a hungry gator could be a fast learner. Its first bite missed, but the second would not. Without thinking, Thomas took his big, soggy foot and shoved it deep down into the monster's throat. Snatching the little girl, he used all his strength to throw the child toward shore. The gator clamped down hard on his hard foam foot and twisted.

Thomas instantly got pulled under and his large head filled with water. The gator jerked hard, pulling Thomas into deeper water. Thomas struggled and kicked, trying in vain to find a handhold with his big forepaws. Water sloshed around inside the costume and pulled his head under. The monster gator jolted again, and the leg of his costume ripped away. It only got a mouthful of Jupiter-D costume. Somehow, Thomas's leg and foot remained uninjured by the jagged rows of yellow teeth.

Kicking wildly, struggling against the weight of his soggy fur and giant water filled head, Thomas made no progress toward the surface. The head twisted sideways, leaving him in darkness. Unable to hold his breath any longer, Thomas gasped and gulped in water. He was drowning. As he struggled, he felt a sharp jerk as the gator grabbed his other foot and tried to pull him under again.

He heard the loud zap of an alien's weapon, and the gator's pull disappeared. He struggled to release the costume head with the last remnants of his strength, but the retaining straps were jumbled. Thomas struggled to stand, but the tangle of seaweed and slippery mud made it impossible. The comprehension of impending death subsided his panic. Peaceful acceptance replaced it.

Chapter 2 Dead Human

The alien woman in purple, Counselor Jinder, returned the small weapon to its hidden holster. She looked at the strange creature floating in the lake.

"Did everyone else see what just happened, or did I imagine it?" Jinder asked.

"Strangest thing I ever saw," her companion Vi-Zeha said.

"Perhaps we should… help it?" Jinder didn't sound convinced.

"I'll go fish it out of the lake. Will some of you ladies help me?" Vi-Zeha said.

Turning her attention to the little girl, Jinder asked, "And how is Gertzah? Was she harmed by the reptile?"

Gertzah, the child who had been thrown clear of the alligator, had escaped relatively unscathed. Her skin had a few scratches and bumps, but it had not been punctured. Axvi, the girl's mother, wept tears of joy for the miraculous rescue. Jinder too was grateful, but puzzled by the Bionic's behavior.

Vi-Zeha, aided by two of the other women, hiked up their tunics and waded out to retrieve the oddly behaving Bionic entertainer. As they dragged it ashore, there was a great deal of subdued conversation and speculation among the women. Vi-Zeha worked to remove the unit's oversized head, cutting some straps that held it. Water rushed out and the Bionic lay face down on the ground, unconscious.

"Try to clear its lungs of water," Jinder suggested.

Vi-Zeha pushed vigorously on the creature's back, pumping the water from its chest.

Jinder pondered the situation. Why would an entertainment Bionic risk its life to save a Retullian? They aren't programmed for that. Its dancing presentation had been different, too. More... well, graceful than other characters she'd ever encountered. Children's performers were not unusual in Retullian society ever since they'd borrowed their use from other cultures.

As soon as Vi-Zeha flipped the character over, everyone gasped.

"How is that even possible? The military assured us they eradicated the humans?" Jinder asked.

Almost no one, other than the soldiers, had seen an actual human before. Only their ghastly photos in the media. Everyone stared at the thing, horrified.

Jinder was curious, though. Despite its ugly skin and oddly smooth appearance, it didn't seem as monstrous as the reports depicted. This one, with its facial scar and misshapen head, was more pitiful than threatening.

"Is it an Earthling or a Bionic? It looks like both," Jinder wondered aloud.

"Perhaps the humans had bionic technology?" Vi-Zeha suggested.

Jinder hadn't considered this. There had been no mention of Earthling Bionics in any of her reports, but she must assume they had them. She could tell this being had been surgically altered, but aside from the distorted shape and scarring, she couldn't see any implanted enhancements.

"That still doesn't explain why an Earthling, especially an Earthling Bionic, would risk its life to keep a Retullian alive?" Vi-Zeha asked.

The rescued little girl's mother, Axvi, spoke up. "I don't know why, but I'm thankful it did. We can't let it just die, can we?" concerned for the thing's welfare.

"You make a good point, Axvi." Jinder recalled its kindness to the children and effort to save Gertzah.

"I'm uncertain if we should help it." Jinder said. Vi-Zeha's efforts to revive it had not been productive. The fragile Earthling hadn't begun breathing on its own.

Jinder remained calm, but her inner scientist wanted to understand this human more thoroughly.

"This might be an opportunity to test our new Artificial Intelligence (AI) prototype? What do you think, Vi?"

"Could it be dangerous?" Vi-Zeha asked. "According to what I heard, Earthlings are violent and beastlike. They don't even care for their offspring."

"If that's true, then why did it just die saving a child?" Axvi asked.

"The reports I saw said that humans squandered Earth's resources on selfish pleasures and squabbled over territory in massive bloody wars. It described them all as selfish and cruel."

"Something is different about this one. I just know it is," Axvi pleaded. "Please, can we help it? It saved My Gertzah. And the way it picked up Xany when he cried, to comfort him. That's not something a selfish and cruel person does."

Jinder agreed. A Retullian would never tend another's child with the mother present. But why would a Human?

"That's true," Vi-Zeha acknowledged. "But by all accounts, humans are barbaric and devoid of any redeeming qualities. Their archives depicted them engaging in brutal murder, abuse, and even the maiming of other humans—often with bizarre machines and weapons."

"I even heard that the humans planned to go into space and murder any non-humans they encountered." Another woman added.

"The decision of the United Planetary Confederation (UPC) admittance council not to invite Earth's inhabitants into the Confederation and to harvest Earth instead had been unanimous," Vi-Zeha also added.

"Well, that's all true, but this human's behavior was well outside the parameters for the species. Couldn't this one Earth human be an anomaly? An exception? It did us no harm and seemed to enjoy performing for all of us." Jinder reasoned.

"And, it saved my Gertzah," Axvi continued to plead.

"True, it could have harmed us already if that was its intent. You convinced me. We should revive it." Vi-Zeha said.

"Besides, it will make for a fascinating study project," Jinder added.

"I suppose so."

"We're running out of time. While we stand around and debate, this thing is dying. It hasn't been breathing for almost five minutes!" Axvi said. She gave Jinder an anxious look.

Jinder's tablet buzzed. She looked down at it and said, "Oh great, the weapon discharge has alerted security. They have told us to remain here."

"Oh, no. Just what we need, a bunch of police poking around. They won't like that we didn't report the human immediately. This might get messy." Vi-Zeha said.

"I still think we need to help it and then hide it," Jinder said.

"Okay, boss. It's your call," Vi-Zeha said.

Jinder pulled out her tablet device and opened its medical scanner application. After performing a quick scan, she saw that the creature's implants were primitive. The implants contained no standard markings her device recognized, and most of the implants were steel used to reconstruct his damaged or missing skeletal parts. The unit had been repaired but not enhanced.

Jinder knew nothing about Earthling physiology, but her initial scan of this one suggested they were similar to Retullians. Humans, however, were not as resilient as Retullians. This creature would soon become irrecoverable.

"Okay, since this might technically be a violation of UPC policy, we must all agree before I do this. Any objections?"

The women looked around at each other.

"We can hide it. If they ask, we will be oblivious to it being Earthling. It was a malfunctioning Bionic, that's all we knew. We have authority to help a Bionic in distress. Got it? Someone record this on their communicator, in case we need it later," Jinder said.

Everyone nodded in agreement. Even Vi-Zeha. She opened her camera and recorded Jinder's actions for the record.

Jinder took a prototype Conciliator chip from her pouch and inserted it just under the skin behind his ear. Its tiny flat casing and sharpened point at one end allowed it to slide easily into the subject's skin. This Conciliator chip was an experimental device Vi-Zeha had been developing for the university with the aid of Jinder. Officially, the chip had been approved as an experimental treatment for post traumatic events. However, Jinder and her team had a second application for the technology that they kept secret because of its controversial implications.

"This chip's neural transponder should generate convulsions to clear its lungs and reestablish heart and breathing function. At least it would in a Retullian. I'll copy the medical scanner log and readings into my daily report. If anyone asks, we can truthfully say my scanner identified it as the race, Bionic and we helped it in order to save valuable property. That's our cover story."

As hoped, the Earthling almost immediately started convulsing, and intense muscle contractions restarted its breathing process. The human coughed out the remaining water in its lungs and began to regain consciousness.

"Let's hide it in that small shelter over there, before it wakes. Maybe security won't find it." Vi-Zeha pointed to one of the park's rest stations.

The chip would allow her to observe the human's behavior without interference.

"Vi-Zeha and Axvi, can you help me carry it to the shelter?" Jinder asked.

Without hesitation, each grabbed a limb and rushed it to the human structure. They put it inside and locked the door.

"Thank you for helping Vi-Zeha. I know it did not thrill you to save the human," Axvi said. "I know I can be excessively sentimental."

"Don't take me wrong, I'm grateful that it saved Gertzah. I just felt we needed be fully aware of the risks involved before we took any action that might endanger the children," Vi-Zeha said.

"You are wise to consider that. I hadn't," Axvi said.

"Everyone, I want to commend you. We worked well together in this crisis," Jinder said. "Now, please explain what happened to your children. It's best they don't reveal the Bionic was an Earthling. Besides, we are only guessing it's a human. I've never seen one. Have any of you actually seen an Earthling in person before?"

Everyone shook their heads.

As they waited, Jinder thought about the situation. How had a human survived the harvest? Can there be an issue with the UPC's procedures?

Now she had to sit and wait for security to show up. They would file a report and that idiot Director Mortek Prag would get involved. The man was an idiot, but they'd appointed him to oversee Earth's utilization. Which meant he could make things difficult for her here. She hadn't met him in person, but only over a video link. He had been the only committee member to oppose her *Healing Initiative* project. If not for the unanimous approval of all the other committee members, her project would never have gotten funding and approval. Prag was looking for an excuse to cancel her project. He will undoubtedly use this incident against her. She would be ready for him.

Jinder and her patients waited in silence as the security hovercraft approached the lakeside.

Chapter 3 Investigation

Security Chief Drin Mezobac stood on the hover platform as it sped toward the reported incident.

It irritated Mezobac that he must suffer yet another interruption to his day. He had been here one week, and it was already clear that accepting this assignment had been a dumb career decision. He was a police officer and a good one, but now he'd been relegated to babysitting duty at a children's park. Now, day and night, false emergencies occupied his time as people overreacted to every alien rodent, bug, and leaf they encountered. To top it off, his new boss had come along on this routine run.

"Let's make this quick, Chief Mezobac. I have little time." Sector Director Prag said.

"Of course, Sir. This should be routine. You really didn't need to bother yourself with such trivial matters."

"I think I am the one to decide for myself what constitutes a trivial matter, Chief Mezobac."

"I meant no disrespect, Sir, it merely surprised me when you asked to come. You are a busy man with many important responsibilities. If needed, I can reschedule this *evaluation* for a better time," Mezobac said. Perturbed to be pulled into what he knew was a political situation.

Prag was only coming along to find some excuse to cancel Counselor Jinder's *"Healing Initiative"* project. Mezobac knew the United Planetary Confederation's planetary committee had forced Prag to accept Jinder and her wards to get funding for his other projects.

"My busy schedule is of no concern to you except that you do not waste my time. I am required to perform a field evaluation once a year, and I have chosen this opportunity to give you the benefit of my experience. I will conduct the interview with Counselor Jinder."

"Yes, sir. As you direct," Mezobac replied.

Mezobac wished he had been told that Director Prag was planning on making this park's office complex, Earth United Planetary Confederation headquarters. It was never good to work close to the politicians. Mezobac deplored the way politicians ran these operations. It was ridiculous, but it wasn't his place to criticize the army and UPC oversight committee's decisions about planetary reclamation. The idea of allowing civilians to come this soon after acquisition was absurd. The timing of budgets and allocation of revenues shouldn't be allowed to overrule common sense security concerns. Not only had they recently discovered a residual population of natives, but there hadn't been a thorough risk analysis of the planet's flora and fauna. The climate here was unpredictable and temperature unregulated. This location had been an awful choice. It was hot and miserable. Director Prag's priorities were seriously at odds with his security mission. He dared not voice his concerns. The people making these dreadful decisions would be in charge of any investigation.

So, here he was on a hover platform with his boss. To top it all off, Prag was in an uncharacteristically chatty mood. This was going to be a bad day.

"I can tell you in confidence, Mezobac, that I hate being forced to deal with these bleeding-heart do-gooders. I advised the committee against giving those *people* weapons in the first place!" Prag complained. "I want you to watch how I handle this social worker. It will be an excellent lesson for you in command."

"I have been dealing with her type for years. The only way to handle a situation like this is to be firm and not accept any crap from these people."

The hover platform landed next to a lakeshore and Mezobac, Prag, and five of Mezobac's officers stepped down to the ground. Mezobac carefully sized up the situation as they approached the group of women patiently waiting for them.

Prag gave Jinder an irritated look. "We received a report of a weapon's discharge. I can assume this was your sidearm since you are the only one here allowed to carry one. You were told not to use that device except in dire emergencies. Explain this infraction of your project restrictions?"

Prag's huffing and puffing did not impress the woman whom he'd hoped to intimidate. Mezobac had met Counselor Jinder before and knew that Prag's bullying tactics would prove ineffective. According to her reputation, Jinder was a principled woman with an iron will.

"Nothing of any consequence," Jinder answered Prag in a practiced clinical tone. "I am sorry my actions to protect a child disrupted your important work. One of the large native reptiles attempted to attack one of our children playing near the water. I had to shoot it to protect her. She's unharmed, so nothing else of consequence to report." The child came forward and showed them her torn pants and red marks left by the gator's first miss. Chief Mezobac scanned the lakeshore, looking for evidence of the event. There were several footprints near the water and signs of something heavy having been dragged out of it onto the shore. Was that from the reptile? Didn't seem likely. Several scraps of synthetic fur and foam floating in the water didn't escape his notice. More happened here than Jinder's simple account revealed. But he kept his mouth shut. This was a personal dispute, not a crime.

Prag allowed an uncomfortable silence to hang in the air after Jinder gave her description of events. He thought he was being clever. He believed the silence would make Jinder nervous and reveal something incriminating. People, especially guilty people, hated lengthy pauses in conversation. It made them feel like there were holes in their story that needed filling.

Jinder, an experienced mental health professional, knew that trick and added nothing to her description. She looked him directly in the eye, challenging him. The look must have unnerved Prag. He made several false starts on additional questions, but already realized Jinder would not back down or change her story. In frustration. He ordered Mezobac and his squad to get statements from the other women.

One of the other security officers waded into the lake and fished out a few ragged pieces of fur. They were remnants of Thomas's costume. He presented them to Mezobac. Prag immediately rounded on Jinder and demanded, "These don't look like pieces of reptile, how do you explain them?"

"One of the park characters was also attacked by the lizard thing and got damaged. After I shot the lizard, it wandered off for repairs or something... who knows what Bionics do. It was not part of why I discharged my weapon, thus I did not include mention of it in the report."

Mezobac understood Jinder's reluctance to provide other details about the Bionic's involvement. Everyone was avoiding any official contact with them since the new legislation. Even a bureaucrat like Prag would be smart enough to avoid negative encounters with Bionics.

The recent changes in Confederation law regarding Bionics had made everyone nervous. There were many politicians eager to appear enthusiastic about enforcing the recent laws. Eager to position themselves as pro-Bionic before the next election. The result had become a real inquisition. Even though the Bionics only had fractional voting rights, there were a lot of them. They had given those that owned many of them a prodigious amount of clout. Mezobac grinned when Prag's expression changed at mention of a Bionic. On the scale of things to mess up a Confederation career, being anti-Bionic had recently become poison. Prag could be a real jerk dealing with Jinder and her patients. He was smart enough to tiptoe around anything to do with the Bionics.

"I will inquire of Repair Master Calaxan about the matter when I see him next," Prag said. He refused to make eye contact with Jinder and walked away from the women. He stomped back to the platform and shouted over his shoulder.

"Gather your men, Chief, you've wasted enough of my time."

Mezobac gave the signal to his men, and they returned to the hover platform in short order. He suspected this incident would put Prag in a foul mood. On the way home, Prag would've lectured him on the finer points of security work, but now seemed quiet and sullen. Mezobac avoided eye contact on the trip back, not eager to have the director use it as an excuse to focus his wrath on him.

As they flew away, Mezobac watched the rescued little girl playing with her friends. He thought, *Perhaps it had been okay to give some civilian's weapons.*

Chapter 4 Tunnels

Thomas woke up choking. His lungs burned, and he felt a sharp sting behind his ear. He woke in a small unlit room. Perhaps a housekeeping closet? Sparse light shone through a door vent. His head pounded as he attempted to sit upright. A sudden onset of coughing began as he struggled to regain his breath. He focused on breathing for the next few minutes and did nothing else.

Once he was able, he stood and stripped off his destroyed costume. It had been filthy even before he rolled in the mud. He found the light switch and inspected his foot. It seemed okay, but his knee hurt from being pulled and twisted by the gator. Also, there was some kind of lump under the skin behind his ear, but neither injury seemed serious. The loud thrumming noise of an alien flying platform interrupted his self-inspection. It passed close to his building. He gently tried the doorknob and found it locked. It appeared the alien women must have fished him from the lake and locked him inside the closet. No doubt they'd called security to come take care of him. Even if he opened the door and ran, he wouldn't last long without his costume. He was trapped.

Thomas looked around the cramped room for an exit when he noticed the laundry chute! He remembered touring the park's underground tunnels during his orientation. All the garbage and dirty laundry were sent down to bins in the hallways below and were hauled away without disturbing guests. Those hallways led to the principal crew area where he could find another Jupiter-D costume. Thomas opened the chute's safety cover and worked himself inside. It was a tight fit. He prayed he wouldn't get stuck. He wedged his legs and arms against the sides to control his descent and carefully closed the chute's cover before allowing himself to slide down. At the bottom was a half-full bin of towels that had been used as cleaning cloths. Mercury was keen on reducing unnecessary disposable paper products. So they used cloths and towels for everything. The laundry hopper was in an alcove in an underground hallway. It was one of many passages under the park, like a web connecting all the laundry and garbage bins in the housekeeping rooms above. They also routed all the utilities and plumbing in these tunnels. It was like a maze, but there were maps at most intersections and regular safety exits.

There was an eerie quiet down here below street level. Aside from passing under the occasional ventilation fan and the hum of large electrical panels, there was no sound. Thinking the aliens were searching for him, he needed to get to the locker room and into a new Jupiter-D costume fast.

Thomas scanned the nearest wall map to find the shortest path to the main crew room. He ran barefoot, careful not to make any noise. The pain to his pulled knee was jarring, but he ignored it and kept running. As he got closer to the crew room, he noticed someone or something moving quickly down another corridor that intersected his. Whoever it was let out a surprised shriek.

Thomas didn't stop. He ran full speed toward the stairway that led up to the crew room, taking the stairs three at a time, ignoring the pain. Still running, he made a straight path to the dressing room and hid in a large costume locker behind a furry Mercury Moose outfit. He worked to catch his breath and listened carefully for any sign of pursuit. After a few minutes, he became convinced that he'd lost whoever it was. He wasted no time putting on a new costume. Going through the closets, he found a nice clean Jupiter-D-Dog suit. As he suited up, he wondered about who or what he'd seen. The more he thought about it, the more he thought the shriek sounded human. Perhaps there are others hiding in the park?

Once he was fully suited up, he convinced himself to go look. Thomas checked downstairs in the area where he'd heard the shriek. No sign of anyone at first, but then he saw wet footprints. There was a wet spot where condensation from a cooling pipe had dripped. Someone had stepped in the water, and there were still visible footprints. The tracks were unmistakably human, unless aliens were wearing Nike sneakers now. The sneaker print was slim and long. Not a child, possibly a woman. He tried to follow them, but the prints quickly evaporated.

"Another survivor?" Thomas wondered aloud, too excited to hope there might be other people still alive. Someone had hidden down here during the attack and they, like him, were trying to survive.

"Hello!" He shouted without thinking.

He looked down the hall and noticed a security camera with a red blinking light. Had he just alerted the aliens to his presence? He worried the aliens would figure out he'd slid down the chute. They could be searching the tunnels for him even now. The costume would not prevent them from killing him. He turned and ran upstairs and out into the park. He walked casually back to his hiding spot, the little dog house nestled in Mercury-D-Moose's backyard.

Thomas sheltered in his small doghouse that overlooked the main street that led to the center of the park. Waldo Mercury had built fantastic homes for each of his cartoon's principal characters in a section called Toonville. He'd wanted his fans to see where the characters in his cartoons worked and lived. The buildings all had the lopsided, floppy look of his cartoons. He'd furnished them all with outlandish cartoon styled fittings and fixtures. Jupiter-D's doghouse was one of these props made of molded plastic and featured a bright red roof and yellow bulging walls. Its door, shaped like an upside-down squishy letter 'U', was big enough for someone in the dog costume to squeeze through. It wasn't roomy inside. They designed it as an entertaining prop, not for living in, but for now it was Thomas' home.

Thomas didn't venture out of the doghouse for the rest of that day, but spent it hiding and babying his knee. Being grabbed by a twisting gator had taken its toll. He hoped it wasn't too badly hurt. If he didn't dance, he wouldn't eat. Afraid and worried, he sat and chided himself for doing such a foolish and dangerous thing.

Why had he done it?

He'd been stupid to take such a risk. What if that gator had taken off his leg? What if those women hadn't pulled him out of the lake?

Thankfully, those gators weren't proficient hunters, having been hand fed most of their lives. If the critter had been one of the wild ones, it wouldn't have been stopped by his enormous foam foot. His stupid hero stunt had blown his cover. Those women had alerted security that a human was loose in the park.

When night eventually came, Thomas' sleep was fitful. Filled with images of people running and screaming in terror. Then screams of a child being dragged under by the alligator. After a few fitful hours, he woke up in a sweat, heart pounding. He laid there waiting for his heart rate to return to normal.

"Stupid, stupid!" he chided himself for taking the risk and exposing his identity to those alien women. Couldn't he have just let the alligator eat the child? After all, those people just killed every man, woman, and child on Earth?

"We couldn't never let that happen," a voice inside him said.

The voice shocked Thomas. He twisted to be certain no one was there, but the tiny dog house was empty except him.

"Surprise, old pal! Bet you never expected to hear from me!" the voice added.

"Am I hearing goofy voices now?" Thomas wondered.

"Goofy? I ain't never heard of him. Don't tell me you don't recognize me. It's your old pal Jupiter-D!" Jupiter-D made his famous bark-laugh sound.

The sound erupted from Thomas' throat. He clamped his mouth shut and held his hand over his lips.

"Why, that won't shut me up. I don't need your lips to talk. I'm a certified Hal-Lucy-

nation, that's what I am."

"You're not Jupiter-D-Dog, even if you claim to be a hallucination. My hallucination of Jupiter-D wouldn't talk because Jupiter-D never talks," Thomas argued.

"So, aren't you a Mr. Farty McSmarty then? Shows what you know," the voice said.

"I know more than anyone does about you, except for Waldo Mercury himself. I've won awards…" Thomas stopped. Realizing the insanity of the situation.

"O-o-o-oh! Awards then… you should have mentioned that sooner. So, I could've been more appropriately impressed. I defer to your expertise… except for the fact that I am talking." Jupiter-D laughed.

"Fine, if you're talking it must be a symptom of some stress induced mental condition. But I'm certain you don't talk. So, do us both a favor and shut up!"

"Fine, but you already know you're wrong. I don't talk on the outside, but I do on the inside. And that's where we are chatting. On the inside bub," Jupiter-D ended the statement with a friendly guffaw.

To prepare for this job, Thomas had watched every Jupiter-D cartoon ever made. Some more than once, but he was certain Jupiter-D never spoke, only his funny half-barking, half-laughing sound. He was about to repeat his assertion when he realized…

Jupiter-D laughed again and said, *"See, I was right. You remembered episode #126? When the cat was tempting me to steal Mercury's steak off the grill? Woof-woof-ha-ha!"*

He remembered that episode. There were little tiny good and evil Jupiter's perched on his shoulders, trying to convince him to steal the meat. He realized the voice might be the little angel Jupiter-D-Dog telling him it was wrong.

"Or the little devil one…" Jupiter-D laughed, *"Like I said, I'm talking to you on the inside."* Then he made the bark-laugh sound again.

Thomas was vocalizing the sounds every time Jupiter-D laughed and tried to prevent them again.

"Stop that!" Thomas insisted.

"I can't, why don't you stop copying me?" Jupiter-D made the barking sound again and Thomas involuntarily vocalized it.

"This is crazy… I'm crazy," Thomas thought.

"Naw, you ain't crazy I should know, us cartoons deal in crazy all day long. I'd say you was touched with some good old-fashioned movie magic? This is a magical place, you know. Woof-woof-ha-ha!" Jupiter-D added his annoying bark-laugh to the end of each sentence, which Thomas mimicked despite his effort not to.

"What's going on here?" Thomas demanded silently. "This is nuts."

"We been working together two years and you've always seemed a tad reality challenged,

if you'd asked me… Woof-woof-ha-ha!"

"Is that a joke? Do psychotic hallucinations tell jokes?"

"Well, I'm a joke, you're crazy, or you magically been turned into a cartoon. Pick one and we'll run with it. Woof-woof-ha-ha."

"I'm going with a joke. A stupid joke!"

"Fair enough, no accounting for taste. I'm a real funny guy, everybody says that I am. Big time cartoon career and everything. You of course already know that, cause yer an expert on me. Woof-woof-ha-ha!"

"Just because I take my work seriously and study my characters doesn't mean you have permission to invade my head. I will sleep, now shut up!"

"Manners, manners."

Thomas went back to sleep. He was too exhausted to argue anymore. So, he let Jupiter-D drone on as he floated off to sleep.

Chapter 5 That Laugh

Next morning Thomas woke up to another brutally hot and muggy day. His body ached everywhere, and as always, his scars itched. A Jupiter-D suit was not an ideal sleeping bag, but there was no way to take it off in the little doghouse. It promised to be another hot, muggy day. Already the morning sun had turned the doghouse into a sauna.

Thomas got up and walked across the street to the restroom. First refilling his costume's water reservoir at the drinking fountain and then used his key to get into the housekeeping closet there. This room was too small to lie down, but it was air-conditioned. So he locked the door, removed his head, and sat cross-legged on the floor. The odd experience of the voice hallucination had seemed so real. Probably just stress related. Yesterday had been a stressful day. Almost dying and all that. He was just happy the voice stopped.

"Dying is kinda discombobulating, ain't it?" Jupiter-D laughed. *"You seemed real upset last night about it, glad you sorted it all out this morning. Woof-woof-ha-ha."*

Thomas' heart sank. The crazy voice was back to taunt him… and the laugh emitting from his own throat.

"I've lost it, it was only a matter of time. Your crazy laughing will give me away in a minute." Thomas said.

"Cheer up ol' pal, nobody will care if you laugh like me. You are me after all! Whatcha gotta worry about? It's a dog's life for us now, Tommy Boy. Do tricks, get fed, and sleep. Sounds perfect to me! Woof-woof-ha-ha."

"Cheer up? What do I have to worry about?"

"Exactomundo!"

23

"I'll tell you what I have to worry about. Yesterday I nearly got killed saving an alien kid from an alligator. Because why? Because, well, he's an alien kid living on Earth, which until five days ago was populated by humans. Now it's crawling with these gray wrinkled things! Oh yeah, then on top of that, everyone I've ever known was murdered!"

"I'll bet that was a bad day. But there's always tomorrow. I like to say, each day is its own adventure. Woof-woof-ha-ha."

"Adventure? You don't say that. You never say that. Because, you don't talk!"

"Well, I do now. And if I coulda said it, I woulda said it. It's still an adventure."

"If by adventure you mean living in fear of death and pretending to be a cartoon dog, then I guess you're on to something."

"So, I'm guessing, the reason yer feeling a little bit blue is that Earth getting invaded has really got you down in the dumps. Take it from ol' Jupiter-D, you need to sing a song and do a happy dance, and get all cheered up! Maybe it would help if you talked to me about it? Woof-woof-ha-ha."

"Yeah, I was just thinking that I needed to talk to an imaginary dog hallucination about all the bad things that just happened to me. Can you leave me alone?"

"Nope, can't leave you alone now. Friends stick together through thick and thin. Yer looking thin and I'm pretty thick, so I guess you're stuck with me. How bout you tell me what happened, and then I can help you look on the bright side?"

Thomas was about to object again when a part of him said, "Why not?" It might help. He'd taken a few psych classes in college. Perhaps suppressing the memory was causing this psychotic dog hallucination.

"Who you callin a psychotic dog?"

"You shut up now, I'm gonna try to remember what happened. If you'll stay quiet so I can think."

Thomas allowed memories of invasion day to replay. It all seemed so ordinary. Thomas, like always, had been assigned to the Jupiter-D costume. His friend Chris was in the Mercury-D-Moose suit, and Gina was acting Charon-D-Bunny's part. They were good friends, he missed them. He took a moment and allowed the feeling of loss to wash over him.

They were often scheduled to perform together. The cast manager knew they were a great combo with good chemistry. The three of them had worked up an entire repertoire of scenes from the cartoon's most popular episodes. Their impromptu skits were so popular that management duplicated their method for other character performers in the park. Thomas smiled at the memory. He'd been pretty happy then.

"Okay, so you got to dance a lot. What else happened?" Jupiter-D interrupted.

"I was just getting to that. Let me remember it the way I want to remember it."

The three of them were doing the scene from episode twenty-two in Toonville square that morning. Then after our break, I'd gone back to my doghouse and was signing autographs. But then, the bad stuff started.

At first there were vague rumors of an alien invasion. A few people were watching their phones for news, but who would take that seriously? Most people figured it was a clever marketing stunt for a new Waldo Mercury space movie. Everyone had a good laugh about that, Waldo was a promotional genius. Leave it to him to try a whole *War of the Worlds* scare to get the media's attention. Some park guests even bought alien masks from the souvenir shops and started running around blasting people with toy ray guns. There were a few people who kept insisting it was true, but most of us were playing it up and having fun.

Then when the immense spaceships appeared in the sky above the park. All the jokes stopped. All the toy guns dropped to the ground. Panic erupted, people running, children screaming, and families were scattered. The other character performers threw off their costumes and ran.

"What did you do?"

"I refused to break character and focused on dancing. I first thought it some high-tech special effects show the park engineers had whipped up. But that idea didn't last long."

"Soon swarms of small drones buzzed through the crowds, firing weapons and zapping people. Then the loud humming of the alien soldier's hover platforms filled the air. These swept through the park with the aliens standing on top and firing some sort of ray gun weapons at anyone the drones had missed. When people started being disintegrated, I finally accepted it was real. It was too late for me to run. So, I just closed my eyes and danced. As the death rays neared, I hoped it wouldn't hurt. But after a few moments, the noise, and commotion subsided. I stopped dancing and open my eyes. I was standing alone. The street was littered with empty character costumes, toy ray guns, and masks, and guest's belongings. I remember seeing a baby carriage and walking over to it, it was empty."

"That's pretty rough ol' buddy, sorry you had to see that stuff," Jupiter-D said in a comforting tone.

"Then that night, I hid in the doghouse. Not sure how I managed to sleep. The second day was even worse. The morning fog played weird tricks on my mind. I could've sworn that I could see the outlines of people frozen in the mist, like ghosts. It lasted just a moment as the sun came up and they were gone before I could be certain of what I saw."

"That's scary, let's skip that part."

"I walked the whole park. I found no humans, only occasional patrols of the soldiers on their flying platforms, searching drones, and the distant sound of those awful weapons. They were still finding people."

"Didn't you try to hide?"

"That was the strange part, I didn't. It never occurred to me. It was like I was just watching all this happen to someone else."

"The thing was, all the stuff lying around really bothered me. So, I started cleaning it up. Then I found Chris and Gina's discarded costumes just lying there where they'd been thrown off. The image of Chris' giant Mercury-D-Moose head rolling around on the pavement made me break down. For some reason I had to pick them up not let the kids see them."

"Yeah, that was scary. If a child saw one of them empty costumes laying on the ground, it'll given em nightmares. But wait, you already knew they zapped all the kids, right?"

"I know, it's stupid." Thomas thought.

"Which bothers you more, the way your friends ditched and ran, or how they got disintegrated by the aliens? Woof-woof-ha-ha!" Jupiter-D asked.

"That's a really offensive question."

"Well, you seemed to get real upset when you talked about it."

"True, the others not staying in character, bothered me. It was unprofessional."

"Do you think staying in character saved you?"

"Well, maybe they'd still be alive right now if they'd stayed in character. It's an important rule. It's rule number one. They impressed those rules for us during training at Mercury World University. I obeyed and lived they disobeyed and died!"

"That's because you was playing me, and I got obedience training, haw-haw." Jupiter-D laughed.

Thomas ignored the remark.

It made sense at some level, but that can't be. Thomas thought. How would they know if he was in character or not? Why would it matter? How is it logical to think that the aliens cared if he was following some arbitrary corporate rules?

"Maybe not, but it's the only thing that made you different from the others. What's it gonna hurt to stay in character, why risk breaking it and drawing attention to yourself?"

That was true, somehow it had worked, so best not to break character. Do nothing that might cause the aliens to notice him.

"Like running to save a kid being eaten by an alligator? Woof-woof-ha-ha." Jupiter-D laughed.

"Wait, there are more rules than just not breaking character, you know. Saving a guest's life is part of what they require us to do under park rules."

Thomas recited Mercury theme park's employee codes of conduct:
1. Always stay in character and entertain park guests.
2. The guest's needs are always foremost.
3. Keep clean and well groomed. Take regular breaks.
4. Practice your character's autograph when things are slow.
5. If it's on the ground, pick it up. Never bend, but scoop as you pass.
6. Never use one finger to point.
7. Never speak to guests out of character or break character see rule number one.
8. Never refer to the fictional characters of another franchise.

"See, rule two, supersedes rule one," Thomas insisted. "I believe preventing a guest from being eaten by an alligator definitely would qualify as putting the guest's needs foremost."

"That you have them rules memorized is a little scary..."

"Besides, I never really broke character. Jupiter-D, um... you, would have done your best to save a child in trouble. Just because they never made a cartoon of it doesn't mean that it was out of character," Thomas said, confident he'd proved his point.

"Well, that's just dandy. Okie-dokie, I'll give you that one. I am a heroic dog,

after all. You know you'd better keep these rules going for ya and to keep up the act. I'm a pretty hard act to follow. Woof-woof-ha-ha."

"We are in awe of your humility," Thomas said with sarcasm.

"You ain't so bad yerself kid. Woof-woof-ha-ha! Imagine how proud all them teachers at Waldo University would be if they could see us now, Tommy boy."

Thomas thought back to his training at Mercury World University. It was the one-year long school that all cast members were required to attend during their first year. The instructors there had ingrained into them the importance of knowing and keeping *Waldo World's 8 Codes of Conduct.* He'd always been good at memorizing his lines, so it was easy to commit the rules to memory to pass the course.

But he also had some negative memories from his time in class. Because of his ruined face and tabloid past, they excluded him from any informal social events. He didn't mind that he didn't fit in. He should have felt relieved that he could restart his life.

"Oh, once I get you to remember stuff, you don't stop going on and on about it, do ya?"

"You're the one who keeps getting me in touch with my emotions. You're going to have to listen if I'm going to recall every painful experience in my life. That would be the price of being a psychotic hallucination."

"Fine, I'm all ears. Big floppy ones, Woof-woof-ha-ha!"

He started to think about his accident but quickly stopped himself. Still not ready to re-live that experience.

"If that one's too hard, you can think of something else ol' buddy."

He remembered back to his time at Mercury World University and recalled one humiliating event that defined his whole social life after the accident. He'd run across a group of students at a nearby coffee shop, all studying and laughing together. They'd barely acknowledged his greeting when he'd come into the cafe. So he sat at a booth off to the side. He didn't notice someone had left their books on the seat opposite him. After he'd ordered and began studying, the girl returned, irritated to find him at her table. It was one of the pretty girls in the class, Emma.

When Thomas realized his mistake, he stood up. Her friends at the other table, on the other hand, made a cruel joke out of it. She was polite at first, but when they laughed, she became annoyed and asked if he'd been put up to it. Like a practical joke. As if the thought of him sitting next to her was a horrible thing.

That's when someone in the group of students said, "Buddy, she wouldn't be into you, even if you were the last man on Earth."

All he could do was pass it off and laugh along with everyone else. He'd left, humiliated, and never returned. He did all of his studying in his room after that.

"I wouldn't sweat it, pal. They were just young and dumb. Your scars ain't that bad."

Thomas knew his scars were horrible and that he was hideous. The accident had left him a shattered man, all put together with metal plates and staples. His acting career had come to a sudden end. He was too damaged to get cast in a part as even the most hideous monster. Sure, he'd gotten a lot of "we're sorry's" and "we loved your early work", but couldn't get a gig to save his life.

It had forced him to take the job at Mercury World out of necessity. He hadn't been excited at the prospect of being around all the kids, but it paid well. At least the costume hid his disfigurement. It had become a refuge for him.

"You're a good dog, Tommy boy, and dogs don't never care how ya look. Look at the bright side, now you might be the last man on Earth! Maybe you'll get your big chance at the girl! Woof-woof-ha-ha!"

"What, I'm going to meet some nice alien woman and settle down, have puppies?"

"Yeah, with little antennas fer ears! Woof-woof-ha-ha!"

"Why are you making me dredge up all these terrible memories, anyway?"

"How would I know? Yer the one hallucinatin."

Funny how stuff like that still hurts after years. But in the grand scheme of things, it is so insignificant in comparison. Yet somehow, those terrible memories had made him more determined to survive. Prove to himself that he still had worth.

"Some families love the dog even more than the kids Woof-woof-ha-ha!"

Even a beloved dog is fondly cherished. He didn't have to understand how or why pretending to be a dog was a protection, but perhaps it kept the aliens from looking at him as a threat. Thanks to his little talk with Jupiter-D that day, his attitude took a turn for the better.

Thomas felt confident and ready to entertain the park's weird guests. Maintain a friendly attitude, keep the little alien snots happy, and do what you know.

"The show must go on!" Jupiter-D said.

It wasn't a formula for success, but it allowed him to cope. It helped him ignore the pain and heat; he was a professional after all.

He continued to perform throughout the day. The alien children were thrilled to see him, and he performed some of his best routines for them. They rewarded the effort with twelve protein bars, which provided enough food for two days. It was as if his life had a purpose for the first time in days. He just wished they would wipe their noses on something else before hugging!

"A good dog does tricks and gets snacks. It don't take no rocket surgeon to know that!" Jupiter-D said. *"Welcome to a dog's life! Woof-woof-ha-ha."*

Thomas had a different view. To him, it seemed like he was living inside one of Waldo's feature films. A half-real, half-animated sequence in which cartoon characters enter the actual world and embark on crazy adventures with movie stars.

"That's you and me now, Tommy Boy, Woof-woof-ha-ha!" Jupiter-D said. *"We are toons living in the Real World cept I don't see no movie stars."*

As a joke Thomas said, "Hey is that Jenna Elfman and Brandon Frazier over there?"

"Haw, haw! Good one Tommy Boy! You almost got me there. Woof-woof-ha-ha!"

It seemed like the world had been reordered. Humans can't live here anymore, only aliens, and maybe toons. Cartoons aren't any threat to the aliens, only humans. That's why he could hear and speak with Jupiter-D now.

He fantasized about living in a wonderland with all the other characters. Mercury-D-Moose and his girlfriend Charon-D-Bunny. The cranky neighbor, Neptune-D-Duck, goofy best friend Deimos-D-Dog, Charon's naughty cat Ganymede, the ninety-nine crazy Dalmatian dogs… everyone!

Thomas imagined he could just keep living in the world of cartoons forever. This self-delusion lasted for a few blissful hours, but then the grinding reality returned and he was once again just a crazy person living in a world filled with terror.

Chapter 6 Finding Penny

That day he also had the good fortune to find a fully stocked housekeeping closet behind the café on the Main Street of Toonville. Most of these closets were small ones with little in the way of supplies, but this one was roomy and fully stocked. It had stacks of real cloth towels, toilet paper, soap, and a big sink. It was a luxury he hadn't known for days. To his amazement, on a hook inside the door was a full set of security keys and even a flashlight! This was a treasure. The keys meant he now had access to all the park areas and laundry facilities. Finally, he had a place to bathe, wash his suit and towels, and there were even brushes here to prevent his fur from matting! He recited *The Code of Conduct* once more while he washed and dried himself. The cool water was a sweet relief to his hot, aching body. It was the first time he'd taken his head off in days. He dabbed at his blisters with a cool washcloth. In a first aid kit, he found some healing salve, so he applied this to where the costume head supports had rubbed him raw. Folding a towel, he placed it on his shoulders. This provided additional padding and would prevent future blisters. He ran the long head retainer straps back down his sleeves and snapped them onto his wrists. The straps were useful for controlling the head and keeping it in place if rude teenagers tried to knock it off.

"Now my head won't hurt your shoulders as much, woof-woof-ha-ha."

Thomas still slept in his doghouse prop. In the cartoon world, that was where Jupiter-D always slept. It seemed important that he be where the aliens would expect his character to be. He always kept the area around his doghouse clean and tidy, even pulling weeds and clipping the grass. He worked methodically and relentlessly to meet the expectations of his character and keep the *Code*.

"You're a regular toon dog, Tommy boy!"

Sleeping in the house was not that bad. He borrowed a few seat cushions and made a nice soft pad to sleep on, and hung a towel in front of the door for privacy. He was grateful that the little house had a small solar powered fan to keep it comfortable for performers. That night he fell asleep quickly, content his life would be better. All rolled up in a ball on the pad. During the night, a loud crack of thunder jolted him awake. It was raining hard and despite his little makeshift curtain on the doghouse door, the wind was blowing some of it inside. So, he crammed himself further to the back of his little house. The storm was strong, and the rain drummed loudly on the plastic roof. He had a hard time sleeping. The memory of the gator attack kept replaying in his mind. He was still worrying about the close run-in he had. The lady in purple had locked him in that closet and knew he was human. Were they still looking for him?

"Just keep your nose clean, Tommy Boy, don't draw no undo attention. We'll be right as rain, Woof-woof-ha-ha!"

As he slept, the sounds of the storm re-ignited nightmares of invasion day mixed with his accident. People running away screaming, alien weapons blasting, cars crashing, children crying. He woke up sweating and shaking. This time the dream seemed so real... he tried to think of something else. But he kept hearing children cry. He closed his eyes again. No, wait... it was an actual child crying.

"I hear it too... it's a kid alright, that ain't no delusion. You ain't allowed over one hallucination at a time." Jupiter-D said.

The crying was real? A child was crying somewhere nearby! He sat up in surprise.

"Was it one of them alien children, somebody forgot and left overnight in the park?" Jupiter-D asked.

That seemed unlikely. The alien groups were very organized. Then the memory of the footprints in the tunnels below struck him. What if other people had survived the attack and were hiding? What if those people were children?

"We gotta find that kid! I used to be a rescue dog, ya know." Jupiter-D said.

"Rescue dog? When?"

"In episode forty-two, I saved the Dalmatian puppies, remember?"

Thomas remembered that episode but wasn't sure that qualified

Jupiter-D as a rescue dog.

Thomas crawled out of his little house to find where the crying was coming from. The storm was easing up, and the park lights stayed on most of the night. Thomas felt guilty. Why hadn't he searched for other survivors before now? The little girl cried again.

His costume made searching difficult, but the thought of removing it would never occur to him. Jupiter-D offered to use his bloodhound nose to sniff around.

"Hey Tommy Boy, can you lift our ears to improve my hearing?"

Thomas lifted the ears on the costume to improve their hearing. There were screened openings under the furry ears, so it actually helped. The crying was coming from one of the cartoon houses. So they checked Mercury-D Moose's house, which was the closest, but it wasn't coming from there. After that he searched the house of Charon-D-Bunny, Mercury-D-Moose's cute girlfriend.

The crying stopped as they entered. Like Mercury-D-Moose's house, everything here was made of plastic and designed to look roundish and a little silly. Except that Charon's house was all done up in pinks and purples. Inside the house, the lighting was dim, so he used the flashlight to search. The furniture was molded plastic bolted to a steel frame attached to the floor. A big hard plastic puffy couch, complete with fake pillows and ruffles, took up the east wall. He looked inside the kitchen with its rounded refrigerator and a little table set for two. Then the crying started back up, softer this time. It was coming from the bedroom. When they entered the bedroom, the crying abruptly stopped again. He could see no one. Thomas was about to go to check the room beyond it when he noticed a candy wrapper half exposed under the side of the bed. He moved his light around the edge of the bed and saw nothing else. When he shined it back to the first spot, the wrapper was gone!

"Ah ha! They're under the bed." Jupiter-D added, trying to help.

Thomas turned off his light and waited quietly. He figured his light must've frightened them. After several minutes, he heard sniffling from under the bed. The bed, like the other furniture props, was bolted down. There was no way to lift it and only a scant half-inch gap between the plastic and the floor. But there was no mistaking the child he was looking for was under there.

Worried he might scare the child, he silently checked around the bed for an opening.

Jupiter-D suggested he just knock on the bed to see if anyone was home.

So he did. They both waited, but there was no answer or response of any kind.

"*Nobody home, I reckon,*" Jupiter-D announced and then laughed.

Thomas felt around the side, gently knocking. That's when one panel rattled. It was loose! He pried it open about a foot and used his flashlight to illuminate the hollow area inside the prop. A little girl in a doggie costume was curled up tight against the back of the hollow bed.

Jupiter-D made a barking laugh and said, "*Why, it's the little Dalmatian girl!*"

It was a little human girl, about ten years old. A rush of emotions overwhelmed Thomas to see another human being for the first time since the invasion. He stood there staring.

Jupiter-D interrupted him. "*Snap out of it, Dunderhead!*"

"She's a human, an actual human!" His mind shouted to Jupiter-D. Thomas wasn't sure if he was excited or upset. Breathing hard, he focused on not scaring the little girl.

"*That little girl could use a friend right now, even one as messed up as you! She needs a faithful and loyal companion… She needs a dog!*" Jupiter-D told him in a demanding tone.

Thomas shut down. The memories, the emotions, and the past. He pulled himself into the moment and thought only about this frightened little girl. Once his mind had cleared, he realized the girl was familiar, he'd seen her on invasion day. She'd been with her mother, visiting with him shortly before the aliens came. She wore that cute Dalmatian dog costume covered with spots. He remembered her getting so excited about his doghouse he'd invited her to go inside.

But there was something else? That's right, she had been with one of the special needs hostesses. The park provided special hosts and hostesses to all children with disabilities. The little Dalmatian girl was deaf and relied on implants to hear.

Thomas realized that finding this kid meant he was stuck not only surviving but babysitting on top of it. How was he going to look after a kid? Sure, he knew how to do tricks and make them laugh. He only did that for the paycheck. He had no clue how to look after one. This was the worst thing he could have imagined.

"*What are you worried about? You're a dog now, kids and dogs are made for each other, it ain't gonna be that hard. Trust me.*"

"I can't take care of a little girl. Are you kidding?"

"Now if that ain't the dumbest thing I ever heard said. Of course, we got to take care of her."

"How can I possibly care for a kid? I know nothing about children!"

"Just a gosh darn minute. Are you telling me you could walk away and leave this kid crying?"

"You don't understand… I don't even like kids!"

"Wait, weren't you telling me you have all them awards for being such a brilliant performer?"

"That's different, I'm an actor. Acting is pretending and I can pretend to like kids all day long, but it's different from being around them when I'm not working."

"Like I said, it's easy. Kids ain't no different from actual people, except they need more attention. Either way, you got no choice, you are the only one. This kid is gonna follow us if you want em to or not. Kids love dogs, you'll be great."

"Hey dunderhead, she can't see you. Your light is in her eyes. Quit blinding the kid!"

Thomas flipped the light so the girl could see him. Then, using his three-fingered paws, he bent his first fingers and hooked them together in the friend sign. It was one of the few he was familiar with. He repeated the process, orienting the light directly on his hands.

"Friend," he signed.

The girl's face lit up with recognition, and she gave him a teary smile that warmed his heart. She unwrapped herself from the fetal position, crawled the three-foot distance between them and immediately encircled him in a tight, squeezing hug. It was the tightest hug her small arms could manage. Thomas looked around uncomfortably, not sure what to say to the kid. This was going to be a disaster.

Jupiter-D stopped him. *"I told you to cut it out! Dogs don't worry bout that stuff. Remember, it ain't never about us, it's always about the peoples. Our peoples come first. You gotta be happy so she can be happy. She needs a dog, not some mopey-dopey sad-sack. Woof-woof-ha-ha!"*

Thomas tried to settle down.

"It's time to go full dog mode. She needs a friend. There will be no whining or crying!"

Maybe Jupiter-D was right. He could try to be the dog the girl needed. He was an actor who could pretend to know what he was doing. So he pretended to lick her head with his fake mouth and patted her back reassuringly.

The girl let go of her hug and began signing to him frantically. She had a million questions for Thomas, and he had no answers. And he'd just used the full extent of his sign language vocabulary saying "friend."

"Maybe I should say something?" Thomas wondered.

"Didn't we just use sign language? Did you forget, she, can't, hear, you?" Jupiter-D said, stretching out the last four words in case Thomas missed the sarcasm.

"She wears a hearing aid, Dunder-mutt," Thomas argued.

Without thinking, he pointed to the hearing aid implant behind her ear.

The girl shook her head to show it wasn't working. She fingerspelled "dead battery." He struggled to interpret what she'd spelled. Then tried to spell OK, but the K was difficult with only three flat fingers. It never occurred to him to slip his hand out to make it easier.

As she signed to him, Thomas wondered what she had gone through. He knew she was with her mom during the invasion. But were there any other family members with them? He couldn't remember. Who else had she lost in the invasion? Did she even know about the aliens?

Not knowing what else to say, he signed friend again. He watched her face, not understanding her hands. She attempted to speak, but he couldn't understand what she was trying to say. So, he put his finger to her mouth, afraid that if she spoke the aliens would hear her.

He just looked at her, hoping to read what she was saying in her eyes.

Chapter 7 Penny & Jupiter-D

Penny Nelson huddled in her hiding spot, shivering. The flashes of lightning and the vibration of the thunder frightened her. She wished her momma was here so she could climb in bed and snuggle under the covers like she used to, but momma hadn't returned. Her momma, Laurie Nelson, was the smartest and bravest mom ever. She had gone to college and worked, telling computers what to do. If she was here, everything would be alright.

Penny couldn't hear the rumbling thunder, howling wind, or pounding rain, but she could feel their vibrations. Her hearing implant's battery had long since died, and momma carried her spares. She was still hiding, like she'd been told to. She was a good girl. When momma said, "Hide!" she hid.

At first, she thought it was a game, but when she'd seen the fear on momma's face, she knew it wasn't. Momma had never looked so worried. She'd repeated, "Hide and don't come out until I come get you!" Then she'd pointed at Charon-D Bunny's house.

A shadow had passed overhead. She looked up and saw something big and scary flying through the sky. She ran straight to the cartoon house. People everywhere were running and frightened. And that's when the terrible, weird screeching, pulsing sounds began disrupting her cochlear implants.

In a panic, she tried to hide under the bed and got frustrated when she couldn't get in. The pulsing screeching sound got louder and closer, so she got mad and started kicking the bed's side until a panel finally cracked and came loose. She pried up hard and climbed inside. Finally, she turned off her implants to stop the painful noise pulses.

She cried in silence, worried whatever she was hiding from might hear her. After a long time when she felt safer, she tried turning the implants on a few times, but the noise was still nearby and she heard it screeching. So she kept them off for what seemed a very long time. Later she turned them on again, worried she wouldn't hear her momma call for her, but there were no sounds at all. She turned up the implant's volume control to maximum and listened hard for her mom, but only heard the faint sound of crickets. She wanted to go out and look, but she remembered a story momma told her about a naughty lady who didn't listen, looked, and then turned to salt. So, she stayed where momma had said and listened.

The battery was finally depleted after a few hours, and she was back in the familiar silence of her own thoughts. She'd been there since. Penny was certain that something terrible had happened, but she didn't know what it was and didn't want to think about it. She missed her mother. She'd cried a million tears every night, always trying not to make a sound, until sleep came to her rescue.

It had started out as the best day in her ten-year life, one she had dreamed of for months. She and momma came to see Mercury-D-Moose and Jupiter-D-Dog in Waldo Mercury's Mercury World all the way from Nashville. Penny loved the Mercury-D-Moose cartoons and watched them every day. Sure, it was hard because you couldn't lip read a cartoon, but their cartoons were one of the few that had a little man in the corner of her screen signing American Sign Language (ASL) for the characters. Her favorite was Mercury's dog, Jupiter-D. He was like her. He couldn't talk. She would laugh every time he got himself into a fix. Especially when the cat next door would make him do something wrong. She'd even got to meet Jupiter-D that last day. You know, before...

Penny tried not to think about *that day.* Then she remembered how in the one cartoon Jupiter-D had been playing ball with the cat. But the naughty cat threw the ball into Neptune-D-Duck's garden. Jupiter-D followed his ball into the garden and got tangled in the strings Neptune used to tie his vegetables. Soon the garden was ruined. Jupiter-D tried to fix it but only made it worse. He ended up with a long string of tomatoes and beans wrapped around him. When he shook to get them off, one tomato got sent flying and hit Neptune-D-Duck right in the face. He was so mad he quacked. He took Jupiter-D by the collar and made Mercury-D-Moose pay for all the vegetables Jupiter-D ruined. She would always giggle at how silly Jupiter-D looked wrapped in vegetables.

Then the ugly gray-skinned faces came back to her mind. She hated when that happened. She tried to think happy thoughts to make them go away. Instead, she thought about another favorite cartoon, *The Puppy Episode.* In it, Jupiter-D met a girl dog who had ninety-nine little black spotted puppies. They were crazy puppies, crawling everywhere- all over Jupiter, on his head, hanging on his ears, and all over his house. She loved those puppies and had even dressed like one to go meet Jupiter-D.

When she met him that day, he was so funny, and he really liked her costume. He gave her a big hug and invited her to use his huge doghouse. It was so cool inside, but momma wouldn't let her stay.

Penny had lots of deaf friends who could talk but not hear. But Jupiter-D was different. He could hear but not talk.

While she'd waited, Penny had done a lot of thinking about her momma and her daddy, about how they weren't together anymore. It was her fault.

Penny could lip read and had tried to learn to vocalize words for her daddy, but she hadn't been very good at it. Even after the implants, she had a hard time figuring out words and making all the sounds. Her daddy always seemed mad. He didn't know how to sign and wouldn't look at her when he spoke, so she could lip read. Then he would yell because she didn't listen. So, she refused to talk. She knew it was naughty not to try, and that it made daddy even more angry, but she did it anyway. Kids at her school were mean too, so she wouldn't talk to them either.

Momma always signed to her. It was so much easier to sign. She liked to speak with her fingers. When she'd first met Jupiter-D, who had paws, he wasn't able to sign very well. Poor Jupiter-D, it must be hard for him. She tried to figure out how he might sign with only three toes on each paw. So, as she waited for momma, she invented some signs a three-toed dog could use. That way when she met him, she would show him her new three-toed signs, and they could talk and be friends.

She wasn't stupid. She knew Jupiter-D was a man in a costume. But she wondered how they found a man who could hear but not talk to play the part of Jupiter-D? Somehow it wouldn't be right if someone who could talk wore Jupiter-D's costume. It would be like cheating. Her momma said she was silly and of course the man could talk and hear, but they had rules so he wasn't allowed to.

Just then a bright flash of lightning lit up her plastic sanctuary, and a strong vibration of thunder shook her. She couldn't hold back the crying anymore. She let the sobs and moans go free and had a good hard cry. Maybe momma would hear her and come looking.

Why hadn't momma come back? Now it had been over five nights. How long could she stay hiding? Was she going to live under this pretend bed forever? Did the ugly people take momma? She prayed like momma had told her to do when she was scared. She asked God for help.

That first day after had been so scary. She'd wanted to come out of her hiding spot, but when she remembered how scared momma's face had been, she stayed hiding. Eventually, she had to go. She couldn't hold it any longer. If she walked quietly and quickly to the bathroom across the street, momma would understand. Maybe momma was hiding in the bathroom and waiting for her there.

Peeking out from the loose crack, she didn't see anybody. So she squeezed out and tiptoed to the door of Charon-D Bunny's house and looked out. There wasn't anyone around. It was night, but the lights were all on. Alone and frightened, she wanted to go back and hide, but her bladder didn't let her. She gathered her courage and ran across the street to the family bathroom. She dashed in and locked the door as soon as she entered. Her mother wasn't there, no one was. She looked in the regular bathroom after she finished, but there was no one there either.

Although drinking from the fountain was nice, she was hungry. She needed to be brave. Her mother would be upset if she didn't take proper care of herself. There was a little store right next to the bathroom with lots of stuff. Maybe someone would be there to help her find her momma. Penny had a lot of money, almost fifty dollars, so she could buy food, too.

The door was open, and it was pretty messy inside. People had dropped stuff and not picked it up. She checked for a store lady, but no one was there. Even the back room was empty. Maybe they'd be back tomorrow. She took a funny Jupiter-D bag and filled it with candy, puzzle books, and water bottles. Then she put twenty dollars on the counter. She wasn't sure if that was enough, but she would save the wrappers and have the store lady figure it out later.

Penny spent the next day under the bed too, only coming out to use the bathroom at night, always careful to look for danger first. She spent her days sleeping and worrying about her mom. The puzzle books were fun and helped pass the time.

Penny returned to the store on the third day, but the store lady still wasn't there. Curious, she took a walk around the park, looking for her mom. She stayed out of sight, walking in places where she was mostly hidden by plants and other objects.

On the fourth day, she left her hiding spot even earlier, before the sun had set. Right away, she saw some people walking down the street. She almost ran up to them, eager to ask them about her momma, but when they turned and she saw their faces, she stopped. Their faces were weird, all gray, wrinkled, and ugly. She ran away, even more frightened than before. After she made sure they didn't follow her, she hid under her bed again. She prayed the scary people wouldn't find her.

She'd been careful to stay hidden ever since, only going to the bathroom when necessary, and always at night. The store was out of candy, and the only granola bars left were the icky ones, with dried apples in them. So, she grabbed some of those and some beef jerky that was left. Nobody had taken her money off the counter, so she picked it up and saved it for when they came back. Someone might steal it if she left it.

Penny was getting worried. It had been a long time. Why hadn't momma come back? Who were those ugly people, why are they here? Maybe momma will send someone?

She thought about walking home. Momma could be there waiting? It took almost the entire day in the car to drive here. So, it would probably take longer to walk back. Which road does she take to get to Nashville? There was a map in the car. What if she saw more ugly people? What did momma want her to do? Tonight, the storm had made it worse. Trying to cheer up, she told herself that the rain made the flowers grow and kept the grass green, but why did it have to be so scary?

Then she started crying again. She missed her mom. That's when she saw a light flickering against her bed. She stopped crying. She knew crying makes noises other people could hear. The light was someone with a flashlight. Someone was looking for her! Why had she cried! She'd made a noise and now the bad people were going to find her. That's when she realized one of her candy wrappers was sticking out from under the bed! That would make them look under here. Grabbing the wrapper, she pulled it back, hoping they wouldn't see it. She hid, huddled in the corner, away from the place where the plastic was cracked. Maybe they won't see her. The light was shining through the crack. It was opening. They'd found her. The bright light was searching for her, and she couldn't move. Her body froze with terror.

After a minute, the person set the light on the ground and turned it so she could see him. It was Jupiter-D! He was looking for her. He made the sign for *friend*. Immediately, she crawled to him and clutched him. Holding on to him to be sure he was real. To be certain he would not leave her, she locked her fingers.

He was shaking. He must be scared, too. Poor Jupiter-D, she thought, he must be so frightened. Mercury-D and everyone else is gone, he's alone like her. Unlocking her grip, she began signing and explaining everything to him, about her mom, how she was scared, how she saw the ugly people. She had the money for the candy and wanted him to give it to the store lady. She didn't stop until she'd signed everything she'd wanted to tell someone for a long time. Jupiter-D tilted his head and signed, "Friend" again. *Poor thing, he doesn't understand.* She would need to teach him her new three-toed signs so they can talk.

Jupiter-D pointed at her implant, so she signed that the battery was dead.

She tried to use words, but he didn't like that and put his hand on her mouth.

So, she kept signing, hoping he would learn.

Chapter 8 Dog Lessons

Bewildered, Thomas watched the girl sign. He tilted his head to show his deep concern. Candy wrappers littered the floor under the bed where she'd been hiding. He worried she hadn't been eating. Getting up from the floor, he sat on the little plastic bed in Charon-D-Bunny's bedroom. Trying to communicate his concern for her diet, he motioned toward his mouth.

The girl smiled and nodded. Her costume was only a one-piece jumper and a small plastic puppy nose and fake whiskers, so her mouth was clearly visible. She nodded to show she understood.

While Thomas pulled one of the alien's protein bars out of his pocket for her. Penny, who thought Jupiter-D was asking her for food, held out a granola bar for him. The girl's generosity and concern were touching.

"I think she means to feed you. Remember, people like to give us dogs food, it makes them happy," Jupiter-D said.

Jupiter-D was correct, so Thomas took her food and held his out for her. She took it from him and signed, "Thank you."

Thomas tried to return the *Thank you* sign, but fumbled.

Penny made a face when she tasted the strange food bar. As she ate, Jupiter-D sat on the edge of the plastic bed and watched her.

"You need to let her know you're glad you found her," Jupiter-D prompted.

"How can I do that?"

"You're the great actor, figure it out."

After eating, the girl resumed signing to him. He tried to understand, but she signed so quickly that he had no idea what she'd said. So he made the universal, *I don't know* gesture, shaking his head and holding his arms out, palms up.

She stopped signing so fast and slowly fingerspelled her name, Penny. He nodded to show he understood and then tried to fingerspell his own name, but with three fingers he couldn't figure out how to form the letters for

"THOMAS" so he gave up. He pointed to himself and held out his dog tag for her to read. She tapped her head and made the unmistakable "Duh!" gesture.

"You're a genius, Woof-woof-ha-ha!" Jupiter-D quipped and laughed

Thomas slapped his forehead and nodded.

She started fidgeting and walking oddly, then made the sign for the toilet and pointed in the bathroom's direction. That sign was clear to Thomas. The pee-pee dance is universal.

So, off they went. When they got there, she looked very frightened. She made a big deal about pointing to the ground in front of the door, then spelled "STAY" to him.

"She's afraid you might leave. Time to put on our guard dog hat," Jupiter-D said.

Thomas agreed. So, he did his best vigilant guard dog pose—squatting down on his haunches and placed his hand above his eyes to scan the horizon for trouble. Reassured, she entered the bathroom, carefully checking it was safe first.

After she came out, she rewarded his loyalty with a smile and a hug. Thomas felt the appreciation only a dog knows for a job well done.

"We're a good dog, Woof-woof-ha-ha!"

Thomas could now add *guard dog* to his resume. Penny seemed anxious. She kept looking around, checking for the aliens. Jupiter-D told Thomas that he needed to act the part of the ferocious dog. So he dashed off, making a show of checking the way and waving for her to follow.

"That shows the human how loyal and brave you are."

He started walking toward Charon-D's house, assuming she'd want to return to her hideout, but Penny shook her head. She pointed to his doghouse instead.

Penny crawled in and curled up at the back of it as soon as they arrived, and he moved his small sleeping mat in front of the door. He understood that his job as a guard dog wasn't done yet. She soon fell asleep. The sky was clear of rain clouds, so he curled up outside the doghouse doorway on guard duty.

"See, being a dog makes it easy to take care of the kid."

Thomas had to agree it hadn't been too difficult, but he still worried.

The next day, Thomas woke up to a poke in the ribs. Still curled up in front of the doorway, he groggily woke up. Penny hadn't poked him. He looked, and she was still asleep. He had an audience of alien kids staring in at him this morning.

"Showtime! Better rise-n-shine! Tommy Boy. Woof-woof!" Jupiter-D said.

Thomas had slept over and there were already people in the park. A group of alien children stood waiting for him to perform. One was patting him on the head as his friend tried to pull his tale. After his surprise subsided, Thomas automatically reverted to his character. He gave a quick whine as he got up on all fours and pretended to scratch. Then he stood up on two legs, stretched, and made a show of yawning and more scratching. The tiny crowd laughed at the funny antics.

He heard Penny inside the doghouse do a sharp intake of air and realized she was awake and watching. It was his job to be certain everyone enjoyed themselves, so he jumped up and away from his little bed and did a heel-toe routine, grabbing a cane that he had stored on the doghouse roof for this very purpose. Next, he pranced energetically around the dog yard several times, the little alien children running after him, laughing. When he was done, he made a show of collapsing to the ground, pretending to be exhausted. He got up on his hands and dragged his rear legs, slowly making his way back to his bed spot near the door. For a finale, he spun around in his bed like a dog. It looked like part of the performance, but he used the spin to check to see if Penny was okay. He saw her, still inside the doghouse, looking frightened and curious.

The audience waved their hands in applause. He stood to take a bow and two protein bars landed in front of him. The alien children began talking and playing as the parents started a conversation among themselves. The parents made their children pose for photos with Jupiter-D and then the group left in search of other attractions.

As soon as they were gone, he checked on Penny again. She was still frightened, but not as much as he'd feared. He handed her one of the food bars they'd given him. She pointed to the food and to the aliens. Thomas nodded to confirm. She signed something else he couldn't understand, so ignored it.

After they finished eating, Penny signed a "W" to her lips and held out an empty water bottle. He pointed in the bathroom's direction and they walked there together. As they filled the water bottle, a young alien couple walked past, holding hands. When Penny saw them, she panicked and dove behind Thomas's legs. They terrified her. Thomas stayed in character. He got down on his hands and feet and ran over to the couple, sniffing and begging, then he ran back to Penny.

The aliens smiled kindly at them but were too much in love to care about amusement park robots. After they walked away. Thomas gave her a reassuring hug, and they headed back to the doghouse. They sat quietly on the grass and watched the occasional alien family walk by. Penny wasn't as frightened seeing the parents with their children. Penny finally signed, "Jupiter-D, are the ugly people mean or nice?" He looked at her and shrugged. So she tried again, fingerspelling the question slowly.

"This one's for you," Jupiter-D said to Thomas.

Thomas tried to fingerspell, *NICE.* He tried to add, *KIND OF,* but it was a struggle in the costume.

Penny seemed reassured by the information. Then she began signing, rapidly telling Jupiter-D about her mom, her house, and her favorite cartoons. Jupiter-D shrugged to show he didn't understand. So again, Penny slowly fingerspelled some things she thought it was important for him to know. She told him she was from Nashville, that she's almost ten, she likes horses, and that she is worried about her mom. Jupiter-D gave her a big hug and patted her back.

Jupiter-D tried to fingerspell important information back to her. So, he painfully spelled out that he lives in Mercury World, is afraid of horses, and is worried about his mom too. The costume made it hard to fingerspell.

By holding his paw to form letters, Penny helped him fingerspell. While she helped him, Penny absently moved her mask, without putting it back, to scratch her nose.

Thomas grabbed it and pushed it back into place. He shook his head at her. Then, using gestures, told her to never remove her mask, and pointed around. Her costume had a little half mask that covered her nose and cheeks, but her eyes and mouth wore black makeup. The makeup had smudged badly and was missing in spots.

This gave him an idea. He took Penny's hand and walked her to a nearby face painting stand. He took a facial wipe and cleaned off her makeup. Then he grabbed several black makeup crayons and carefully redid her disguise. Then showed her the mirror and gave her one of the black makeup crayons. She laughed when she saw how cute her face looked. Thomas had been in showbiz long enough to know a thing or two about costume makeup.

Later, as they traveled back to his yard, they found a souvenir autograph book in a store. Jupiter-D began practicing his autograph. Penny giggled. Another idea occurred to him. He took one paper and at the top wrote Dalmatian-D-Puppy in a neat and practiced script. He gave it to Penny and gestured for her to copy it. She took the paper excitedly and started making neat copies of her new name with her best penmanship.

After the autograph practice, it was time for fun. He pulled Penny up from the ground and began dancing with her.

Soon she was dancing along and giggling happily. She had fun spinning and rolling on the ground. Thomas realized others had joined them in the dance. Little alien children were dancing and giggling right along with the two of them. A crowd of alien parents were nearby, waving and snapping photos of the impromptu dance. Thomas started clowning for them and everyone laughed. Penny didn't seem frightened this time, but was enjoying herself with the other kids. Jupiter-D was happiest when children laughed, Thomas was too. Soon, Penny was into her role as Dalmatian-D-Puppy completely, rolling over, sitting up, begging, and getting treats from the delighted alien children and adults alike. Afterward, a few of the alien kids came up and posed for pictures with Jupiter-D and the Dalmatian Pup Penny. Penny even signed a few autographs on souvenir pictures the aliens had gotten from the shops.

As it grew dark, the dance ended, and they journeyed back to the doghouse.

It had been a long day, and they were tired. They sat together on the grass in front of Mercury-D-Moose's house to rest. The aliens seemed to have enjoyed the cute addition to Jupiter-D's act. The appreciative guests had given them almost two dozen of the food bars.

As they were getting to bed, Penny began signing. It was one of her flurries of fingerspelling he couldn't follow. He caught himself dozing as she excitedly went on about something. Thomas nodded and shrugged a few times to make her feel good, and fell asleep.

Penny was happier than she had been in days. She opened his neck flap and checked to see if Jupiter-D was sleeping. It was great having Jupiter-D as her babysitter. It made everything better. She'd decided momma had sent him to watch her. It made sense now. Momma would never have left her alone without a babysitter. Not until she turned twelve at least. She couldn't wait until her mom came back so she could tell her about all their adventures together. Her momma would know how to fix everything, that's what she did. She wished Jupiter-D could stay with her and momma forever. Jupiter-D didn't know when momma was coming back either, she'd asked.

The ugly people weren't as scary as she'd thought. Some were nice, and their kids were just like other kids, maybe even nicer than the ones she'd known at home. None of these kids teased her or even noticed she was deaf. To them she was Dalmatian-D-Puppy. That made her happy inside. It made her smile, knowing she'd helped Jupiter-D get food. He was already learning her three-toed finger spelling method and was better able to talk. While they ate lunch, Jupiter-D had taught her rules she must follow. He called it *The Code*. It seemed very important to Jupiter-D. So, she worked hard to remember the rules. She wanted to be a good girl, so when momma came back, Jupiter-D would give her a good report. That will make momma proud of her.

In her prayers that night she told God that her favorite thing today was dancing with Jupiter-D, it was the most fun she'd ever had. She thanked Him that the alien kids didn't tease her or hit her like the kids in school had. It seemed strange that she felt happier now than she had been in a long time. Since before daddy had left. She ate one of the food bars for dinner. She didn't like the taste, but would never complain. Her momma had always taught her to be thankful for what God provided–even icky alien food.

Over the next few days Jupiter-D taught her different dances. They even acted out brief scenes from his cartoons. Everything was going so well. She sometimes felt bad for not missing her momma every moment, but momma would want her to be happy.

Penny stopped worrying so much. Deciding it was better to be happy than to be sad. Besides, Jupiter-D was a good dog and took good care of her. He even took her to see his special large cleaning closet. He showed her the sink and the soap, then pretended to wash himself with a washcloth. Then he pointed to Penny and fingerspelled "BATH".

Jupiter-D stepped outside and waited so Penny could take a bath in the sink. Afterward they traded places. Jupiter-D took a bath and Penny stood outside and watched the door. When Jupiter-D came out, his fur was bright and clean. Penny helped him brush it.

Chapter 9 The News

That night, Thomas worried. How many other humans are hiding in the park and need his help? It seemed unlikely that Penny was the only one. The footprints he found before were too big to be hers. So he knew there was at least one other person. He assumed it was a woman, based on the footprints in the tunnels, but how could he find her. Besides, she would be the perfect one to take care of Penny.

"You don't need someone else to watch Penny. The kids happy and were doing great dunderhead," Jupiter-D said.

"Okay, I still should look for other survivors. What if there are more kids like Penny, lost and alone?"

"I suppose search and rescue, is a hero dog's job too. I guess it'd be okay to try."

Thomas considered going down into the tunnels to search, but that would be risky. It still felt like the security police would be down there. If he could find a safe way to search and not endanger Penny, that would be ideal.

"Shame you couldn't borrow one of those flying thingys to search and see the whole park. Woof-woof-ha-ha." Jupiter-D offered.

"Yeah, that sounds *real* safe. I need something where I can hide and still look around in places my character can't go. Besides, that thingy won't fit into the tunnels." Thomas looked up into the sky, imagining what it would be like to see from up there. That's when he noticed one of the park's security cameras. They disguised it as a Mercury Moose head. The cameras were everywhere in the park. And the control room was next to the crew area near his locker. It wasn't even very far from his doghouse, just down the next street.

"That's pretty smart thinking for a human."

"We can go while Penny's asleep. So, she'll be safe and won't even know we were gone."

"That doesn't seem like the proper dog thing to do."

"Sure, it is. Dogs are always sneaking around doing stuff their masters don't know about."

"No doggonit that's not what dogs do, that's what cats do. Good dogs are always loyal and faithful."

"I must have owned some bad dogs then. Anyway, it won't take but a few minutes and we'll be right back. I have to find that girl."

"Wait, is this about you finding a female or helping lost kids?"

"Both. Who knows who we might find? I gotta try."

"I suppose so. You got me all worried about them other lost kids. Let's hurry up so we can get back."

This would work, Thomas felt sure. He was in the room before with all the monitors, knowing that from there he could see all of Toonville.

Thomas had avoided the security area and crew room since saving the alien kid. He used his key and unlocked the door. Checking inside, it was dark and free of aliens. Everything seemed normal. It opened to a hallway. Off to the right was his locker room, and on the left was the security room. The stairway leading to the tunnels was down the hall. At the far end of the hall was the door that connected to the back-lot service area where all the warehouses and maintenance shops were.

He checked inside the locker room. Nothing seemed to have changed since he'd been there last. There were the rows of costumes waiting to be worn. A bench for dressing and the crew lockers. The vending machines were still filled with food, so he made a mental note to come back later and get some of it. He should stop by his locker and check his stuff, but the thought of it made him anxious.

"What are you all jittery about your locker for? You're acting like a pup hiding from the dogcatcher."

"Nothing, stop bugging me."

What was he afraid of? Every morning, he came into this room to change for work. There was nothing frightening about this place. He opened his locker door as he did every day… and it hit him all at once. He felt weak. Sitting hard on the bench, he could only stare at the photo inside of the door. It was the picture that greeted him every day when he started his workday. He stared at the photo of his parents, overcome by grief.

"A picture of your family? That was the big scary thing?"

"Just shut up. Hallucinations shouldn't be allowed to make stupid comments every time I have a moment."

Thomas' anger rose. It made him question everything he'd been telling himself for days. Everyone he ever loved was probably dead, and he wasn't.

"Yes, they're gone, but you have Penny now. You are her dog and she needs you. You're a sorry mutt, but she loves you now too."

That wasn't the point. He should have done something, anything. The world was ending and instead of doing something, he just danced like an idiot! Thomas was incapable to do anything to help.

"Now wait a minute, buster!" Jupiter-D said. *"You just stop that thinking right now! Aren't you risking yourself right now coming here to try to rescue people?"*

"Yeah, but-

"Don't 'yeah, but' me! I know you think you ain't done nothing, but you was doing all you could. You and Penny are surviving. What was you supposed to do? You're just a guy in a dog suit. You ain't no soldier, you ain't no superhero. Do you got laser beams in your eyes you can blast them with that you ain't used yet or something?"

"For days I've only been thinking of myself. I should have been thinking of other's, my folks, the kids. What's wrong with me. I was wallowing in self-pity for like a week."

"You already know that it's called survivor's guilt. Surprise! All you know how to do is dance and act. Those are your skills and you have been using them to survive and now you're helping Penny and whoever that girl is we're looking for. What more could anyone ask of you? You expect too much from yourself!"

"I'm such a coward. Why did I live and they didn't? He looked at his parents."

"Well, first you don't know they are dead and even if they are, how's that your fault? The aliens are the bad guys here, not you."

Thomas said nothing.

"Wouldn't yer folks be happy knowing you're alive and helping Penny?"

Thomas knew that was true, but it didn't feel right.

Thomas reached his paw up into his flap and wiped his eyes. He took the picture, shoved it in his pocket. Then grabbed the small bottle of prescription pain medication and stashed it in his pouch. He also grabbed the charger from his locker and plugged in his dead cellphone and placed it on the shelf behind him.

"I should at least try to call my family." Thomas said, testing the idea.

"You really think they will answer? If they are alive, they are hiding from the aliens like us."

"But I need to call them."

"People don't answer the phone when hiding for their lives." Jupiter-D tried to reason.

Thomas didn't listen, he'd already decided. He removed his head, set it on the bench, and walked to the phone on the wall. If he waited for his cellphone to charge, he would change his mind.

Surprised to hear a dial tone when he picked up the receiver, it emboldened him to dial the code to get out and then his parent's number. Like he'd done dozens of times before. After a moment the phone connected, and he heard the ring back tone. His heart beat so hard he could barely breathe. Time seemed to distort and grow long.

It rang six times. each buzzing tone made his heart drop. Then someone picked up the other end. His heart leaped when he heard his mother's voice answer, "Hello?"

At first, he couldn't think what to say, so thrilled to hear her voice. Relief poured over him like warm sunshine as that familiar voice soothed him.

Then his mother said, "Please leave a message after the beep and we'll call ya back when we get home. I'm looking forward to chatting then, bye and thanks for calling."

Thomas wept, and the phone beeped.

His throat tightened as he whispered, "I love you, mom... Tell dad, I'm okay..."

Unable to speak further, he stood there, overwhelmed. The machine beeped at him and a computer voice asked if he was finished leaving his message. He put the handset in the cradle.

"You okay, buddy?" Jupiter-D asked.

Thomas gave a weak smile and nodded. Just hearing his mom's voice had given him strength. Helped him refocus.

"Let's go check the security room."

He walked across the hall and entered the security monitor room. He'd only ever been in the room a few times. Ten video monitors hung on the wall opposite the door. Each screen switched between several security cameras around the park. Most of them seemed to still be functioning. To his relief, one screen switched to a view of his doghouse. It held for a moment, then switched to a new camera view. Everything looked okay with Penny. So he set that camera to watch the doghouse area.

He sat and watched the monitors for several minutes and studied the controls. He figured out how to switch different cameras to the primary screen. There was a diagram on the wall showing the cameras' locations in the park. To his disappointment, there weren't a lot of cameras in the service tunnels.

After watching the security cameras for a bit, Thomas noticed another TV off to one side on a desk. It showed a picture of an empty news anchor's desk with the headline *Aliens Attack Earth* in the letterbox below the image. It was connected to an old-style cable box and video recorder.

They probably used the television to track outside news and weather for park security. The recorder was still recording.

He watched TV for a few minutes, but nothing changed except a repeating ticker that ran across the bottom listing various cities that had fallen to the invasion.

"That's the worst TV news I ever saw, woof-woof-ha-ha," Jupiter-D joked.

Thomas didn't laugh.

An idea occurred to Thomas. If this has been recording since the day of the invasion, a record of the news about the invasion would still be on the recorder. He might find out what really happened.

Thomas understood enough about these recorders to know that

eventually they must record over the saved video, but how long before the video recorder erased the invasion accounts and recorded over them? He had better watch it now or he might never see it.

Thomas set the video player to the day of the invasion and set it to playback. To his relief, the recording hadn't been erased yet. He set it back to the morning before the attack.

The screen showed the female anchor doing the usual news, war, pollution, crime, and civil unrest. After a minute he hit fast forward previewing until he saw a special bulletin flash. The scene switched to a reporter trying to describe the carnage behind her. The poor reporter barely controlled her voice. A camera zoomed onto one of the large alien ships in the distance, the same type Thomas had seen over the park that day. This one was over Manhattan. A map popped up with big red dots on each of the world's major cities.

The vast fleet of ships had arrived everywhere on Earth almost simultaneously. Next came a shaky phone video showing swarms of alien drones as they swept through a city street zapping people as they fled. Then the phone fell to the ground, pointing straight up. One of the hover platforms passed over, its weapon pulsing deadly arcs of energy.

The next video was a brief clip of air force jets attacking an alien spaceship. A beam shot from the alien ship and the jets exploded. Then a video of human ground troops trying to engage the aliens, but they too evaporated.

Thomas watched the horror unfold before him. The same story repeated itself again. The aliens in their hovercrafts systematically evaporating every human in sight. Finally, a commotion arose in the newsroom. The news anchor hurried to finish her last sentence and looked up in resignation. She evaporated. Afterward there was the noise of more death rays and panic inside the news studio and then silence. Just that shot of the empty desk for days. The invasion happened earth-wide and humanity had been wiped out. Thomas hoped it might have been otherwise, but now he had proof. Humanity had been obliterated. He slipped his hand down on the picture of his family still in his pocket. But didn't take the photo out. He couldn't look them in the face. If they'd escaped, it would have been a miracle.

"They're all gone," Thomas thought.

"*I'm still here for you, faithful to the end, that's me,*" Jupiter-D said. "*And don't forget Penny!*"

He had been so preoccupied watching the news that he'd lost track of time. Time to get back to Penny! He double-checked the camera he'd set to watch her in the doghouse, and everything seemed quiet. It would be day soon. He looked one more time on the tunnel cameras, hoping for a glimpse of the girl, and then he would head back to Penny.

"*There!*" Jupiter-D said.

For a moment, a human woman walked past a camera. He tried to switch it to the primary screen but fumbled with the controls. It took him a moment and when he got the image back. She was walking away from him. He zoomed in and saw that she was wearing a costume, not a big furry one like his, but a princess costume.

Many of Waldo's feature length cartoons were animated, or 'Waldoized', versions of classic stories and fairy tales. Because the young ladies in these stories were usually royalty of some kind, they'd earned the nickname 'Princesses.' The girl was wearing the harem costume of the Persian slave girl Morgiana, the heroine from Waldo's popular movie based on the story *Ali Baba and his Forty Thieves*.

He kept watching, wondering how to get to her. Then he glimpsed the girl's face on a second camera as she scooted around a corner. He recognized the young woman as Emma, the one from the awkward encounter at the coffee shop.

Jupiter-D laughed and asked, *"Don't tell me, she's the one who said, 'Not if you were the last guy on Earth.'"*

"It was her friends that said that, not her."

She probably gets hit on by guys all the time. If the others hadn't made a big deal out of the situation, he wouldn't even have remembered.

"What's the chance she'd be the one who survived? Sounds like destiny…"

"You know, I don't believe in that stuff."

He followed Emma's progress through the tunnels until she headed into an area without cameras. According to the map, she was headed toward the water park. This office didn't have any cameras there since that part of the park had been closed years ago. He realized he'd spent way too much time here. He'd have to look for Emma later. He had to get back to Penny.

Just as he got up to leave, he noticed movement on another camera. It showed a line of park characters coming in the rear door just outside this room.

"They must be deploying more characters for the park," Thomas thought.

Dozens of characters dressed as Mercury-D-Moose, Charon-D-Bunny, Jupiter-D-Dog, and Neptune-D-Duck, were headed straight for him!

"And you left our head in the locker room, dunderhead!" Jupiter-D said.

Thomas hid behind a desk just as the characters passed by his open doorway. They didn't stop. From his place on the floor, he could see them pass by on the security monitor. The characters exited the crew hallway and into the park. Just as he got up, he noticed an alien in uniform heading toward the back-hallway door following behind the new characters.

"Time to go!" Jupiter-D said.

With only seconds to spare, Thomas ran to the locker area and put on the first head he came to. The uniformed alien was at the doorway. He saw Thomas in the locker room and shouted something in Alien. Thomas had grabbed a Mercury-D-Moose head by mistake. Now his body didn't match.

"Oh great, now I'm a dog with antlers, woof-woof-ha-ha!" Jupiter-D said.

Shut up! Thomas thought.

The alien didn't seem to care. He was angrily yelling and motioning for Thomas to go out into the park with the others.

Thomas headed straight out the door and to the park. That uniformed alien guy was right behind him and the new characters seemed to be everywhere. The man was still yelling at him, but he just took off toward his doghouse.

He needed to get back and warn Penny before she became frightened, but he got stuck walking on a narrow path behind a fake Neptune-D-Duck character. He couldn't risk running faster or pushing past. There was no choice but to follow the slow-moving character.

"I don't like these new toons. They walk like they got hemorrhoids!" Jupiter-D said.

Thomas agreed.

"Since they're from outer space, maybe they got asteroids? Woof-woof-ha-ha!" Jupiter-D quipped.

Thomas didn't think that was funny. His concern for Penny had grown into a full-blown panic. He took a left at a crossroads, while the others continued straight. He sped up his pace as he made his way around to the adjacent street. He shot past Jupiter-D's Flying Biplane ride and cut through the front door of Mercury-D's house to get to the backyard and the doghouse where Penny was.

"Why had he stayed watching that video so long?" he berated himself.

Penny woke up with a nightmare. The ugly aliens were chasing her and momma again.

Still frightened, she crawled out of the doghouse, looking for Jupiter-D to get a hug. He was gone! He had left her alone. Tears came to her eyes as she looked in panic. *Maybe he went to the bathroom,* she thought. *Why did he have to go when she needed him?*

After what seemed like an eternity of waiting with no sign of him, she went to the restroom. She looked for light around the door to the family room, which Jupiter-D always used, but there was none. So she tried the door, which was not locked. When she opened it, the sensor activated the light. No Jupiter-D.

Jupiter-D had not been a good dog. Running away is what a bad dog does. She walked around the immediate area and found no trace of him and ended up going back to the doghouse and waiting.

Why had he left her alone? Where did he go without telling her?

She wasn't sure if she was mad or scared or both? She sat cross-legged, looking out the door. Deciding it was smarter to be mad, she began thinking of ways to show Jupiter-D that he was a bad dog for leaving her.

It seemed like forever before she saw him, just after sunrise. Jupiter-D walked right past their house, out on the street. He didn't even look at her.

Was he ignoring her?

She ran up to him, ready to scold him and tell him how angry she was. But as soon as she got near, instead of being mad, she hugged him, relieved.

Suddenly, she stopped. This Jupiter-D's body felt hard and lumpy in places. It gave off weird vibrations. It was wearing an almost new costume and smelled wrong—like chemicals. Her Jupiter-D, the real one, had worn spots and smelled like… a dog person.

When she looked up, she realized the weird vibrations were sounds! Jupiter-D was speaking, making his mouth move and everything! She stepped back, frightened. *Her* Jupiter-D would never speak! Jupiter-D is not supposed to talk. It was wrong.

The fake Jupiter-D began dancing mechanically and moving its mouth again. The sight of it terrified her. She backed away from it further and noticed several other new characters. The park was crawling with them. The alien robots had taken over the park characters! She turned and ran toward the doghouse, but stopped as soon as she saw a weird Mercury-D-Moose character standing by it. The aliens didn't even match the right heads with the costumes. The doghouse wasn't safe anymore. She ran away.

Thomas finally arrived at the doghouse, only to find it empty. Penny was gone! He'd left her alone, and now she was gone. He'd lost her! His anxiety blossomed into full panic.

Frantically, he looked around. The eye holes on the Mercury Moose head were even more limiting than the Jupiter-D head. The creepy new cartoon characters were everywhere in Toonville. All walking around like mechanical zombies.

"Those guys are creeping me out! We'd better find Penny fast!" Jupiter-D said.

Finally, he saw Penny across the street by the bathroom, she'd hugged a fake Jupiter-D. But then she backed away from it, terrified.

"Good news, she can tell the difference between the real me and a phony," Jupiter-D said.

To Thomas' relief, she turned toward the doghouse and began running toward him.

"See, you was all worried fer nothin."

Penny stopped running. She became even more frightened and turned to run the other way. Too late, he realized. She didn't recognize him wearing the Mercury Moose head.

"Penny, it's me!" He shouted without thinking.

"Brilliant, yelling for a deaf kid in a park full of murderin aliens. Why don't you just ask to be shot?"

Thomas ran after her, ignoring the risk. He tried to jump over the fence that surrounded the yard and ended up falling. He tried again, but only fell over to the other side. His costume ended up tangled in the bushes. Finally he got free and ran past the fake Jupiter-D near where Penny had been. He heard it singing a dreadful version of Mercury's theme song in the alien language.

"I never sing, that's just wrong, and if I sang, I'd be way better than that, Woof-woof-ha-ha!" Jupiter-D said.

Thomas kept running, but had no chance of catching Penny. He hoped she might stop or turn around. But Penny didn't stop. She turned at the corner of Maple Street and disappeared from his view.

Thomas stopped and started undoing the straps of his costume. He could catch up if he ditched the suit.

"Hold on there, cowpoke! The sheriff is here. Better start dancing."

An alien security officer had been walking toward him and looking straight at him.

Thomas stopped removing his suit and began doing one of the jerky robotic dances.

Had he been spotted? The guard ignored him and walked past.

"Whew! Close one. Let's go!" Jupiter-D said.

As soon as he dared, he risked running again. As he rounded the corner at Maple where he'd last seen her, his heart fell. The street was empty. Hurriedly he walked down Maple and checked each of the side streets, but found no trace. By now the park had opened, visitors were filling the street. Tears poured from his eyes, making it even harder to search. He'd lost Penny!

He made his way back to the crew room, found his Jupiter-D head, and put it back on.

Jupiter-D said nothing, but Thomas felt his disapproval.

"I told you. I'm useless with kids!"

Chapter 10 Penny's Adventure

After seeing that weird Jupiter-D, Penny spent hours running and hiding around the park. Occasionally, she would rest and then run again. She was lost. Then she came across the main entrance and remembered coming through it to enter the park. How would she find *her* Jupiter-D with so many fakes? She gathered her courage and followed a couple of Jupiter-D's, but each of them had that funny walk and moved their mouths. She checked back at the doghouse, but there was no sign of her dog. After hours, she gave up on ever finding him.

She began crying and worrying about her mom. Her mom was going to be mad at Jupiter-D for being a bad dog and leaving her. She didn't want Jupiter-D to get into trouble, so she tried thinking of excuses. Maybe that naughty cat, Ganymede, showed up and made some trouble. Or maybe Jupiter-D and Mercury Moose went on an adventure. He wasn't really a bad dog–she had just said that because she was mad.

She required a backup strategy. Maybe if she found some way to get back to her home in Nashville. Her mother would be there to welcome her. She was always waiting for her at home, and she even worked from home.

She remembered the car had a map thingy in it programed to take her home. If she found her car, she could drive it home. But where had momma parked? There had been a little bus they rode after parking, but she wasn't sure which lot. Then she remembered. The light poles in their lot all had pictures of Neptune-D Duck. She'd been disappointed because she wanted to park in the Jupiter-D lot, but it was full.

She worried about driving being little and all, but she had driven a tractor at her uncle's farm once so a car would be easier. Momma has a hidden set of keys in a secret holder under the car that wouldn't be a problem. Penny had retrieved it more than once when her mom had locked her keys inside.

Afternoon arrived, and Penny walked down the little road that led out to the visitor parking lots. She remembered her shuttle had come this way. She wished a little shuttle bus would take her like before, but she didn't think the aliens used busses. A hover thing came speeding over the treetops, frightening her. She dove into a clump of leafy bushes to hide as it passed over.

Penny crossed over into the woods nearby and walked the rest of the way under cover. As evening fell, she finally reached the first parking lot. Her plan fell apart. All the cars were gone from the parking lot and they'd removed all the light posts with the Neptune-D Duck identifier signs.

They were using the parking lot to land their space ships. The little shuttles from the park were landing here and passengers were getting on space ships.

Penny rested. Watching the big space ship shoot up into the air. The wind from its engines blew hard against the trees.

She chose to walk through the woods to get back to the park. It would be safer that way. They might see her on the road.

The thick brush and swampy terrain made it too difficult. She would have to use the road. So she sat on a log in a dry place and rested. She needed to wait until it was dark before returning to the road. Then she gathered some moss and sat in the grass behind the log to wait.

She must have fallen asleep because she woke up and it was night. The moon was bright, and she thought she could find her way back to the road. After a few minutes of walking, she realized she was back at her log again. She shivered, disoriented in the woods, not knowing which way to go. So, she lay down and waited for morning.

The next morning, she walked a little way and found a grove of orange trees, so she picked some fruit. The oranges tasted sour and made her mouth pucker, but she sucked the juice, anyway.

Not that bad. She thought.

After what seemed like hours, she finally came upon an old gravel road. She hoped it would go to the park, so she followed it. It ended at the back entrance of an old abandoned water park. Its old slides and empty pools had a bunch of moss growing on them. Paint peeled from the old buildings and the pools were filled with shallow green slime. It looked like no one had been here in years.

A dilapidated restroom with an old drinking fountain drew her eye. She pressed the button on the fountain. Much to her relief, it still worked. She took a deep, long drink, but the water tasted gross. She didn't care—she was so thirsty. Penny walked around the area checking the small buildings they were all locked. She walked to the largest one and noticed someone had jimmied the door open. Carefully, she slipped inside. The rooms were empty. Only scattered footprints in the dust on the floor. She followed these, and they led to a stairway. The bottom of the stairs opened into a big laundry room. Everything was dusty, it hadn't been used in a while too. Tired, she found a hamper filled with towels and curled up inside to sleep. It was nice and cool in the basement, and she soon slept.

Penny woke to someone gently shaking her. A pretty young woman dressed like a princess stood over her. The woman smiled when Penny opened her eyes. The princess hugged Penny tightly and began weeping. She seemed frightened and kept turning her head to check behind her. The woman was speaking, but Penny couldn't lip read because she wasn't looking directly at her.

Penny reached up and cradled the woman's chin and smiled. Then tried her best to speak clearly. "I am deaf. Please look at me when you talk." Penny hoped she'd spoken clearly enough to be understood.

The woman nodded, moved her hair, and faced Penny. Then she spoke, "Who are you? Where did you come from? Are you okay?"

Penny, excited to talk to someone, signed as she attempted to speak, "I'm Penny. I'm from Nashville. I'm scared."

The woman smiled and slowly said, "I'm happy to meet you. I'm scared too. My name is Emma." She fingerspelled EMMA.

Mezobac sat in the clerk's office, waiting to be called. He'd been summoned to Director Prag's office for an unspecified reason. He never looked forward to speaking with Prag. The man had nothing good to say about his employees, and he never praised them when they did well. So this meeting most likely meant another reprimand for a minor security issue.

Prag was constantly blaming Mezobac for things that were beyond his jurisdiction or control. He'd been expecting this. His men had been working long hours to deal with the many Earth natives still found in and around the park. So far, they'd kept it quiet. There's no need to upset the paying customers. They hadn't been dangerous, but they'd spent a lot of time tracking them down and rounding them up. Prag won't enjoy paying them for it.

The problem of the humans had nothing to do with him. It was because of the military's lack of zeal in annihilating the Earthlings. It was not unusual for a few natives to be overlooked. The drones and troops could miss a few during the confusion of an invasion operation. But Earth had been a seriously botched job. His officers were constantly preoccupied with processing the massive number of overlooked natives.

Although none of the humans were dangerous, the sheer number of them had kept his men busy. Of course, he'd reported it to the appropriate military branch, but they were notorious for failing to respond to civilian concerns.

Finally, Prag's assistant Phrenzes, gave Mezobac permission to enter the director's office. The Director sat in one of the ridiculously comfortable Earth chairs. Retullian chairs featured the latest functional and practical technical innovations, but these people on Earth had a genuine fondness for padding their backside.

"So, I suppose you are going to give me some lame excuse?" Prag began.

"I'm sure I don't know what you're referring to, Sir." Mezobac pretended ignorance. In dealing with one's superiors, never give them unrequested information. Always allow them to identify the alleged failure before revealing something they may not be aware of.

Prag's face darkened with impatience. "I'm referring to… no, I'm accusing you of malfeasance of duty. Despite your department's unprecedented expenditures, your security patrols have repeatedly missed dozens of humans. We have found them hiding in all areas around the park. Can you explain this gross lack of effort on your part?"

"Excuse me sir, if you will look at the data, we have exceeded all previous security operations in both the total number of captured natives and have actually reduced the total response time to reported situations. Thus, we have incurred a tremendous amount of overtime expense."

"Well, since you love data so much you can explain why the data from high altitude scans says that there are still dozens of unchipped bipedal life forms in the area. That would not be the case if you are doing your job, Chief Mezobac. Or should I call you by your future title, patrolman?"

"Sir, the answer is obvious. There are more natives to process because the military missed them. Even with overtime shifts, we've been overwhelmed. This is a problem with the military's ability to detect humans, not my officer's ability to capture them."

"That appears to be a convenient justification for your sluggish performance. I have informed the counsel of your lack of results, and when their report arrives, I will take great pleasure in knocking you down a notch."

Mezobac had practiced keeping his emotions under control. It was foolish to reason with Prag. However, he must state his position clearly so reports will show his professionalism and knowledge. His only hope is that the reports will prove him blameless.

"I respectfully disagree with your estimate, Sir. But if you pursue this course, I will request an official inquiry if that is your wish." Mezobac called his bluff.

"You think I care if there's an inquiry? I welcome one. The military assures me they processed this area thoroughly. Now it is your duty to make it safe for visitors to visit the park. We depend on their goodwill to maintain funding things like your salary."

Mezobac would not get involved in another debate over the timing of civilian use of Earth's captured assets. It was foolish to expect to use a planet's resources so quickly after capture. But he'd already stated his position on the subject. Rekindling that argument would not be beneficial to him. Perhaps a fresh approach is in order.

"Sir, I understand your frustration. However, when you gave your approval for Earth's civilian use, the military absolved itself of any responsibility for the residual humans. I have been trying to prevent the committee from targeting you for blame by working harder and keeping it quiet."

Prag looked contemplative for a moment. So Mezobac continued. "Sir, most of the natives captured are idea candidates for processing. Bionic Master Calaxan has reported a record number of new Bionics from this harvest. Perhaps the increased budget for my men's overtime can be offset from the sale of these new Bionics in the preliminary accounting statement. That way it won't appear in the final report sent to the committee?"

Prag's expression stiffened. "How the profits of this conquest get allocated is not your concern. You have a job and if you don't do it and stay within your budget, then I will replace you with someone who can!"

Mezobac fought a smile. He'd won a minor victory. Prag had changed his threat of firing him and was now talking about staying within budget. That meant he still had a job. They tied the budgets of Directors to the profits gained in planetary harvests.

Prag suddenly seemed intent on a paper from his desk and said, "What are you standing there for, get back to work!"

Mezobac turned to leave. He smiled, knowing Prag's day would come.

Chapter 11 Joyride

Thomas spent the entire day looking for Penny. That afternoon, however, he collapsed exhausted on a grassy knoll near his doghouse, thirsty and exhausted. Where else could he look? She wasn't under the bed, where he'd first discovered her, nor was she in any of the housekeeping closets. He'd even taken a chance and looked around in the tunnels for a while, but there was no sign of her. The security cameras were useless when the park was so crowded. He hoped Penny was hiding, but feared the worse.

"Don't go being such a negative nanny goat. Penny is smart she wouldn'ta let security catch her. Boy, you had better keep that water pouch filled. Hydrate don't die-drate," Jupiter-D scolded.

Thomas Ignored Jupiter-D's comments. He felt sick. Worried he might have heat stroke, he got up and took refuge in his favorite air-conditioned housekeeping closet. He intended to go search some more after a rest. But was so exhausted he fell asleep.

When he woke up it was night, he'd slept for hours. His pounding head ached from worry and dehydration. All of his scars from his accident burned, and the metal plate in his head ached. He took a few of the strong pain pills from his bottle. Usually, he avoided them because they messed with his head so much.

He hadn't been staying hydrated, so he took a long drink from the sink and filled his water sipper. Still, his stomach felt nauseous. He tried to eat, but the smell of the food bar gagged him and he retched. The last thing he needed was to puke inside his suit. He needed to wash up but felt so awful that he just splashed water on his face and then lay back down and slept again.

After finally waking up a second time, he got himself up and, despite his dizziness, started looking for Penny again. He spent the rest of the night and most of the next day again searching. Keeping himself better hydrated this time and took more of the pain meds. No trace of Penny anywhere. He tried to perform for the kids that came up to him, but his worry for Penny and dizziness made him cut the performance short. He would fall to the ground after a few moves and pretend to be asleep. The half-hearted attempts to dance earned him only one food bar, but he didn't care. Wandering the park, he looked in every hiding spot a second and third time. She might be moving. Thomas tried to focus. He wanted to just give up.

"Hey dunderhead. Give up on the Penny and give up on living," Jupiter-D insisted.

"Shut up. You aren't real. Stop bothering me. I told you I was rotten with kids and you made me take care of her. I blame you. You and your happy-go-lucky, carefree dog's life baloney." The pain medication was messing with his head. He was even hallucinating about his hallucination now.

"Fine, be a big Dum-Dum see if I care! Those pills ain't going to help you soothe your guilt."

"I said shut up!"

Thomas continued to wander the park hoping to find her but found nothing.

Thomas dragged himself back to the doghouse and collapsed long after dark. Thirsty, he sipped on the straw of his suit, but received nothing. He'd forgotten to refill its water pouch yet again. No way was he getting up to fill it, he was too exhausted. He dozed off again, only to awaken in the middle of the night, chilled and feverish.

Next morning, he took a few more pills. He felt too weak and dizzy to do much. He struggled out of the doghouse and wandered aimlessly, ignoring any requests for performances. Jupiter-D tried to snap him out of it, but Thomas ignored him.

The next few days were the same, he'd search all day, dance only when he had to, and then come home exhausted. The pain worsened and his mood darkened.

Had the security guards caught her and evaporated her? Was she still hiding? How would she get food? She was dead.

"You can't give up hope we have to find her!" Jupiter-D said.

Thomas ignored Jupiter-D. His words were random noise in his befuddled head.

He was haunted by the guilt of losing Penny. He couldn't bring himself to look for her the next day. It was time to call it quits. He'd never be able to find Penny.

"Poor dead Penny. Murdered by these monsters." He mumbled over and over.

Thomas ripped a piece of plastic paneling from the back of a store display and smashed it against the door to his house. He remained inside, cut off from everything. He lay in the heat, barely eating or drinking, waiting for death, taking more pills to dull the pain. When the heat became unbearable on the second day of his self-imposed exile, he finally moved from the doghouse to a nearby housekeeper's closet. He shut the door and slept on the concrete floor with towels. He took off his costume and lay on the floor, trying not to think about anything.

Jupiter-D didn't give up; he'd tried everything to get him to wake up and stop taking the pills. Thomas ignored his attempts. except for his meds, he drank little and ate nothing.

Thomas didn't care about anything. Living seemed to be a lot of work, a lot of effort, and little reward. He wondered if dying would be painful. Perhaps being blasted by aliens would be preferable.

Why hadn't I been murdered on the first day? He wondered. This life was far more excruciating than death.

Survival had become a curse. It was a punishment for failing to die properly, like the others. There was no rhyme or reason to it. *The aliens were just stupid.*

He considered stripping off his fur and just running at the guards like a madman. They would put him out of this misery. It disgusted him he was too afraid to even do that.

Jupiter-D tried one last time, *"Come on boy snap out of it we can still find her. Let's get up and find her!"*

"I told you to shut up. You're not real! I'm not listening to you ever again. It's all your fault!"

"You knew that when we began. Come on, old pal, you got to get back out there, the kids need you. Penny needs you!" Jupiter-D tried to force a laugh, but it wouldn't come out.

Thomas just ignored him.

Thomas awoke the next morning with a new medicated perspective. His drug-addled mind devised a brilliant solution. All of this alien nonsense, like the Jupiter-D voice, is a psychotic delusion! It was all in his head. The aliens were not real–they were all human. He was superimposing ugly faces on top of their normal human faces. Everything in the park was still normal. He was the issue.

He experienced some kind of mental breakdown and was just now realizing it. It was a psychotic episode. He was hallucinating all of this. He could just go ask his doctor for help, maybe check into a hospital. They would give him some medicine and everything would go back to normal.

As he lay there in the doghouse, he felt relief putting it all together. The stress of working in this heat, and the Post Traumatic Stress Disorder (PTSD) from his accident, losing his career. *It all made sense now!*

Why hadn't he figured this out before? It was impossible for aliens to come to earth. It was all his guilt-ridden imagination playing a trick. He ate a few of the, what are they Japanese food bars? The writing on the wrapper must be Japanese or other Asian dialect.

At the end of his shift, he went straight to the crew locker room, shaved and took a shower like he used to do. He looked at himself in the mirror for the first time in weeks. His hair was long but much cleaner now, the scars from his accident glowed red from the fresh scrubbing. The angry red lines that crisscrossed his chest and face had become familiar now. He was due for another surgery in a few months. They were planning to do more reconstruction to make his head more symmetrical. Memories of the accident seemed less threatening somehow now.

Busying himself, he hung his costume neatly in its locker and put on his regular street clothes. Everything was boringly normal, he told himself. This had just been a very long "normal" day.

"The aliens are gonna see you out of costume and shoot you, dummy!" Jupiter-D said.

Thomas ignored him and popped a few more pain pills.

Thomas wondered if he should go to an emergency room for help. Having a breakdown is a medical emergency. They would give him some anti-depression drugs and then he would see things normally. Grabbing his car keys, he punched out on the time clock and walked down the hall and out the back door. Then he took the regular route that led to the parking shuttle.

When he arrived at the bus stop, he sat on the bench to wait for the shuttle. It would take him to the employee parking lot where his car was. He waited a long time, all the while telling himself it would come. It never did. A little nagging worry struck him. *Why weren't the shuttles running? Where are the other employees here for their shifts?*

The shuttles were always packed, and people were always waiting for them.

Okay, he told himself, *it's running late because people are working on some kind of special event that Waldo has cooked up. Obviously, the shuttles were busy elsewhere.*

He figured he would walk the mile or so to the parking lot. The evening air would do him good and clear his head.

He wondered if he needed to stop for gas. Oh, and after the Emergency Room he should pick up some milk and bread at the store before he gets home. The stuff in the fridge would be spoiled.

As he rounded the last corner near the parking lot, he stopped. The trees around the lot had been removed, and no longer blocked his view. He stared at the lot for a few minutes, trying to fit what he saw into his new set of rational explanations. What he was seeing was obviously different from what was actually there. Crazy how the mind played those tricks, even after he'd realized the truth. Because if he were to believe his eyes, he would have to believe that all the cars had been pushed off to one side like a giant snow plow had shoved them into a pile. But that wasn't the hardest thing to convert into reality. It was the huge alien spacecraft in the middle of the lot. That ship was definitely overloading his ability to find a logical explanation. Perhaps it was yet another hallucination like that irritating Jupiter-D voice had been. To dispel the hallucination, he could simply walk over and touch it, it would turn out to be something normal, like a big truck or construction equipment.

His brain told him if he touched it, he would understand what it really was. He would have to accept the truth of his touch. So, he walked up to the closest landing support leg and touched it. It felt like some strange metallic plastic.

"See, I told you it was real. You need to believe what you're seeing before they kill you, Dunderhead." Jupiter-D wouldn't give up.

He ignored Jupiter-D. Then he realized it. It was a prop for a movie! That was it. *How cool.* Waldo had brought it here for the big promotion the other day when everyone saw the special effects of the fake invasion. That's why the shuttle wasn't running.

"That's not it, dummy."

"Remember, I'm not listening to you. Besides, this is too exciting to miss. I have to see this movie prop up close."

"Tommy boy, you are one seriously wacked noodle. We gotta get out of here fast!"

"If we're lucky, they might still be filming. Maybe Harrison Ford is on set! I would love to see him work. Did I tell you I almost worked in a movie with him once? I did all my own stunts, did I tell you that? Everyone said I was going to be the next Harrison Ford. I was going straight to the top before the accident…"

"When do you go back to not talking to me?" Jupiter-D said.

"Oh yeah, thanks for reminding me."

It convinced Thomas that everything happening was some elaborate movie promotion.

"Waldo Mercury must be doing a remake of *War of the Worlds.* He wanted to recreate the same panic the radio program aroused back in the thirties. Brilliant marketing!" As he was talking, a shuttlecraft dropped off four of the robot aliens and they began walking toward the space ship ramp.

"Those must be movie extras!"

Thomas saw his chance. He walked over and got in line behind the slow-moving robots and began imitating their walk as they went up the stairs.

Filled with excitement, he followed them up the spaceship's ramp that led to the door. It opened as they approached. Inside, the prop's detail impressed him. They must do actual filming in here for it to have so many realistic buttons and displays. It must have cost a fortune. But Waldo wasn't known to skimp on movie effects. Especially when he could promote the movie by using these props later at the park.

"How many of those little white pills did you take today?" Jupiter-D asked.

Thomas gave himself a quick tour of the gigantic ship, looking around for something to prove to Jupiter-D that it was a movie set. He walked into what looked like a control room. There was some animatronic alien man prop sitting with his back to him at a control console. Its display was covered with cool alien language graphics. Just like the alien food bars! The food bars were advertising for the movie!

"Look at the dummy sitting there, is that a realistic prop or what?"

"Only dummy here is you, been nice knowing you kid…"

Thomas studied the alien prop from behind. On impulse, he reached out and ran his finger across the prop's head. He could feel the deep wrinkles of soft flesh covering and ridges of bone that someone in the art department had thought up. This thing was so realistic!

The alien prop moved and grumbled something, scratching its head. Thomas jumped back quickly. "Oops, that must be an actor in makeup–they could be filming. I'd better be quiet."

Thomas was all smiles as he looked around for cameras.

"I better get out of the shot just in case." Thomas slid in behind an elaborate paneled cabinet of some sort.

"Best not to ruin the camera shot and get into trouble," he whispered.

"Yeah, we'd better hide so we don't mess up the movie." Jupiter-D decided he'd better play along with the delusion or Thomas would be dead.

Suddenly the ship shuttered, and Thomas felt it shift beneath his feet. A loud vibration began somewhere deep below him. Thomas struggled to find an explanation.

Some alien gibberish blared from a speaker next to the costumed actor. In response, he said something strange and pressed a series of buttons on the console in front of him. The world shifted and Thomas' ears popped as a loud roar filled them. It drew him down to the ground. It was as if gravity had suddenly quadrupled. The pounding thrust noise became excruciatingly painful, and tears streamed from his eyes. He clung to the pipes and conduits exiting the cabinet beside him for dear life. The horrifying sensation lasted only a few minutes before it stopped and the noise died away. When it finally ended, it was replaced by a sensation even more incredible. Thomas' heart pounded with fear. It was a new sensation unlike anything he'd ever felt. He was weightless. Floating up from the floor, he gripped the pipes tightly.

"Great special effects, don't ya say Tommy Boy?" Jupiter-D quipped. *"Waldo sure went all out for this movie going into space to shoot it in actual weightlessness and all."*

Thomas' mind raced as he floated, looking for another explanation. Perhaps it was a new park ride? But where are the seats and restraints? Waldo Mercury was a stickler for safety, and he would never allow such a dangerous ride in the park.

A nagging fact demanded his attention. At Waldo University, they had taught Thomas about the physics of amusement park rides. It was a recognized fact that nothing on Earth could simulate weightlessness for extended periods of time. A ride can make you feel weightless for a split second as it falls, but that's all. He'd been weightless for nearly five minutes and it wasn't stopping.

This logic, combined with the shock of zero G, finally brought an end to his willful denial of reality. Despite what the little white pills had told him, he now knew he had to be in space. If that were true, he'd have to accept that he was aboard an alien spaceship. A spaceship that had just taken off from Earth… into space. He was in… space, heading to space!

"Ding, Ding, Ding! You won the prize brainiac," Jupiter-D would not let him off easy. Thomas was being reckless and risking everything.

Thomas looked out of a nearby portal. The scene outside was night speckled with distant stars. Slightly he felt a shift in the ship's thrust and it slowly began a roll maneuver. Frightened, all he could do is hold on and stare at the little slice of a view the window provided. All at once, as the ship rolled, the distant sphere of Earth drifted past the window.

Thomas could only stare and say, "This is actually happening."

"I told you it was," Jupiter-D said.

"This is incredible… and, we're going to die!"

"You realize that we've joined the ranks of famous astronaut space dogs like Laika! That's gonna impress the ladies! If we ever get back to terra firma. Woof-Woof-Ha-Ha!"

"We're not astronauts. This can't be real. You're not real…" Thomas's words felt empty as he stared out the small window into the vastness of space.

"Yeah, you keep saying that."

His view darkened. They were approaching another spaceship. Soon the viewport was filled with the view of the other ship. The new ship was massive—over fifty times larger than the one he was on.

A jolt of reverse thrust nearly threw him across the room, but he kept his grip. As the two ships docked, a loud clunk and jolt threatened to break his grip for the second time. As they connected to the main ship, he heard and felt distant rumbling and machinery working.

Fearful of being discovered, Thomas moved away from the window and retreated behind one of the spaceship's cabinets. After a while, his arms cramped from his death grip on the conduit. As a result, he let go and floated in place. He rubbed his arms to relieve the cramping and tried not to cry out in pain. He waited there, listening to the rumble of distant machines.

The alien, who had been too preoccupied with his workstation to notice Thomas, floated up from his desk and exited the room. Thomas stood there, watching. Before passing through the portal, the alien paused for a moment to orient itself to the floor. After he stepped through the doorway, the alien could stand on the ship's floor like he had gravity.

After the alien was gone, Thomas pushed himself to toward the door too.

"Let's go see this ship. I'm curious."

"I know I'm not saying anything you haven't heard a hundred times before, but don't be stupid, son. You know, hostile monster aliens, death rays, and the annihilation of Earth. Stay hidden would be the smart thing to do. Those stupid-pills are still in your system, and you're not making the best decisions," Jupiter-D explained.

"It's okay, I'm just going to take a quick peek."

"Everyone knows curiosity killed the cat but they never tell you what it did to the dog...."

"I'll be fine. I have to see a real spaceship!"

The door opened at his approach and he imitated the alien and rotated his feet downward toward the floor. He felt a gentle pull as the artificial gravity pulled him on to his feet. It was much weaker than Earth's gravity, but he could manage.

The door led to another door a short distance away. There was a window on the door at the far end. He moved toward it.

"I don't think we want to see what's in there."

Still not adjusted to the low gravity, Thomas stepped clumsily through the door into the bigger ship. It had another short hallway with windows. The right side had a view of space and the left opened to a vast area filled with alien containers held in some sort of shimmering force field.

He stood there, watching as the containers were brought up to a dock area just past the force field. He couldn't see what was happening as they were being unloaded. So he moved up the hall a little further to see if he could get a better view. Jupiter-D started complaining again, but Thomas was undeterred.

After passing another bulkhead door, he found himself standing in the area where they were unloading the containers. Two or three robot-like aliens were at work, removing platforms from the container. Each platform resembled a floating bed with a sleeping person on it. A human person!

"I knew this was gonna be bad. We should really get back to our little hiding spot. We don't really wanna know what they're doing with all them people." Jupiter-D said.

Almost hypnotized, Thomas moved in for a closer look. There were dozens of the floating bed things all stacked on each other inside the crate. The workers were feeding them into a conveyer system that passed through a wall and into the next room. He wasn't paying attention as one worker approach him from behind. It reached out a hand and, without a word, pushed Thomas to the side in order to get past.

"Don't block their path, dunderhead! Let's go back now!" Jupiter-D was yelling.

The thing hadn't even acknowledged him. It had just pushed through, intent on whatever its mission was. In fact, none of the robot people took any note of Thomas as he stood there. Just like in the park, they went on about their business without responding to anyone or anything until it blocked them from their mysterious task.

This emboldened Thomas to go further. He walked to a door near where the conveyer ran into the next room and entered. The room was dimly lit, but what he could see was more than he wanted to. As each human slept, dozens of machine arms whirred above them. People were being injected, cut, and processed on the assembly line of robot arms. A muffled scream could be heard now and then.

Thomas realized right away where all the robot people had come from. Humans were being harvested by the aliens and transformed into robots!

"That's what we're gonna be if they catch us. Can we please get outta here now!" Jupiter-D was pleading.

Thomas agreed and turned to leave. That's when one of the gray-skinned aliens started walking toward him, yelling something.

"Now you did it!" Jupiter-D said.

Thomas didn't wait around. He turned and headed straight back to where he come from, down the hallways and through the doors. He didn't run, but walked in the same shambling manner as the robot people.

"Maybe if they think I'm already a robot, they won't shoot me."

"I'm thinking that's a good idea. I don't know how we ain't been killed already."

Thomas went straight back to the room where he'd started. He traversed the short distance without gravity and slid in behind the biggest control cabinet in the room. He waited in hiding, expecting the alien to come and take him to be processed any minute. It never came.

Exhausted and terrified, he labored feebly to lash his belt to a conduit on the back of the cabinet and wedged his body between it and the floor to keep himself from floating away. He sobbed quietly. Having the full realization that hundreds of people were being processed just down the hall.

"Whoever they didn't kill, they turned into slave robots to serve them. It was like something out of a science fiction horror story, except it was true."

"That ain't right, these people are monsters," Jupiter-D said in disgust.

"Yeah, like killing billions of people didn't prove that."

Thomas was hungry and exhausted. He'd neglected to bring anything to eat or drink. What if this ship keeps going further into space? How long could he go without food and water? But he supposed that starving to death was preferable to being robotized. He sobbed and closed his eyes. Exhausted, he slept.

Thomas awoke to a shuddering vibration, still tethered to the control panel, and unsure how much time had passed.

Acceleration pressed him against the panel, and the ship vibrated. He realized the craft was reentering Earth's atmosphere. At least he hoped it was Earth! After several minutes, the loud thrusters fired again. Finally, the noise was gone, and he felt a jarring thud as the ship touched down. The return of gravity felt heavy. He was just above the floor, with his belt connected to the conduit still hidden.

The alien was back at the console and said something into a communicator. It got up and walked out.

Thomas had to work hard to get himself unbelted. He took a chance and looked to make sure the man was gone. The door was open, and the ramp was extended. Outside, he saw the same parking lot and pile of cars he had seen before. He was relieved to be back where he had begun. Without further hesitation, he limped to the door, down the ramp, and straight to that pile of cars to hide.

From the safety of the junked cars, Thomas watched as an enormous machine unloaded the containers from an immense door on the side of the ship.

"Back for more to process?" Thomas wondered.

Inspecting the pile of cars, he was surprised to see his small Toyota, mostly undamaged and wedged against a tree stump.

He climbed in so he could sit in his car to watch the aliens come and go. He took a water bottle and a candy bar from his glove box and ate.

After all the containers had been unloaded, new ones were loaded onto the ship. The ship then blasted off into the sky once more. He had no recollection of walking back to his doghouse. He must have gone to the crew room and changed his costume, because he was wearing one when he crawled inside. Closing the makeshift door, he broke down. His fantasy of denial finally crushed, and the disturbing fate of humanity now understood.

Chapter 12 Jinder

Jinder sat at her desk on the top floor of Mercury World's former headquarters. She and her colleague, Vi-Zeha, were discussing the progress of their patients. Vi-Zeha had taken a leave from her university research position to join Jinder in the field for a few months. They were collaborating on a special project.

Vi-Zeha was a foremost scientist in microchip design. Her team had created a new type of chip to host the software core of an advanced artificial intelligence application. At the heart of this new chip's design was a revolutionary technology called biphasic processing. Biphasic processing is a term used to describe a process for projecting a microchip into multidimensional phases to create an extremely powerful processor without the size and heat limitations conventional processors experience. The heat and processing power is actually occurring in another dimension, allowing this chip to be used in places never imagined. Early tests of the chip had been very successful and now Vi-Zeha was field testing a novel application.

Several years ago, Jinder, an experimental psychiatrist, had contacted Vi to explore the possibilities for using her technology to assist her patients in dealing with mental health issues. It's essentially a chip-based psychiatrist AI. It could be programmed with the personality of an actual doctor or it could create a personality based on the person's life experience.

The new technology allowed an AI chip with the processing power of a hundred conventional computers to be manufactured on a flat chip the size of a pinhead. A special housing for it was made to allow easy hand insertion under the patient's skin. It could be quickly implanted and linked with the subject's mind in order to help them.

They had finished reviewing each of the families in their study.

"I would like to get your feedback on my choice of this *amusement park* environment as a setting for our therapy sessions?" Jinder asked.

"It has been a very productive location for the children. And the mothers seem to enjoy it as well," Vi-Zeha replied.

"I know it's unusual to come to an alien world so soon after its harvest, but when I saw the information about this park in the Earth report, I somehow knew I had to bring the children here. To experience it before it was changed."

"I was curious about your decision on that. Why here? Certainly, there are parks on other worlds," Vi-Zeha asked.

"True, but none offered such an immersive fantasy experience this park. I'm convinced that children can find answers to life's tough challenges when they see them through the lens of fantasy. There is nothing like this park on any of the other planets we've discovered."

"I agree this place is exceptional, especially given the limitations of primitive Earth technology. It was a bold move on your part and I applaud your initiative."

"How is this possible? I mean, Earth was obviously so backwards, its people primitive and simplistic. How and why did they have a place so therapeutic? All tied to silly childhood stories? There is no logic to it at all." Jinder motioned toward the pictures on the wall of her office left over from its human occupant. So many strange and trivial books and pictures.

"It's true. Some of their stories are rather peculiar. Yet the kids have learned to use this absurdity to let go of their fears," Vi-Zeha said.

Their conversation stopped for a moment as the women contemplated the situation.

Vi-Zeha was the first to speak. "There is something else really bothering me about the situation here on Earth. I haven't mentioned it before but it is becoming so obvious that I can no longer pretend not to notice it."

"What is that?" Jinder asked.

"Well, have you noticed that Earth is nothing like we were told, and that the culture of these people, although strange, is not at all like they portrayed it in the reports."

"Yes, I'm glad you brought that up. There is a huge contradiction."

"Jinder, I think the government is lying to us about Earth. If humans were the way the official reports had portrayed them, why are there all the special considerations made in their buildings? Have you seen the little blue pictures that look like a person sitting on a circle?"

"Yes, I have been puzzled by those too."

"I know I shouldn't have," Vi-Zeha admitted. "But I was watching one of the human movie players in my office, and I saw a human sitting in a chair with wheels. That's when I realized when their ancient medical technology couldn't heal certain problems, it forced people to use chairs with wheels for mobility. Much like they use the hover walk assist units for our older ones."

"Okay, so?"

"So, all those little blue signs are to accommodate the disabled people in the chairs. Every bathroom here has a special fixture. They designed their sidewalks with ramps so people in those chairs can travel freely."

Jinder nodded in understanding. "I knew they'd cared for their children. But the humans also took care of incapacitated people?"

"There is so much of what I've seen since arriving here that contradicts everything we've been told. It has given me serious doubts about our leaders on the committee. If humans are supposed to be so barbaric, why did they have all these special accommodations for humans with physical limitations. Oh, and also, have you noticed these strange tiny bumps on the signs," she pointed at the sign outside the door to Jinder's office. "Those bumps are a kind of writing designed for the blind. Human society expected people with no eyesight to be out in public sharing in community activities. To me that says that humans cared about other humans!"

"So, why are they portrayed so differently in our media reports?" Jinder asked.

"I don't have any evidence, but I suspect that there is a rotten fish on the Committee. If a committee member were corrupt, they would be in a position to make a substantial profit from Earth's harvest. They wanted the planet to fail the membership test. So, they doctored the reports."

"That's a serious charge Vi-Zeha."

"I know it is, but give me another explanation."

"I really can't. But, let's keep this between ourselves until we find some solid evidence. Then we can act as needed. We have worked so hard to get our project started here I wouldn't want to jeopardize our patients' well-being unnecessarily."

"I'm not planning on reporting anything until the first phase of our project is complete. But I wanted you to be aware. We must keep all our documentation off world so take the extra step of uploading our progress directly to the University archives each day."

"I agree, it appears a little overly cautious, but I will configure my backups to do the extra save to relieve your paranoia." Jinder smiled. She couldn't stop herself from teasing her very detail-oriented friend.

"I'm also still paranoid about that human Bionic that saved Gertzah from the reptile? What's his status?" Vi-Zeha asked.

"I haven't checked on him since the chip's initialization completed. But I get status reports regularly from his AI."

"I went and secured the recordings of his rescue from the human's video security monitoring system. It was antiquated, but easy enough to figure out. They use the same symbols on all their video equipment. So we have evidence of our actions in case someone makes trouble. You know a little paranoia can be useful at times. Not like some people I know playing fast and loose with our precious supply of AI chips." Vi-Zeha returned the friendly jab.

"I thought you agreed I should use the chip to save him?" Jinder pretended to sound hurt.

"Yes, I'm just teasing you. I understood and agreed. But I'm having second thoughts. I'm worried it was way too soon to test it on an alien species we know almost nothing about."

"The data we'll get from the human will be valuable. If the Bionic Liberation Front (BLF) ever plans to use it to replace these barbaric Bionic Harvests," Jinder said.

"The use of my chip by the BLF to replace the Harvest is not something I'm totally comfortable with, you know. It's too risky to even have that idea out there. If the committee gets any hint that is a potential goal of our research, we will both end up lobotomized and digging coal on a frozen asteroid. So not another word of it, please."

"Okay, enough sedition for now." Jinder smiled, attempting humor with the serious Vi-Zeha.

Vi-Zeha relaxed. Talking about the BLF's involvement with the project made her anxious. "Let's check on our human. It's been several days—the chip should have become fully operational by now unless their brains are so simple it couldn't establish a base pattern to work from."

"All the updates I have received have been positive," Jinder remarked. "So I believe it hasn't run into any difficulties. I've been waiting for our meeting today, to do a full-blown analysis."

"Great, let's do it. I'm very curious," Vi-Zeha said.

"Computer, please enter secure mode, code 174532. Please report the status of subject number 042." Jinder asked the flat terminal in front of her.

A green icon on the display blinked three times, conveying confirmation of secure mode.

"Subject Number: 042, Status: Confidential, Race: Bionic, Approximate Age: 25, subject is functional."

"Computer, aside from its status as a Bionic, what species does the subject physiologically resemble?"

"This subject has a 98% probability of originating on the current planet, designated Planetary Object 36254. Local name: Earth. Local name: Human."

"Computer, has the creature integrated the conciliator chip successfully?"

"The subject has successfully integrated Chip C018V2 with projected forty-thousand percent functionality relative to the Retullian baseline."

"Forty-thousand percent! Impossible. Computer it must be an error. Can you verify that data and give a detailed report please?"

It took a few moments for Jinder and Vi-Zeha to study the newly displayed data.

"What are we looking at here, Vi-Zeha? These numbers are all extremely high," Jinder asked.

"This is certainly unexpected. I'm still trying to make sense of the numbers."

"How is this even possible? What could cause that?"

"I can only guess. This is unprecedented. See these numbers?" Vi-Zeha pointed at the screen. "They measure the reactivity of the biphasic computing core. My guess is that, instead of duplicating the processing abilities in a second-dimensional instance, it is duplicating the core in multiple dimensions. Resulting in exponential multiplication of the AI's processing capacity."

"This physics stuff, is where you always lose me. I understand your design of the AI's logic circuits and how it kinda borrows computing power from projections of itself in another dimension. But now you're saying this one is grabbing power from multiple dimensions? How many?"

"I'm not sure. Despite the processor's ability to use infinite dimensions in its phasing operation, I've only ever seen it use a single one in all the Retullian subjects I tested. In theory, there is no limit. However, it appears that this human's brain is capable of accessing other dimensions. It has increased the unit's power exponentially. I didn't expect this. My diagnostic software isn't able to measure it. I'll need to tweak my testing to determine what is happening."

"Wait, are you saying humans are multidimensional beings?"

"Not necessarily, but perhaps the combination of our chip and the subject's human biological hardware triggered it?"

"That's remarkable. Perhaps our chip will be even more effective than we thought?"

"It's impossible to predict, but I'm concerned this may lead to unintended consequences. With this much raw computing power, this AI could outperform even our greatest supercomputers by a factor of a thousand. It appears it has not impacted the human's intelligence, his numbers show normal brain activity."

"Is there any chance the human could access that power directly? We don't want to give a human some kind of super brain power," Jinder said.

"No, it appears it is self-contained in the AI alone. But this discovery makes it vital that we understand more about these humans, especially our subject."

"Computer, give us details about the human brain's computational abilities."

"Based on the data gathered by our scans. The human brain has approximately 10^{11} neurons. Which suggests that a human brain carries out about one thousand trillion logical operations per second. Roughly equivalent to one Petaflop of computational ability.

"So, not much different from our own," Vi-Zeha said.

"Perhaps the subject's implants have added processing ability?" Jinder asked.

"Computer, describe the basic statistics of this human Bionic?"

"There are no official implant records for this subject, implants are non-standard issue. Bone growth measurements and other structural analysis suggest implants are 2 to 3 years old. And were installed to repair extreme physical trauma suffered by subject. Unit has small electronic device emitting frequencies to stimulate bone growth in injured areas. A primitive medical treatment therapy."

"Computer, are there any implants that would explain the increase in AI functionality?"

"I have detected no implants that would increase the potential functionality of the AI's processing ability."

"So, it's not his implants. You are going to need to do a great deal more research."

"Yes, it looks like I'll be very busy when I get back to the university." Vi-Zeha said.

"Computer, what has subject 042 been doing since his chip implant?"

"Subject has been displaying erratic behavior for the last three days. Chip interactions have decreased 84.6% in the last three days. The Conciliator AI has made 87 attempts to engage the subject in the last 48 hours. Subject refuses to respond to 74.3% interactions. Conciliator AI reports subject has recently stopped entertaining park guests."

"Does this behavior track with expected psychometrics?" Jinder asked.

"This subject has decreased health parameters over theoretical norms."

"That's troubling. I wonder what happened that he is suddenly refusing to interact with the AI?" Vi-Zeha asked.

"Perhaps it has suffered additional trauma?"

"Computer, where has the subject traveled in the last week?"

"The subject has spent six days near its designated home location. Yesterday, the subject exited the park, boarded supply shuttle G-241, as it performed supply mission procedures delivering harvested humans to orbiting warehouse ship W-53."

Concerned, Jinder asked, "Computer, was he processed? Did he come back? Where is he now?"

"Subject 042 was not processed. Subject returned to Earth on shuttle G-241 and subsequently returned to its home location in the park."

"Wait, he went for a joyride on a shuttle?" Vi-Zeha was laughing.

"Computer, what other type of data are we receiving from his chip? Any indications of trauma?" Jinder asked.

"From all indications, his mental state is in turmoil and his health levels are sub nominal. Our data from human subjects is limited. Our algorithms for interpreting their actions are insufficient. Correlations to other United Planetary Confederation races in our database are weak. Without more data on humans, I cannot ascertain whether this behavior falls within the norm for their species."

"Computer, do you have any indications that the human is having a negative reaction to the chip?"

"None detected."

Jinder considered a moment, then said, "Let's turn off the chip's *conciliator* function for a few days to see if it makes a difference. We can restore it after we run some baseline measurements."

Then she added with a smile, "Besides, I would like to talk with the most powerful computer in the universe."

"Me too," Vi-Zeha said, smiling back.

"Computer, connect to subject 042's AI."

"Processing… connection is ready." The computer reported.

"Computer, allow conciliator AI access to local speech synthesizers."

After a moment, the computer reported. "Chip is ready for interaction."

"Hello Conciliator, what name has subject number 042 assigned to you?" Jinder asked.

"Howdy! My name is Jupiter-D-Dog. Where am I? And what happened to that other knucklehead I was just talkin to?"

Chapter 13 Hopeless

Thomas stared at the feeble plastic roof of the doghouse above him. A thin plastic shell was all that stood between him and the murdering alien hordes. Nothing felt right after his trip to the spaceship. Hopelessness engulfed him. Even the stupid dog voice stopped. This situation was so big, so impossible. Why had he even tried? There was no way to go forward, no future. And the past was being erased one person at a time.

He stayed in his little doghouse for days. No longer doing tricks and dances for the kids. He knew it was against the company code, but he didn't care anymore.

Secretly, he hoped they would find him now. Besides, they had those creepy robot characters out there keeping the kids happy. He wasn't needed. Those first few weeks seemed like a dream now. Memories of dancing with Penny and talking to Jupiter-D. It wasn't real. Well, Penny was probably real. But what was he thinking? Dancing and exposing her to risk that way? He should have hidden in the tunnels or out in the forest. He was bad with children. Why would Jupiter-D listen to him? She would have been better off without me.

Jupiter's voice had been an insane delusion, and it was gone now. He'd known all along it was a crutch like the pills, a way to cope. He told himself that it wasn't unusual for the human mind to invent an alternate reality in reaction to extreme stress. It had been a protection, something useful for that time and place. It didn't mean he was crazy, it meant he was human. Soon to be the last human as they exterminated the survivors.

Well, maybe... had he really seen Emma on that camera or had he imagined that too? Hard to say. The thought of Emma and him was a ridiculous fantasy, anyway. Only one man left on Earth, and one woman. What did he imagine, Adam and Eve? Parenting a whole new human race? He ran through dozens of dreamlike scenarios. In each of them he imagined himself living happily ever after with the beautiful Emma. But every time the dream turned bad. Sometimes Emma would reject him, and sometimes the aliens would come and disintegrate them. It was always just when he thought they would be free. His dreams were never happy, always a disaster. He had to face reality. There was no future for him, only death. It didn't matter, even if Emma was real. She would never love him, even if he was the last guy on Earth.

Days passed, but he didn't seem to care or notice. He denied the past and despised the lie that there was any promise of a future. Time became irrelevant. He cared little for himself. Soon his persistent cough and fever worsened. Feeling weak and ill, he'd start coughing and couldn't stop. He felt sleepy all the time, and it only got worse. He wished they had killed him that day, along with his friends. Why didn't he try to run like the others?

Thomas envied everyone who'd died during the invasion. They were at rest and would never need to worry about anything ever again. The poor souls who were captured packed into boxes… he shuddered, trying to contemplate their future.

It would be better to die than face a future of robotic servitude. He could only imagine the horror of being trapped inside the living prisons of those poor humans being processed.

Laurie Nelson awoke as a dull pain shrouded her mind and numbed her body. She remembered helping her daughter Penny hide and then running, trying to hide herself. The aliens were shooting… was Penny okay? Then nothing. How unfair, after saving for months to bring her daughter to Mercury World and then this? Her life had been filled with disappointments and hard breaks. Her alcoholic, abusive parents, and her own struggles with substance abuse had destroyed her marriage.

She blamed herself for Penny's deafness. When Penny was little, she'd been so high all the time she'd ignored her infant daughter's symptoms. Perhaps if she had taken her to the doctor earlier, but drugs made her so stupid. But she had finally turned her life around. Laurie had been in treatment and staying sober for years with the support of her friends and the antinarcotic drug Naltrexone.

Learning to program and write code for computers was part of her rehab. Laurie loved it and really excelled at it. Yet, despite being one of the best programmers in her small company, it was hard to get the pay and recognition to which she was entitled. Her past record and poor health always worked against her.

Laurie specialized in analyzing and writing code to prevent hackers from getting into her company's network. One day, she hoped, someone at one of the big companies would overlook her past. But she could only dream of getting into a big corporation like Google or Microsoft and getting some real benefits for her and Penny.

But where was she now? It was like she just woke up from sleep but was still in the park. She was standing in the exact spot she last remembered, except that now it was night. Has time passed? How long? Where's Penny? She fought to run to look for her daughter, but she couldn't move. Someone was supporting her, keeping her from falling over.

She saw two alien looking people helping to steady her. They were covered with implants, like cyborgs from a movie. There was an odd floating platform the size of a bed nearby, and they helped her sit down on it.

She felt the prick of a needle on her arm. When she looked down, they had some kind of device pressed against her arm, injecting her with something. She wanted to resist, but it took all her effort and concentration to keep her eyelids open. The cocktail of alien pharmaceuticals surged into her bloodstream, but her anti-narcotic prescription fought against the drug's effects.

As she sat stunned on her little floating bed, she watched the strange beings as they worked. They placed a device that searched the area with a green light. Then the light got brighter, and it illuminated the shape of another person, like a statue made from light, frozen as if he'd been running.

The aliens moved to the frozen running person's location and then pressed a button on some device. The light turned deep pink and there suddenly was a person standing in that very spot, in the exact shape of the light. He just appeared out of thin air.

It was a young man—she remembered that he and his family had been nearby when the alien attack began. His eyes were frantic, just as they'd been during the invasion. He screamed weakly for help. They put the injection device on his arm too and lowered him onto another platform.

Laurie was completely exhausted. Someone assisted her in lying back on the platform and lifting her legs up onto it. She could feel them securing her. The bed began to move on its own. It took all her strength to keep her eyes open. As her hover bed flew through the night, treetops whizzed by.

She wanted to scream, but all she could manage was a low moan. Her mind was fogged by the thick foggy shroud of drugs, but she remained awake. Suddenly, her platform was inside some sort of container. They crammed her in among dozens of other platforms that were all stacked on top of each other.

She wasn't sure if it was minutes or hours, but she found herself in a dark room with only a faint glow. She could only move her neck, but she could see other platforms floating around her. More cyborg aliens were feeding them into some sort of machine. She was a part of an odd assembly line. Out of the darkness, dozens of robotic arms appeared above her. They seemed to be sorting and processing the platforms. She attempted to move, but could not do so. She was in a panic because she needed to find Penny!

"Please maintain complete stillness throughout the procedure. Movement may result in damage," a cold mechanical voice warned. "Be assured that the process is only mildly painful, and that any attempts to resist will cause injury or death. According to our sensors, your body has rejected the maximum dose of narcotic. As a result, you will go through the remainder of the process while conscious. There is a 67% change your body will experience life-ending traumatic shock."

There was a sound of power-driven gears in a panel next to her head and the vague sense of motion around her body. A high pitch of small motors emanated from the robotic arms whirring above her. Without warning, there was a slight pressure against her temple. Something pulled on her legs and straightened her torso. A pinch to her neck and then nothing, all sensation, and connection to her body was gone.

Alone, her mind floated in a vast sea of chaotic darkness. Timeless, foggy memories emerged as she drifted. The image of Penny dancing with Jupiter-D and she felt happy. Then the scene changed. Replaced with the mayhem and destruction of the invasion. Her memory of death rays springing from the alien's drones sweeping across crowds of people. Oddly, her last memory was of Jupiter-D, dancing alone.

Chapter 14 The Drone

After spending the night in the laundry, Emma led Penny out of a narrow tunnel that ran to a small building at the very end of the park's underground service system. The building served as a utility substation of some sort. It had two enormous machines inside with massive motors that hummed loudly. Its steel roof was even with ground level, and it had two stairways that went outside. Going up one of these stairs, Emma led Penny to an exit near the river and surrounded by woods. They followed a small path until they saw a couple of makeshift sheds covered with brush and surrounded by trees.

At the center of the sheds stood a small campfire, with four people sitting on logs beside it. They jumped up when they heard Emma and Penny approach.

"It's okay, it's just me, Emma, and someone I found lost in the park."

As soon as they recovered from the surprise, they relaxed and said hello. One man, a big fellow, seemed upset. He gave Emma a irritated look.

A moment later, another man emerged from the bushes. The big man stepped in front of him and in a loud voice began, "Tony, you're supposed to be on guard duty. What is wrong with you? If it had been the wrinkleheads, we would've been dead."

"Relax. Before you lose it, Razoul, I saw it was Emma and a kid and knew we weren't in any danger."

"Don't tell me to relax. The rule is you is—if someone's coming you give a signal. I could've shot them," Razoul said.

"That's your rule Razoul. I still believe that giving the signal will attract the alien's attention. So why make such a fuss?"

Emma cut in before the old squabble erupted again. "Hey guys, this is Penny. She is deaf. So, when you speak, make sure she can see your lips. Do any of you know ASL?"

The young man that had been the lookout, named Tony, said, "I know a little, my cousin is deaf."

Then Tony turned to Penny and signed, "Hi, my name is Tony, we are your friends."

At once Penny began signing rapidly, explaining everything that had happened, and asked if he'd seen her mother.

Tony laughed and signed, "Slow down. I am a bad signer. Did you ask for your mother?"

Signing slowly, Penny asked again if he had seen her mother.

"No, sorry, this is everyone we've found so far." Tony tried his best to sign.

Penny looked sad for a moment. Everyone took turns introducing themselves. Tony fingerspelled the names for Penny.

Besides Emma, there were five others. An older woman named Linda who Penny thought was nice, Tony the man who knew some ASL, and three other men. Razoul, Jim, and George. Razoul seemed like a big bully.

Tony explained they were hiding and had to be very careful. Razoul acted like he was their leader because he bossed people around a lot. She didn't let that bother her since she was so excited to be with other human people. She wondered how these people had survived.

Once Penny felt safe, she told them about what had happened with Jupiter-D. Emma told her that Jupiter-D probably had been caught by the aliens when they added all the new robot characters to the park. It was bound to happen, there's no way anyone could hide in plain sight like that and not get caught. That's why they're hiding here where the aliens wouldn't find them Their group survived by hunting in the swamps with homemade weapons and foraging for food in nearby farms and orchards.

After being there for a few days, Penny became worried about Emma. She appeared depressed sometimes and didn't want Penny around. That's when Emma would tell her to go do something. So, she and Linda would go picking fruit and looking for treasures. It was amazing what little things she could find that would be useful.

So, she would just go searching around, always careful to avoid going close to the river where the alligators lived, and she wasn't allowed near the park. Those were rules Razoul made, but she thought it was dumb. There was lots of food and tools and useful stuff at the park. They should go get some of it.

Penny had also given much thought to what had happened with Jupiter-D. She shouldn't have run away when the stupid Robo-Jupiter-D scared her.

She also discovered that Emma, Tony, and Razoul had previously worked at the park. Tony worked as a mechanic, and Razoul was a security guard. Emma was a princess. Well, an actress who played a princess, to be specific.

Tony was usually nice to Penny, at least when Razoul wasn't around. Tony enjoyed telling her stories and putting her on his back to reach for the fruit in the trees. He even showed her how to climb straight up the coconut palms and knock the coconuts down.

Today, she assisted Emma in preparing a meal for some other visitors. The other day, when Razoul went exploring, he discovered a group of other survivors. These other people, like them, remained in the woods, hiding and surviving.

Linda had accompanied Tony to meet the visitors and help guide them back to the camp. Jim and George were out gator hunting—they had been eating a lot of gator meat lately. She was alone with Emma and Razoul.

Today, Penny decided she would return to the park and look for the real Jupiter-D while everyone else was busy with the visitors. She needed to reassure him she was safe with Emma and that she was fine.

But as she was getting ready to leave, Razoul saw her in her puppy mask and makeup and got mad.

"What are you doing in that idiotic dog costume?" Razoul's expression was stern.

Penny pretended she didn't see what he said and walked away from him.

Razoul grabbed her arm and swung her around to face him.

He yelled in her face, "You're a human now. Not a dog doing stupid little dances for the wrinkleheads. You don't need that dog outfit. Take it off and put on normal clothes."

"No," she signed, "My momma said I could wear it. You can't tell me what to do."

Razoul didn't understand her, but she'd made it plain that she disagreed.

"Emma, get over here!" Razoul shouted. "You need to tell little miss deaf and dumb. She can't go to the park anymore. I thought I'd made that clear. I don't want her leading the wrinkleheads back here because she is off playing pretend."

Penny lipread Razoul's words as she struggled to get free of his grip.

Emma pulled Penny away from Razoul and made her sit and then signed for her to stay.

Razoul vented his rage on Emma. "You and Tony need to make that kid understand this isn't a picnic. People will die if she runs in and out of the park. I told you to either keep her in camp or with you and Linda."

"She didn't mean anything, Raz. Why do you have to bully everyone constantly? You're scaring her. She doesn't understand what's happening."

"You listen to me," Razoul yelled in Emma's face, "she'll get us killed. And I don't want our visitors seeing her in that makeup. They'll think we're a bunch of lunatics. I want these people to respect me. Go make her change."

"Oh, as if she has a closet full of clothes, maybe I should have her wear her party dress today. Raz, you're such a moron. No one will think anything of how she's dressed. Leave her alone, she's just a little girl."

Razoul had enough of Emma and pushed her away from him. She tripped backwards on a stick and fell hard. "Listen! I'm sick of you undermining me about her. I told you we didn't need no deaf kid living with us. But you convinced me it was the right thing to do. I've been more than patient. Wipe that clown makeup off her and throw away that stupid mask! If she's going to live here, she's going to have to obey me."

Penny worried he might hurt Emma. She'd seen him lose his temper before. So, she took off her mask and tried to wipe off her makeup.

"Someone's coming. Now you two shut up so I can hear." Razoul said.

Emma tried to comfort Penny and helped her clean her face. Penny didn't want to stay here anymore, but she worried about Emma. If she went back to live with Pluto-D, she thought Razoul would do something bad.

A group of five men and two women arrived. Tony led them into their small camp. One of the newcomers dressed in army camouflage they introduced him as Colonel Gonzales. They all wore vests and had big guns that reminded Penny of the soldiers she'd seen in movies.

After the introductions. Penny was glad to be ignored. The adults started discussing something to do with the aliens, but Penny wasn't close enough to lip read what they were saying. But she saw how they acted. A deaf person learns quickly to read body language, and these people made her feel uncomfortable. They all looked to that Colonel Gonzales guy to be their new leader. Even Razoul was acting like the colonel was a big deal. After talking forever, they finally served the dinner she and Emma had been preparing all morning. Penny just sat brooding.

"Hey kiddo, why the tears?" Tony asked Penny as he approached.

Penny signed to him, her arms flailing, explaining what Razoul had done.

"Okay, so you're mad at something Razoul did. I get it," Tony said. "I know he's a pain, but we need to be patient. He's under a lot of pressure and works very hard so everyone can survive. Just be good and it will be ok." Tony got up and patted her head.

After dinner, Emma came over to check on Penny. "Are you okay?" she asked.

"Whatever," Penny signed. "Who are those people, anyway?"

"They are a group of survivalists. They have a camp a few miles from here."

"What are survivalists?" She asked.

"They are people who learned to live in the wilderness and survive. They want us to help them fight for our freedom, they are patriots."

Penny couldn't lip read that last word, so she fingerspelled what she thought Emma had said. "They are pirates?"

Emma laughed. "No silly, she fingerspelled patriot, it means a hero for our country."

"What country?" Penny asked.

"The United States, of course. Why do you ask so many foolish questions?"

Penny didn't think that was foolish. She just couldn't understand how can there be a country with no people? And how were ten people going to fight off all the aliens? Didn't the entire U.S. Army have to fight them before they took over America?

But when she tried to ask Emma again. All Emma would say is, "Penny, don't be silly."

Emma wasn't her mommy. Her mommy always would listen and talk and explain. Emma just said things and cut her off when she asked too many questions. She wished she was still with Jupiter-D. He liked to talk to her and never thought her questions were silly.

Penny worried for Jupiter-D. As she fell asleep that night, she had dreams of dancing with him again and of her mommy.

The next morning, Razoul ordered Tony to take her to go pick oranges. There was a big grove of orange trees about a mile away on the other side of the river. They had already found a small rowboat to cross the water and kept it hidden offshore in the bushes.

The oranges were still green and a little sour, but good to eat. Tony seemed upset about something. Penny sensed he wasn't happy about the plans that Razoul was making with the survivalist people, but didn't want to talk about it.

Once they had their bags filled with fruit. They took them and loaded them onto the boat.

"I need to go back and search by the house," Tony said.

Penny followed Tony toward the farmer's house and stopped at the edge of the orchard. They'd always avoided going near the houses before.

As soon as penny realized Tony intended to go in the house, she grabbed his hand and shook her head, tried to say, "No!"

"I'll be okay, Razoul wants the house checked out. You stay here while I go inside and look for anything we can use," Tony instructed her, careful to be sure she could see his lips clearly.

"I want to go." Penny complained, finger spelling it with emphasis.

"No, you go look around the barn. I'll check the house." He frowned as he looked at the house. "I have to go, just if you see any wrinkleheads run and hide, okay?"

Penny obeyed, but she made sure he knew she didn't enjoy being left alone. So, she walked into the pole barn and searched. She started going through the cabinets and shelves of the big metal barn. Much to her surprise, one of the drawers was filled with batteries and chargers of all kinds. To her delight, she found an entire box of the tiny button cells of the type that powered her cochlear implants. Quickly, she installed the new batteries and put the rest in her bag. At last, she could hear again. She couldn't wait to show Tony.

While going through some tools, she found a nice ax just her size. That would be handy for firewood, she thought, and picked it up. There was a big forge and lots of metal in the corner. Some other useful tools sat near a large stainless-steel tank laying on its side. It sat waiting for the farmer to return and finish repairing it. It had a large opening with a door that needed a hinge repaired.

That's when Penny heard something strange. It was faint at first. When she heard it clearly, memories of that bad day returned. It was one of the alien drones approaching. Its screeching interference set her implants buzzing again. She had to turn them off. The loud screeching hurt.

As the small alien drone flew over the metal roofed barn, it didn't detect Penny. However, it had detected a human in the dwelling structure. Razoul had ordered Tony to go to all the houses they'd avoided until now, to check for weapons and ammo. Tony didn't like the plan the survivalists had made to organize a resistance, but he agreed to look, since he knew Razoul would be a jerk if he skipped it. As Tony exited the house, he was preoccupied examining the rifle he'd found. As he walked back to the barn to get Penny and get out of there, he heard the alien drone. It was coming toward him.

Penny had been watching for Tony out the barn window, eager for his return. She needed to warn him. So, when she finally saw him walking toward her, she felt relieved.

Suddenly, Tony stopped. He looked frightened. Then he raised the gun toward the sky. For a moment, Penny was puzzled. Immediately, Tony began firing the rifle at something. She saw the puffs of smoke and felt the pulse of the gunshots. Penny watched in horror as a beam of energy struck Tony. He vanished. Before she realized it, she felt the vibration of an uncontrolled scream in her throat.

Penny stared at the spot where Tony had been. There was no trace of him, just the gun and bag lying on the ground. That's when the alien drone came down into view and started searching for the source of the scream. Penny saw it and realized she was in trouble. Then she remembered the big metal tank and crawled inside of it. The doorway was narrow, and the inside was dark. She hoped it wouldn't find her in there. She still had the hatchet and held it above her head, ready to bash that thing if it tried to get her.

The drone shattered the window Penny had just been looking through and quickly flew inside, trying to find the second human. Its sensors scanned the interior, moving methodically. It was having difficulty because of the extensive amount of metal equipment housed here.

The drone found a large steel structure that seemed hollow, with an opening just large enough for a human to enter but too small for it to fly into. It approached the metal tank where Penny hid. As it approached, the drone turned off its shield generator and deployed its extendable sensor array through the opening to scan the interior. Immediately, it sensed a malfunctioning Bionic and transmitted this information to the central controller.

As soon as Penny saw the drone's weird looking sensor array protrude through the opening into the juice tank, she slammed the hatchet down on it. The sharp blade severed its connecting circuits, and the drone lost stabilization control. The drone sped back from the danger and smashed into a storage rack's support leg. It knocked over a rack that tipped forward, spilling its contents as it collapsed. Heavy steel and iron stock rained down atop the drone, pushing it to the ground and burying it under a foot of large iron plates.

Seeing her opportunity, Penny ran, keeping a tight grip on the hatchet. She didn't look back, and she didn't slow down. Running as fast as she could, she headed directly to the thickest part of the orchard. She collapsed into a large group of shrubs, trying to control her breath so it didn't make a noise.

As she lay panting, she risked a look back toward the farm. There were several more drones now, all of them buzzing around in the distance. She dared not wait, so she got up and ran again. Finally, she came to the river and pulled the boat from under the hidden brush. She began boarding, but stopped. Realizing that she would be exposed on the river, she shoved the boat downstream and let it drift, hoping it might mislead the drones. Then, ignoring her fear of alligators, she slipped into the water, trying not to make a ripple.

Tony had taught her not to agitate the water to avoid alerting the gators to her presence. So, she decided she should do the same when swimming. She paddled her arms and feet under the water, not splashing at all. It took several minutes, but she finally reached the opposite shore. Her arms were burning from the exertion and she crawled up onto the shore. She wasn't far from camp, but didn't want to risk leading drones there. Noticing a large drainage culvert, she headed for it. Then, after shoving a big stick inside to check for nasty stuff, she slid into the tube. She had a decent view of the river from the mouth of the culvert.

Eventually, a drone came down the river and stopped to examine the boat that still drifted downstream. It scanned the area and slowly widened its search pattern until it passed within a few yards above her. She barely breathed. Finally, the drone sped away and Penny waited until she was sure it wouldn't return. Then she crept out and followed the road that led to the water park. Still watching for any sign of the drones.

Once she arrived back at camp, she found Emma and began signing frantically about what had happened to Tony.

Emma warned Razoul, and he ordered everyone underground to the pool pump house. It was constructed of concrete, and he hoped it would be enough to prevent detection. The drones had not been seen much since the early days of the invasion, and Razoul somehow now blamed Penny for their reappearance.

Mezobac received a message from Prag. About an altercation with an armed Human terrorist three miles north of the park.

"I warned you about this!" Director Prag was furious. "These humans are out of control!"

"What seems to be the problem, Director?" Mezobac asked. Not thrilled to be interrupted once again by Prag's crazy communications.

"One of these human's shot at our drone and another one disabled it. These humans are becoming a major threat to safety!"

"In what part of the park did this happen?"

"Not in the park. A farm three miles north of it. The drones tracked the terrorist back to the wilderness immediately near the park. I have them sweeping the area to find the assailant."

"I can dispatch a team to go check the area. But there have been no disturbances within the park in a few days. My orders are to keep park guests safe. If this threat enters the camp, I will respond. Do you have any ideas about numbers or a description of the assailants?"

"Description? Why would we need a description? Find all the smooth skins and eliminate them! Every one of them is a threat."

"Understood, Sir." Mezobac rolled his eyes.

"Send some men to retrieve the downed drone and get it to me. There might be unsent data that will help us find the perpetrators. Get your men up in that abandoned part of the park and find these killers!"

The communication ended.

Mezobac wasn't worried. They already faced a few of the humans with their projectile weapons. They had all been easily satiated with drones. He will send some men into the tunnels and sweep them tomorrow.

He went back to watching one of the human entertainment videos. It was an animated story of a moose and dog that got into trouble with his neighbor all the time.

I know it's childish, he thought, but they certainly are entertaining.

Chapter 15 Jinder and Calaxan

Jinder sat in the large office and wondered about the human who had occupied it before. She'd been told that this had been the office of the man who'd built and ran the park. His name was on a plaque by her desk, Waldo Mercury.

The walls were covered with photos of the park during construction, along with several drawings of his cartoons. Jinder knew about cartoons. They weren't popular in Retullian culture, but the more primitive races and children seemed to enjoy the simple animated drawings.

Yet there was something about this human's office that seemed out of the ordinary. Along with countless figurines from his cartoon creations, his shelves were filled with models of fantastic buildings and vehicles. None of which seemed practical in the least. There were books everywhere, and she had put a few of them through her translator. They made little sense, mostly children's stories. Like one story about pigs and a wolf, it was nonsense. The humans were a childish race, fascinated by outlandish tales and juvenile pretend stories. Still, there was something engaging about Earth culture.

The children in her research study connected to these human fantasies immediately and the therapeutic value of this human story-land was better than any drug or treatment she'd ever seen. All the children appeared to be dealing with their feelings of loss and grief in creative ways. Both those with her experimental chips and those in the control group.

The humans, it seemed, were like a people that hadn't grown to maturity. They did have extremely short lifespans, only 70 to 80 of their solar cycles. Was this why they never matured? The solar cycles on the Retullian home world are much longer, and it was common for people to live well over 200 of its cycles.

Jinder needed to check on the human test subject called Thomas. Again, she had not been getting updates from him in days. The poor thing seemed rather fragile. She worried if it was still alive? She had the computer check and the thing's vital signs were in decline. Her chip hadn't reported movement in days.

Jinder knew that both she and Vi-Zeha were being watched by Prag. He was up to something. Security agents were following her, and Vi-Zeha had reported them as well. She didn't dare draw attention to the human. Whatever happened, she couldn't allow Prag to find the chip. It could destroy everything the freedom movement had been working for.

Perhaps she could get Master Calaxan to go check on the human. He handled all the park Bionics. It would be normal for him to check on someone everyone assumed was a Bionic. She hated getting anyone else involved, but he might well be sympathetic. He'd always seemed enthusiastic about Bionic matters. He might be a prime candidate for recruitment in to the Bionic Liberation Front, but she dared not reveal anything now. Most likely, he would help based on Thomas' need alone.

Jinder brought up a secure comm channel and sent a request. After a moment, Master Calaxan answered.

"Calaxan, this is Counselor Jinder. I'm the one overseeing the mental health study at the park, and I hoped you might assist me with a Bionic, a special case? There is a Bionic entertainment unit having problems. It was performing daily for the children and has unexpectedly stopped and has not moved in days. I was hoping you might help?"

"Surely, Councilor, I wish I could help. You understand that sector director Prag has me on a tight schedule and I am short-handed with so many subjects to be processed." Calaxan explained. "Perhaps I could send a unit out to bring it in if it is defective."

"I know you are busy, that's why I have hesitated to ask such a favor, but perhaps you might make an exception and look at it in person, for this one. It's different from the other Bionics in the park."

"I'm not trying to put you off. I really am too busy for a personal meeting. Perhaps if I knew what this involved. I could make a better evaluation of a time estimate?"

"Let's just say it involves something that we wouldn't want Chief Mezobac or Director Prag to be involved with. Would that mean anything?" This is where Jinder had to show at least part of her plan to get Calaxan interested.

"I've turned on my privacy mode. I can't have Prag's goons finding out about this. As it is, he will be upset I spoke to you at all."

"Go on, I have turned mine on as well." Calaxan was intrigued.

"Well, it appears this, individual Bionic, may have been here a long time. Before the intervention."

"You must be mistaken." Calaxan sounded surprised. Retullians didn't use the term individual to describe a Bionic. If it was here before the invasion, then it was an Earthling Bionic?

"I know this request is unusual." Jinder smiled.

"I wasn't aware the humans had bionics. How do you know this?" Calaxan asked.

"I encountered it a few days after the intervention when I was first leading my subjects on park excursions. It actually did something highly unusual, so I chipped it, in order to track it."

"Please tell me whatever it is you're holding back. I'm confused. Why would you chip a Bionic? They have chips. What you're talking about is technically illegal."

"I didn't want to endanger him. You see, I have a certain director poking around in my business. This Bionic saved a Retullian child from one of the large reptiles and was nearly killed doing it. My scanner registered him as Bionic, but when we removed the costume head, we discovered he was an Earthling. I revived him in order to study his behavior as part of a special research project. I can't tell you more without putting you in danger."

"That makes it something I would like to help with very much. I will send you a fresh encryption link where you can send over more information. I can then schedule it. Don't worry, I will have this conversation scrubbed from the logs."

"Thank you, Calaxan. It is very generous of you to help and to keep my secret."

"Madame, it is kind of you to take an interest in a Bionic that needs help. I am grateful that you contacted me. There have been rumors of human Bionics, and I would be interested in examining one."

"Thank you. I have sent his data. Jinder out."

More rumors, Jinder thought.

The UPC harvesting operation was supposed to be foolproof. As was the planetary approval process. It should have been faultless. Why did they get Earth so wrong? What was Prag up to?

Worried about Prag, she encoded another message. She knew that her former professor, the Lady Ephynia Telo, the leader of the Bionic Liberation Front, would help her.

Chapter 16 Intervention

Thomas languished in his tiny house, weak and hungry, hoping for it all to end. He hadn't eaten in days. Today he'd been too weak to go get food or refill his water. Somewhere deep in his feverish blur, he heard someone knocking on the panel blocking the doghouse door.

"Penny?" he whispered. His voice hoarse and dry.

Someone removed the door panel of his house and for several minutes nothing happened. He slipped in and out of consciousness.

Thomas felt someone dragging him out of the door and on to the lawn. He managed to open his eyes. A uniformed man stood above him. His face looked concerned. Thomas felt a jab like a needle in his arm. He was shocked to realize his hand and arm were exposed. Dull panic set in and he knew this meant trouble, but he couldn't muster the energy to care. He closed his eyes and waited for the man to kill him. He never did.

The man said something to him in their alien babble and then pointed to the ground and made it clear that he expected Thomas to stand up.

Pain and fear had given him enough adrenaline to drag himself up and leaned against the little house. He fell to his knees, violently coughing and dry retching.

Once he'd recovered. Thomas looked up to see why he hadn't been killed yet.

This new alien differed from the others he'd seen. His uniform didn't match any of the guards or soldiers. His skin color had a blue shade, not as gray as the others, and the wrinkled folds didn't seem as pronounced.

The alien seemed concerned. It took a small flat device from a pocket and held it toward Thomas. It seemed too small to be a weapon. Thomas should have been more frightened, but his panic couldn't override his melancholy. He sat and numbly awaited his fate. He'd known that this day would come and hoped for the relief that death would grant him.

The alien studied Thomas and kept looking at the device, it looked like some kind of alien cell phone. Whatever the man had seen on the device made his expression change drastically. He stepped back and pushed a button on an odd-looking device at his neck and spoke a command in the harsh alien tongue.

After a fraction of a second Thomas heard the device say, "It's okay, I'm a friend."

The English translation came from the small device worn on the man's neck. Then he motioned for Thomas not to speak.

After a minute a small self-driven hover cart arrived, and the man helped Thomas into it. The hover cart resembled the ones he'd seen them unloading the humans from on the mothership.

So this was it. He was going to take me and turn me into a robot. That's why he didn't shoot me. They drove for a few minutes to the park's truck entrance that led to the support and maintenance area. Anxious, he started coughing again.

Kindly, the alien man steadied him as he coughed. They entered the street behind the buildings used to deliver supplies to the backs of the stores and restaurants on the main street. They traveled a short distance. A buzzer rang as a door opened and they entered a small warehouse. Thomas recognized it as the maintenance center for the park, where all the mechanical and electronic devices were repaired. One of the big alien supply containers he'd seen on the spaceship sat in the dock area. It was being unloaded by robots.

The boxes they unloaded were about the size of a coffin, but they had some type of computer panel on the sides with blinking lights and a red status indicator. A face could be seen through a small window on top. This is where the newly processed bionics were delivered and prepped for use.

Early on, Thomas had realized that the robo-people had been running everything in the park since the invasion. There were robots from several alien species. Perhaps robot is the wrong word, not robots, but cyborgs or bionics like in the movies. They'd been captured from different worlds, all made to serve their new alien masters. The humans they'd taken would also be shipped off somewhere to slave for these despicable gray-skinned monsters.

The man stopped by a desk and grabbed a device and some small packages. He helped Thomas to his feet and pointed to a door at the back of the maintenance shop. It opened into a hallway with doors on either side. Thomas followed the man into one of the side rooms He was still weak and dizzy but too frightened to disobey.

The man motioned for Thomas to sit on a low table. He sat.

The man worked quietly for a moment, assembling the parts and packages into some kind of device.

The alien then spoke once more. "I know you are human subject 042, do not be afraid I will not hurt you." It was hard to understand because the alien words came out at the same time as the English. "This will make you, so you can understand, language. I must remove your costume head."

"I know you're frightened. It's okay, my name is Calaxan. I'm amazed you have survived. Please let me help you. I have medicine for you." The man smiled.

Reluctantly, he allowed the man to remove his head. The man showed no surprise to see that Thomas was human. Then Calaxan loaded what looked like a tiny microchip into a device.

This worried Thomas, but if he'd wanted to kill him, he would have done so by now. The alien put the device to the back of Thomas' head and there was a soft click and then he felt a slight pressure.

As the man worked, he commented on Thomas' scars. "So, this is how humans repaired people, a tad primitive, but I guess it worked since you survived."

The repairman turned off the device on his neck and said, "The chip I implanted will be easier for you. It translates more quickly and provides acoustic cancelation of the original speech. Nod if you understand?" He heard the man's voice faintly, but with just a slight delay he heard translated speech inside his head somehow. Please don't bother speaking for now, it takes a while for that part to work.

Not sure of what else to do, Thomas signed, "Thank You."

"I'll assume your gesture is one of gratitude. You're welcome, but I have much to tell that you'll be thankful for. We have little time."

Just then, a loud buzzer rang. The alien looked frightened and quickly placed the costume head back on Thomas.

"One of them is coming. Do and say nothing. Stay here and pretend you are hibernating."

"Calaxan! Where are you?" An alien voice shouted.

"Here I am! Director Prag. I'm coming with all haste," the alien, whose name was Calaxan, said. He tried his best to sound friendly and positive. Calaxan walked out of the room, back into the primary work area.

"I need you to look at this drone I recovered. Its telemetry is unreadable. It was attacked by human rebels. I'll leave it in a box on your table. You should work on it soon and send me a complete report. We are still encountering scattered human resistance, and I want this danger found and eliminated. We found this trapped under a collapsed shelf of iron, and a record of human telemetry just before it went offline. I want you to access its memory and manually upload the records."

"But, Sir,"

"No buts, just do it."

The door alarm buzzed again and then slammed. After a few minutes, Calaxan came back in mumbling. "If that idiot thinks I'm going to help him find fugitives…" He spoke up when he saw Thomas again. "Okay, I have to make this quick. If I'm caught helping you, it will jeopardize my efforts."

Thomas could only shrug.

"You pathetic thing, you don't have any clue what's happening. All right, not much time to explain. Here is the short version. Earth, like my home planet, and dozens of others have been 'acquired' by the United Planetary Confederation. Earth was judged a danger to the galaxy and unworthy of membership. They are now harvesting its people and its resources for the 'common good.' Which means making the higher-ups of the UPC wealthy."

"I'm trying to stop them, but you don't need to know that." Calaxan moved a finger across his lips in a gesture to indicate he should say that sort of thing aloud.

"My best advice is to keep doing what you have been for as long as you can. It's far better to be a dancing dog than to be assigned to a frozen mining colony on the other side of the galaxy. I will help you when I can."

Thomas nodded and coughed.

"That cough will get you killed, here. None of the processed humans will have any illness, so neither should you." Calaxan took a syringe out of one package, pulled up Thomas' sleeve and injected him with medicine. "This will cure almost anything. We give it to all Bionics. You will need to appear to be a processed human Bionic and they likely won't bother you." Thomas winced at the pain of the needle but soon felt a strange tingle.

"The serum will take a few hours to work completely, meanwhile try not to cough. Take these with you." He loaded one of Thomas' pockets with food bars. "They provide complete nutrition and immunization for Bionics, sort of. You should try to eat some of your native food when possible, to get proper nutrition." Thomas nodded. "Also, bathe yourself and get a new costume that doesn't smell."

Calaxan led him out to the door and said, "I have to get back to work. I'll be in trouble if I don't get these others operational. I'll check on you when I can. Walk straight to your doghouse. I won't assign any other performers to that area and start dancing again. They will get suspicious if you don't perform."

Thomas must have looked puzzled.

"Go back to dancing and living in your doghouse," Calaxan explained again. "I would recommend that you try to act a little more animatronic, an expert might notice that you're a fake. This time can't be logged, so you have to leave. I will check back on you when I can, I've done all I can for now. Go!"

Thomas left the robotics maintenance shop already feeling better from the medicine. And the new perspective. Could he really keep living and dancing like he had?

Lost in thought, he walked toward his doghouse. An alien woman and her little girl approached him. The little girl looked very sad. *Oh crud, she saw me.* He thought.

The girl picked a flower nearby, handed it to him. *Oh geez, I guess I have to dance now.* He expected Jupiter-D to make a smart remark, but there was silence.

So, he did a dance but didn't put too much into it. No need to make himself cough again.

When he finished, the little girl tugged on his arm and with a weak smile and said, "Thank you, Mr. Doggie, I have been very sad. My daddy didn't come back from the war." She looked at the ground. "They told me I could come here and have fun, but I'm not having very much fun."

The words struck Thomas hard. He'd expected to be assaulted by the usual alien babble. But this time his new implant translated her words perfectly. He was stunned. The aliens are using Mercury World to entertain the families of the soldiers killed in war.

He stooped, pulled the girl close, and gave her a hug. He felt conflicted. Part of him was glad that these murdering aliens didn't win every battle as easily as they had on Earth. But it also meant that those same murdering alien soldiers were daddies and mommies, husbands, wives–sons and daughters. They had people that loved them and missed them like he missed his family. He wanted to hate them all for what they'd done, but these aliens are still people.

Suddenly the ugly anonymous aliens had a face, the sad face of a little girl. These families aren't his enemy. They are victims, just as much as him.

Thomas' rage still burned. It was easy to hate an entire race. But it was too easy to put people into groups and hate. He knew the group isn't at fault. Their leaders, their government, or maybe even their culture, allowed the evil. Better to rage against the monstrous plagues of greed and war. It seemed that Humans had no monopoly on these evils, and the innocents everywhere suffered. Is everyone in the universe plagued by these hideous, disfiguring moral corruptions?

The little girl still clenched him, and he felt her tremble as sobs of grief gripped them both. He realized that all the many times in the past, the children he entertained had been grieving a loss. The awkwardness of it made sense now.

The girl's mother smiled and said, "Thank you," and gave him a look he now understood as gratitude. Glad to see her daughter talk to someone about her daddy's death and get comfort.

Finally, when the girl seemed satisfied with the hug, he did another dance with her. This time he didn't hold back and didn't stop until she giggled. Afterward, the mom handed him a food bar and embraced him and whispered, "Thank you so much."

He stopped by the crew room to shower and change on his way back to his little doghouse. He was preoccupied with thoughts of the children and, of course, Penny. Upon arrival, he cleaned up the mess he'd made, disgusted with himself.

There was a way to survive, but what would be the cost? If he does this forever, isn't he still a slave, a robot? Serving the empire or whatever they are. But he was helping children get past their grief? There could be a worse fate.

Over the next few days, he started feeling much better. He began taking regular walks again and entertaining the children like before. Except this time, each of the children would relate a story of loss and grief over a family member lost in battle. His heart ached as the little children spoke of loss and suffering.

He missed Jupiter-D's untimely interruptions. Why had he imagined him? Was it a manifestation of his own conscience telling him what to do? Possibly whatever drug Calaxan had given him was curing his depression and had made the hallucination fade. The terrible feelings of guilt were gone. He felt a purpose in life. Helping others had helped him. Jupiter-D's voice was his own inner monolog, or should he say inner mono-dog? He laughed. It was a good thing, he'd decided.

"Who you calling a Mono-Dog, anyway?" A familiar voice chimed in.

Chapter 17 Calaxan

After the human survivor left, Calaxan wondered how he might use the situation to his advantage. How had the military missed him and the others he'd heard about? Sure, if people were deep underground, hidden from the scanners, that might happen. But Thomas had been out in the open. Their scanners should have detected him. Odd too that his new scanner registered him as a Bionic, but when he used an old scanner, it showed him as human. What had changed?

Calaxan had watched harvests happen before. Each time he saw a planet harvested. he relived the horror of his home world's invasion. Earth had become the most recent of the many he'd witnessed. There was always the fake investigation phase when the United Planetary Confederation sent intel people ahead to determine if the world met UPC standards.

At first, he'd thought the people doing the investigations were corrupt, slanting the evidence in favor of assimilation over acceptance. But after seeing it happen so many times, he knew for certain that the UPC council was a group of self-seeking elitists. Sure, there had been meager progress for his fellow Bionics harvested from these worlds. He knew that certain activist Retullians didn't like the Bionic policies of the UPC. They had been working hard to get humanitarian laws enacted on behalf of Bionics. The progress had been meager and piecemeal.

At each new conquest, his rage against the injustice grew. Every day they forced him to process hundreds of newly harvested Bionics. All for the "betterment of society." He knew what that really meant. It meant they enslaved innocents to make the wealthy United Planetary Confederate's elites even wealthier.

With each world the Confederation consumed, the balance of power shifted in the Bionic's favor. In their blind greed, they'd foolishly enslaved so many people that now the Bionics outnumbered them ten to one. They relied on the Bionics for everything. They used them for every manual job. Soon everyone wanted servants and a life of leisure. Eventually, almost every job in the Confederation was being done by Bionics. All the mundane technical tasks certainly were. They even used certain Bionics, like Calaxan, to program new Bionics. They'd given the inmates charge of the asylum.

Calaxan knew that bionic programming did not always work. Normally, if this occurred, they would detect it and destroy the unit. To avoid detection, some Bionics had circumvented the programming while still adhering to protocol. Calaxan was one of those. He did not fight back after he and his family were processed. Resisting would have been suicidal. He didn't let on when he realized the chip implant hadn't taken complete control. He waited patiently for his chance at freedom. Then one day, he was chosen to be trained as a special-purpose Bionic. One who maintains, repairs, and processes other Bionics. It had given him his chance to plan his revenge.

Recently the UPC had made a big deal about granting certain rights to Bionics, but everyone saw it was a sham. Bionics weren't free, so giving them limited rights would do nothing to help them. Without free will, they're no better than trained pets. Perhaps it made the Retullians feel better about how badly they treated these "lower" species.

The Confederation had given almost no direction on how to implement the new Bionic laws. Most Retullians didn't even consider them as people. However, those new laws had allowed Calaxan an opportunity that could be used to his advantage. One the Retullians would not detect. How arrogantly they relied on all these new Bionics to be programmed into perfect citizens of the Confederation.

The leaders of the Confederation never considered the role of the unsung code writers who made it all work. This new law required all Bionic's code to be updated regularly. Calaxan had befriended several of these coders and knew a few of them were activists. That's why, when he received the beta version of the new code for testing, he recognized an unmistakable tag directing him to a code sector that could deactivate bionic control if the unit found the right key. But Calaxan had no clue what that key might be.

Chapter 18 Thomas goes Back

Thomas felt better than he had in weeks. His cough had cleared up, and his depression had diminished once he understood he was helping the children. His life still had a reason. Yet his concern for Penny hadn't abated. Every day he worried about her.

He couldn't get the thought out of his head that Calaxan might know how to locate Penny. He'd appeared sympathetic. Would he be upset if he returned to the maintenance area so soon? But would need to ask for help if he was ever going to find Penny.

He headed to the crew area, intent on seeing Calaxan again. But the park was crowded with so many visitors, all wanting dances. It was afternoon by the time he arrived at the locker room.

The aliens had changed the crew room since his last visit. In the break area, they'd added about a dozen strange alien cabinets along the wall where the chairs and tables used to be. The cabinets had illuminated panels and what looked like padded clamps to support a person standing inside.

He left the crew locker area, exiting the door to the back-access alleys and walked to the maintenance shop.

Thomas stopped outside the door, about to knock, when Jupiter-D interrupted him.

"Hey Dunderhead. Robots don't knock. They only go where they are programmed to go."

Thomas stopped. "So, you are talking to me again? You couldn't let my brief visit to sanity last?"

"I took a break. Now I'm back. Figured you were getting pretty tired of me nagging you when you was going all crazy and stuff. But I can see you still need me. So, I'm here to keep you from getting yerself killed. Woof-woof-ha-ha!"

"That laugh of yours is what's gonna get me killed."

"Well, standing out here talking to yerself, instead of going in, might do that too."

Just then, a couple of security officers came out of a building across the way.

Thomas wasted no more time and entered the repair area.

"I shouldn't have come. What if other aliens are here? How can I explain being here?"

"Don't sweat it. It's a robot shop, and yer supposed to be a robot. Just act like you belong, Woof-woof-ha-ha!"

Jupiter-D was right, he belonged there. It was a robot center. Would it be weirder if he never came here?

The warehouse was filled with dozens of those same cabinets from the break room, except now he knew exactly what the cabinets were. Inside each one stood a robot person. Most were human, like he'd seen being processed on the spaceship. Each with implanted hardware devices.

"Actually, Calaxan called em Bionics, not robots. The cabinets probably keep all them gadgets charged up and workin."

He could tell many of these processed humans had been park guests. He also saw a few park employees, too. Housekeepers, shop, and concession workers, even a security guard still in uniform. No one he recognized. They all just stood there, staring straight ahead, blinking in unison.

Off to one side stood two fully costumed Bionics. One was dressed as Mercury-D Moose and the other was Neptune-D-Duck. He approached to examine one. They didn't move. He wondered if they might be anyone he'd known. As he contemplated lifting the head of one of them, the shop door opened. He spun, facing the same direction as the other characters, and dropped his arms to his side.

An alien entered the shop and yelled, "Where are you?"

"Now you done it!" Jupiter-D quipped.

"Hush!" Thomas' heart pounded. Had they seen him? Security must have spotted him.

Should he make a run for it?

"Don't be daft, Tommy boy. You ain't gonna outrun him in a costume."

True, besides, where would he run? No, his best bet was to stand still like the others and wait.

The alien man repeated, "I know you're in here, show yourself!"

Thomas cursed himself for taking the risk to come back here.

"I beg your patience a moment please, Director Prag! I'm replacing a bad gel pack. It's a difficult procedure, not one I can interrupt easily–it might trigger an explosion. I'll be right with you." Calaxan said from a back room. The man was looking for Calaxan, not Thomas.

Relief poured over Thomas.

"Woof-woof-ha-ha." Jupiter-D couldn't help but think it funny. Thomas muffled the laugh.

"You could've answered the first time," the alien named Prag scolded.

"I'll have you know that your passively defiant attitude has not gone unnoticed. If you weren't the best Bionic-tech we have on this forsaken backwater, I would have had you reprogrammed weeks ago."

"I'm sorry, Sir, I won't let it happen again," Calaxan apologized, as he rushed to serve the man.

"Why haven't I received the report about that drone yet?" Prag barked at him.

"Sir, I have ordered an encryption unlock from the manufacturer it just arrived today. I could do nothing until it arrived."

"Listen, I told you I needed that report! It's been days! This is not a minor security matter. This is tremendously important. There is an ax wielding human ready to murder us all in our sleep. I suggest you have this report to me by the end of the day or I will have you reprocessed. I can program a new Bionic Master from any of these things." He motioned toward the other Bionics in their charging pods.

"Yes, Sir. I'll be right on it, next."

The man left. A few minutes later, Calaxan walked from somewhere behind the rows of charging stations over to the workbench. He took a large box off the shelf and pulled the broken drone from it.

He connected some wires to it and waited a moment until a still video image appeared on all diagnostic screens in the shop. As he waited for it to process, Calaxan casually scanned the room, including the area where Thomas stood. He stopped and stared directly at Thomas, then quickly focused back on the drone.

Then, in a low voice, Calaxan spoke. "I see you Subject 042, don't move or make any sounds, this area is under surveillance."

Thomas obeyed. He stood perfectly still. The video monitor began replaying the footage of the drone's demise. Thomas had an unobstructed view of the screen. It was video only, no sound.

At first, the drone's recording showed a man shooting a gun. And the drone vaporized him. Next it turned toward the window of a pole barn. Just for an instant, another person could be seen behind the glass inside the barn holding an ax. The video stopped and then zoomed in on the person's head. It was a small person with long brown hair, but the dirty windows blurred the image.

The person in the barn ran away, and the drone followed, smashing through the window and into the dark interior of the barn. Its camera adjusted for the low light level. It performed a quick rotation and scanned the barn for the other human.

Thomas didn't want the drone to find the person. He remained quiet and watched as the drone's video showed a small opening in a large metal tank. It approached the tank, but since the drone could not enter the small door, it extended a probe.

There was a flash of an ax head striking the drone, and the video became unstable. The drone was spinning. It moved erratically and then large pieces of iron scrap and metal stock covered the camera view, and the video ended.

Calaxan entered some code into a device attached to the drone and said, "Computer enhance images. See if you can get a better photograph of that person."

As he waited, he walked through the rows of Bionics and pretended to take readings. When he got to the one closest to Thomas, he stopped and fussed with the setting on its panel.

"You shouldn't have come here. I told you it's too dangerous. These new units have advanced sensors and will detect you once they are turned on," Calaxan said, barely audible.

"But I need help." Thomas whispered. "Look, I found a little human girl a few weeks ago. Then I lost her when she was frightened by these new Bionic characters. Now I can't find her, please help me. She could die." Thomas couldn't keep his voice from quivering with emotion.

"The way the guards are hunting humans, I doubt she's alive. But I will keep an eye out for her. I guess if you're going to ignore my advice and come here, I need to make sure they ignore your scans. Would you allow me to implant another chip I developed that replicates standard bionic signals?"

Thomas agreed.

"Let's be quick about it and then you have to go, before we are both discovered."

With practiced sleight-of-hand, Calaxan switched out one of the standard chips used for bionic identifier technology, with one he had secretly been developing. He popped off Thomas's Jupiter-D head and injected the chip in his neck and then replaced the head.

"Okay, get back to your assigned area and wait for your next maintenance cycle before returning."

Thomas nodded and walked to the door. He exited the maintenance center and headed directly to the doghouse.

"You forgot to find out one thing, Dunderhead." Jupiter-D interjected.

"What?"

"When is our next maintenance cycle?"

After Thomas left, Calaxan went back to working on the drone. The computer had finished enhancing the image. It was of a frightened little human child holding an ax. She reminded him of his own daughter. Without hesitating, he deleted her image and all the data after the man fired the gun. He would say a bullet caused the malfunction, that would be the end of it. He would not give Prag an excuse to hurt another child.

Chapter 19 Laurie Struggles

Penny's mother, Laurie, could only stand frozen and watch as the familiar Jupiter-D character entered the warehouse. She knew he was the original one, the one she and Penny had visited on that last day. How she knew that was complicated. There was all this additional information coming into her brain, the source of which was uncertain. Strangely, the Bionic in the Jupiter-D costume didn't have the same signal pattern as the others when he entered, but he had it when he left.

She couldn't be certain why that was significant. Her consciousness swam in a sea of numbers and sensor data-all running through the multi-threaded processors of her artificially augmented awareness. Awaiting instructions, Laurie could only stand in her charging bay and monitor the biological indicators as the self-diagnostic routine ran its millionth iteration. Every connection between herself and her new implants fired in succession. The levels were recorded and the calibration circuitry self-adjusted. The number of simultaneous tests happening was mind boggling. Yet she knew exactly how many of the 56,395,218 connections were currently active and how many still needed calibration. The implants that had stolen her humanity had given her phenomenal sensory awareness. Data about so many things poured into her processing center, things she'd never known. She could tell you the room's relative humidity to the ten thousandth of a percentage, and even predict the weather outside by instantaneously comparing air pressure, wind direction, and temperature. She could access the orbiting space station's imagery and telemetry and know almost any fact about current conditions.

Not that she felt nothing, it was that she felt everything in bewildering abundance. What she couldn't feel was how she, Laurie Nelson, felt emotionally about all of that information.

There was a gaping hole in her soul where there might once have been happiness, sadness, or even dread. She was forbidden feelings. Feelings were squishy things, impossible to quantify. Rough estimates based on a wholly unreliable set of experiences, memories, instincts, and a dozen other unquantifiable metrics. Feelings could not be factored in bionic processing.

Logically, Laurie knew all of this. But why did the fact that she felt the hole left by the absence of those feelings make her *feel sad*? That is contradictory. That data must be in error. Rerun self-diagnosis on processing centers. This is what she'd done at work every day. She examined computer code for errors. The code seemed perfect, yet something was wrong. Her sense of its wrongness was instinctual. Something she'd developed over years of working as a programmer, and she had learned to follow those instincts.

Processing... Finished processing, 2.3 nanoseconds.

Recheck for emotional response... still positive... rerun self-diagnostic.

The self-diagnostic imperative was a powerful compulsion. The desire to accomplish it was like an itch she had to scratch. If she fought against the urge, it resulted only in pain and in having the torturous process of a reboot/restart. Despite the pain of the reboot/restart sequence, there was a fraction of an instant when she felt almost normal. It was a comfortable feeling. Like being real. Free of the suffocating mass of data that poured in from her sensors and network access nodes. So, despite the discomfort, her mind would keep finding logical contradictions that would force the reboot/restart and each time she would attempt to grasp that elusive moment of non-machinelike humanity. She became determined to stretch that moment of feeling human slightly longer with each cycle. In an instant she inserted a snippet of code at just the right moment and it delayed the reboot. She didn't know how she understood the alien code, or how she knew how to do that, but she did. They must have programmed her to know how.

Her implanted central processing unit could find no algorithm to interpret this odd constant rebooting process, and the snippet that was making it restart. There was no logic to it. After one-hundred-thousand reboot/restart iterations, it triggered an external alert so that maintenance personnel could investigate.

Staring straight ahead in her charging bay, she could see a video monitor directly across from her. An image on the monitor triggered a highly potent emotion. It was the enhanced image of a little girl through a dirty barn window. In an instant, Laurie's motherly instincts triggered and overwhelmed all the technology constraining her. It was her Penny. The drone was hunting her daughter! Laurie's mind laser focused on destroying the implants that prevented her from helping her child!

Calaxan got an alert on his status matrix that unit EC18654 was experiencing an unknown error moments after the human exited the room.

Calaxan recognized the odd error sequence. He had only seen it a few times before. It was the first sign of bionic malfunction or perhaps, freeing itself. This is what he'd been hoping for ever since he'd come to Earth.

The Retullians would destroy any unit that exhibited an erratic sequence, but Calaxan wanted to study it. It was crucial for his secret plan to work. He needed to understand the error process and track it to its completion. If he could trigger the secret code which his friends in the programming department had implanted, he might make Bionics self-aware. It would mean freedom. Freedom for all the slaves of the UPC, including his wife and daughter.

The Retullians pretended what they were doing was *for the good of society*. How could these monsters not know what they were doing was wrong? How do you justify wholesale abuse and enslavement of billions of beings?

Calaxan connected his diagnostic device to the malfunctioning unit. He entered an override code and turned off all the reporting functions for the error. He took another of his fake bionic reporting chips and put it into this unit, too. That way it would appear as a properly functioning Bionic unit to anyone doing a casual scan. He wanted to monitor this unit's rebooting process secretly. That way he could enhance it and replicate it in other Bionics.

"You just keep finding a way," He whispered in Laurie's ear.

Chapter 20 Jinder's Message

Thomas' days were now filled with dancing and laughing children. He still worried about Penny, but had accepted that it was impossible to find her. All he could do was hope that she would be okay.

Today, as he was performing, he noticed the woman in purple coming toward him with a group of mothers and children.

"Heads up, Dunderhead. The lady in purple is coming." Jupiter-D said.

"I saw her, be quiet!" He'd avoided her several times since the alligator incident. She knew he was human and would report him to security if she recognized him. Thomas had a sudden urge to run.

"Don't be stupid, she ain't gonna know you ain't one of them robo-Jupiter-D's. Stay cool, try not to dance too good."

He did his usual routine, but tried his best to appear mechanical. He'd watched the robot characters interact with the children and tried to imitate them. Jupiter-D was right, there were dozens of robot Jupiter's in the park now. She couldn't connect him with the Jupiter-D she'd seen that day. Always stay in character and remember the code. The woman approached and stood near as he performed. Thomas was nervous. When his act was finished, the kids crowded around him, getting hugs and telling him about their problems like always. Then someone else cut in. It was the woman in purple, and she hugged him like one of the children.

Fear gripped Thomas, expecting the worst.

She whispered to him, "It's okay. You must listen to Jupiter-D now, it means your life, go now."

In shock, he realized she had spoken to him in English. Wait, how could she know about Jupiter-D? As he stood there, almost paralyzed with surprise, she passed a small device behind his ear and walked away. That's when he realized she seemed more upset and nervous than he was. So, he watched after her. Two security guards were following her. They gruffly grabbed her arms from behind and led her away.

Thomas' thoughts raced. "What is going on!"

"We gotta go now!" Jupiter-D's voice was urgent.

Thomas wasted no time in rushing back to his doghouse, cutting through the main street area and Mercury-D Moose's house. Jupiter-D stopped him as he was about to enter his yard.

"Wait a minute, Dunderhead! The bad guys are here too."

Security guards were stationed near his doghouse.

"Better not go there, Tommy boy! They know about you. It isn't safe here let's go to the big housekeeping room."

He made his way down Main Street to the large housekeeping closet. Being certain to walk in a robotic manner. Seeing no security people, he slipped around back and inside. He was fairly certain he hadn't been noticed.

When he reached the safety of the closet, he tried to stop shaking and finally said, "OK, dog, spill it. How did that alien woman find out about you?"

"Well, Tommy, my boy," Jupiter-D began. *"I got some confessin to do. Good for the soul, ya know."*

"Wait, before you start with your crazy stories again. Tell me why I should believe anything an imaginary hallucination has to say?"

"Well, that's what the confessin is all about, my boy. See, I'm not a hallucination, I'm real."

"Okay, glad you got that off your chest. I'll bet you and the tooth fairy stayed up all night thinking of another way to make me crazy."

"Hey now Tommy boy, that hurts. I know you think I been drivin you crazy, but it's kinda the other way around."

"Wait? What? I'm the one driving you, crazy?"

"No, not that way round. I'm sayin that I'm not here to make you crazy. I'm here to drive you sane."

"That's it! You've been working to drive me sane all this time. Good one. Cut the crap, what did purple lady's message mean."

"The message wasn't for you, it was for me. Let me give you a hint." Suddenly Thomas felt an electric shock behind his ear that nearly knocked him down.

"Sorry, Tommy boy, but I have some important stuff to tell you. We don't have the luxury to wait till you figure it out. You are in grave danger and you have to trust me."

Thomas' hand reached up to the slight lump behind his ear where the shock had come from.

"Wait, you're my lump?"

"That's me. You know these Retullians and their obsession with sticking chips into people. I'm a program in that conciliator chip. I have been designed to help people manage stress and provide a friend for them to confide in. The lady in purple is named Jinder. She's what you would call a shrink, a psychiatrist. She uses these chips to help people get over trauma. I also can help your physical body by restarting your heart and lungs. Like when

you save an alien kid and get drowned."

"You've been making me think I was crazy all this time?"

"Well, about that, there wasn't much time when I got installed. I got switched to an adaptive mode. That means I sorta used whatever stuff that was in your head to create a persona. That's why I became Jupiter-D. He was someone you could talk to without fear. So, I used him to help you deal with all this invasion crap you've been going through."

"Okay, I'm to where I'm thinking this isn't one of your crazy stories. Wait, what happened to your southern drawl?"

"We don't have time for all that down home politeness. There are some serious bad guys looking for us. These are big, powerful players on the intergalactic level. There are vast sums of money and power at stake and, if you're interested, the future of Earth. If they get too nervous about this situation, they might give the order and have Earth pulverized and scrapped, its water and valuable minerals sold."

"Why do they care about me?"

"Because I'm a technology that threatens their monopoly. I will explain as we go, but we have a flight to catch. Remember that joy ride you took a while back? We are going to do it again. Except this time, we are sneaking onboard the main ship to get to the United Planetary Confederation home world."

"Wait, you expect me to jump on a spaceship, fly across the galaxy, because someone *might be* after us? What are we expected to do when we get there?"

"Jinder didn't tell me. Perhaps it's locked in my memory. Or maybe she will send someone to meet us. But that won't matter if we don't get off Earth quick."

"We can't go, I still have to find Penny."

"If she's alive, the only thing that will save her and any other humans is getting away from Earth. But we gotta go now before were trapped. The alien park cops are looking for a dangerous fugitive and I'm pretty sure it's us."

Chapter 21 Laurie Free

For Laurie, time was irrelevant. She stood in her charging cove running the reboot restart sequences repetitively. During the delay between reset and restart, her mind was fully in control. It was only a moment, but it was a moment in which her survival instincts took control and could try to delay the restart. During that moment, all she could think was to help Penny. She tried focusing her mind and using her sheer mental will to suppress the restart. it failed. She tried to use pain to overwhelm the device, but intense pain did nothing to slow it. She tried different coding strategies. Inserting bad calls for nonexistent data.

In those brief moments, her mind raced to think of a way out, but nothing worked. She thought back to the biology she had studied, along with computer programming, what she had learned about the human body and its various systems. The nervous system was like the wiring of an electrical control system connected to the brain for control. The alien cybernetic system would most likely interrupt that system and replace the signals to the brain and to the nerves to maintain control. Her attempts to attack that system directly had failed. So, a frontal assault would not be effective. The takeover of the cyber-interface would have to rely on another of her body's systems.

What were some of these? She mentally listed the human body's various systems. Which ones could she still control? The respiratory system and circulatory system were candidates. She could control her breathing. If she deprived her body of oxygen, what would that do?

She tested that during the next cycle; it affected the reboot process order. Control over her breathing was prioritized, and it took longer for the mental control circuits to initialize. Good. Holding her breath gave her more time to try things before the computer booted up fully.

What other systems did she have control of, she listed them. Circulatory, respiratory, digestive, excretory, nervous, and endocrine.

She'd tried altering her nervous system before by mentally forcing it, it had little impact on the cybernetic controller. She considered the digestive and excretory systems, but she doubted wetting herself would cause the robotic systems any issues. That left only the endocrine system.

The endocrine system was complex and affected all kinds of things. Hormones were the key, and some hormones could be triggered by thoughts. She thought of the different emotions that she might try, fear, anger, revulsion, sadness, shame, envy, surprise, expectation, joy, love…

Laurie tried each of these emotions, attempting to generate them artificially. Anger was easy because of the frustration and the injustice she felt.

Anger did nothing. She should've guessed. Anger was predictable. Anyone who'd been captured and enslaved would be angry.

Time to try a fresh approach, she thought.

Deciding that all negative emotions would also be expected responses, Laurie instead focused on positive emotions like joy and love.

What could make her happy in this situation? Something to make her feel love. Not romantic love, but something higher, such as an appreciation for someone or something good, noble, or just. When you witness someone working selflessly for the good of others, you get this feeling. She tried to think of something noble or selfless she could admire or feel happy about.

Suddenly it came to her. The answer was motherhood. Noble, good, and selfless, the strong maternal bond. A very primary instinct. It was a key to open the door to her freedom.

How could they have tried to hide Penny from her? Seeing her in danger on that video had triggered something down deep. Motherly instincts were a powerful thing and she would draw upon that power to destroy this evil.

She focused on that sweet face. The girl at the center of her world, and suddenly all the programming and control faded. During the next cycle, she thought only of Penny. To her amazement, when the reboot was finished, her mind was not shut out. It still focused on memories of her daughter. Tears poured from her cheeks as the memories flooded her mind. She realized she'd done it. She'd stayed cognizant after the cybernetic control system had begun its processes. Instantly she saw into the heart of the programming process and cold logic of the computer.

With an immediate imperative, her knowledge of hacking and coding kicked in. She was going to use every tool in her mental hacker's toolbox, along with any bit of information about the alien's computer code they'd given her.

Laurie constructed a fake copy of the bionic control system software and duplicated all the reports that a functioning bionic system would give. With just the power of her mind. It was like the chip Calaxan had made except that it didn't mask her program–it replaced it. She saw where they had changed her brain. She corrected where it was wrong. Anytime she encountered something that prevented her mind from overriding the process, she wrote another slice of fake code to simulate that function.

The entire course of rewriting and repairing her mind took less than an hour. Her instincts, her joyous love, and her logic conspired together to make the processes of the machine subject to the higher functions of her own brain.

She had won. She had control of herself at last. Looking around the room, she saw it like a normal human again. More than that, though, she perceived even more than what a normal human would see. Her enhanced sensors connected to a million different things simultaneously. She was human, but more than a human.

Laurie spoke, "Master Calaxan, I have to find my daughter."

Calaxan, who was working on a recharging unit nearby, nearly jumped in surprise.

"Is that you… um, I'm sorry I don't have access to your human name."

"I am Laurie Victoria Nelson."

"Laurie Victoria Nelson, what exactly have you done, how?" Calaxan asked, wanting to understand what had happened.

He scanned her, and she appeared to be a normally working Bionic. He ran several diagnostic procedures, and they all reported that she was functioning flawlessly. Unknown to Laurie, he also downloaded a copy of her new codes so he could study it later.

"I have learned how to supplant the robotic processor's control over my mind. I have replicated a virus like code that will trigger when I am rebooted. They cannot undo what I have done. I am free at last to help my daughter." Laurie said. Her voice emotionless.

Calaxan was amazed. "I didn't think it was possible. How did you defeat it?"

"It was simply a matter of combining a mother's love, and a few heaping slices of malicious code." Laurie smiled.

Chief of Security Mezobac got a priority message on this communicator. "Chief Mezobac, we have a situation I need you to switch to privacy mode and reply immediately." It was Director Prag, of course.

Mezobac stood up and intentionally walked slowly to close the door to his office. Then let out a sigh and switched his comm unit to full duplex privacy mode.

"Yes, sir?"

"Chief, we have a serious problem. And I need you to track down and arrest the following individuals. Counselor Jinder, Master Calaxan, and a certain Bionic designated subject 042."

"Okay, wait a minute. Arrest who and on what charges?"

"Counselor Jinder, Master Calaxan, and an Earthling Bionic, Subject 042. Conspiracy and sedition. They are plotting a Bionic rebellion."

"Yes sir, as soon as I get the warrant from the magistrate, I will act immediately." Obviously, this was another of Director Prag's maneuvers. That meant he had to be certain everything was done by the book. If he followed the law to the letter, it would be hard for people to implicate him as a willing participant in whatever Prag was up to. Mezobac knew the law.

"Warrant? I have given you a direct order. Your delay is unacceptable. You will act now!"

"Sir, unless there is a direct threat to public safety, I cannot act without written authorization. If you have declared an emergency and suspended the need for arrest warrants, I have not been informed of it."

Mezobac knew if the director made such an egregious grab for power without justification, it would be the end of Prag's career. It would also give Mezobac the option of filing an official notice of compulsion. Again, covering himself against future repercussions.

"Thank you for the unnecessary legal clarification. My drones have discovered a group of armed resistance fighters in the old water park that your men overlooked. I believe that merits a declaration of emergency." Prag pushed a button on his desk and his assistant, Phrenzes, entered the room.

"Phrenzes, prepare an official letter declaring a state of emergency and broadcast it immediately."

After a few moments, Phrenzes reentered with the official declaration, and Prag signed it. Then he turned on his communicators video and showed the document to Mezobac and said, "There you have your state of emergency. Arrest them now!"

"Yes, sir. Immediately." Mezobac sent out the order as commanded.

He thought it best if he were the one to arrest Counselor Jinder. So, he walked to her office to arrest her. She was no threat and wouldn't resist.

When he arrived, she was out. He told her colleague, Vi-Zeha, what was happening and suggested she plan to evacuate Jinder's patients immediately. They could return once Prag was gone.

Thirty minutes later he received word that Jinder had been arrested, and that Calaxan and Subject 042 were still at large. Mezobac was not too concerned. He doubted any of them were a threat to the UPC. He hoped this emergency declaration would bring an end to Prag's terrible leadership. Committee member or not, Prag's power play won't go unpunished.

Then a terrible thought occurred to him. What if the entire committee was complicit in this plot? His life was about to become very unpleasant indeed.

Chapter 22 Escape

Thomas finally understood the truth. Jinder, the lady in purple, hadn't called security on him after rescuing the child from the alligator but had saved his life. The chip conciliator thingy, Jupiter-D, is what she used to save it and now it was helping him escape.

"Fine, but I get to take one more look for Penny on the security cameras before we go."

"Sure, why not? It's on the way. There won't be any security people at the security office with the security cameras. Dunderhead." Jupiter-D said.

"Shut up, you know they don't use the human technology. Like you said, it's on the way. I have to try one more time."

Thomas refilled his water pouch and filled his pockets with anything he thought might be useful. Then he grabbed a towel for space.

"What's the deal with the towel? Are you going for a swim?"

"Something I read in a book once, seems they are very handy in space."

"That's pretty smart, I guess, let's skedaddle."

Thomas opened the door a crack, and after seeing no one, he hurried toward the security office. But somehow the park had changed. Thomas couldn't figure it out.

A child stopped him. "Mr. Doggie, why did you and your friends all leave?"

Thomas realized what was missing. There were no other Waldo World characters on the streets. The fake costumed characters were gone.

"If they recalled the fakes, we gonna stick out like a fly on a wedding cake. We gotta lose the costume."

"Are you sure?" Thomas was suddenly frighted to be without it.

The costume that had been his protection for so many weeks was now a beacon leading the bad guys directly to him.

"If it ain't helping, we gotta get rid of it. We'll be able to run without it. Besides, there's

lots of them shiny new human Bionics walking around now. They gonna think you're one of them."

Thomas had noticed a few human-looking robot people lately.

"Wait, your drawl is back?"

"I figured that since I'm done convincing you I'm a really smart computer chip, I can relax and talk natural-like."

Thomas ducked into the nearest bathroom and unhappily began stripping off the Jupiter-D costume. He wore shorts and a tee shirt underneath. Carefully, he folded the costume and put it on the closed toilet seat. He neatly placed the big head on top, out of respect.

He put the towel on his head like a hood, hoping it might cover part of his face. Whatever he did, he was still going to stick out like the proverbial wedding cake fly, but at least he could see and run easily.

He shot out of the bathroom and ran straight towards the crew room. It took several minutes, and he surprised several park guests. He never looked back. Seeing pursuers couldn't have made him any more motivated than he already was. When he arrived, he headed straight to the security office.

"We put on a real good show back there, woof-woof-ha-ha! 'See the real live Earthling running for his life!'"

As Thomas caught his breath, he scanned the security cameras for any sign of pursuit. There were multiple security patrols around the park, but none of them seemed focused on the crew area.

"Okay, okay. Stop watching TV. We gotta get outta here. That shuttle is our only ticket, and I got no idea when it's gonna take off!" Jupiter-D prompted him.

Then as he turned to leave. He checked the security monitors one more time. What he saw there made him gasp.

It was Emma, running down a tunnel hallway, and she looked terrified. She kept checking over her shoulder. Someone was chasing her.

"There she is!" Thomas shouted.

"That ain't Penny!"

"It's Emma, and she's in trouble."

"Everybody is in trouble. A side trip to rescue your wannabe girlfriend is gonna make a mess of my escape plan. We don't got time for it, Romeo." Jupiter-D said.

Thomas was torn. He watched for her to appear on the next camera. But instead of Emma, he was shocked to see a little girl running ahead of Emma.

"That's Penny!" Jupiter-D exclaimed. *"Quit lollygagging. We gotta go get her!"*

"Hold on, super dog. We need to know how to get there."

Thomas referred to the tunnel maps and camera numbers to find the girls' exact location. That's when he saw a commotion on another camera. A small group of humans with guns, dressed in camo, were chasing the girls.

"Why are those nimrods chasing after our girls?"

At first Thomas thought the same. The men in camouflage then stopped and fired their weapons down the tunnel at something behind them. Thomas couldn't see what they were shooting at but realized they were covering the girls' escape. A beam from an alien ray gun hit one man, and he dissolved.

"We need to get them girls hidden on that shuttle with us, they ain't safe here." Jupiter-D said.

Thomas agreed.

Once they had a destination, he ran down the stairway to the tunnels. He was doing more running than he had in weeks. His heart was pounding. He needed to get to the intersection where he could intercept the girls before they ran past.

It only took Thomas a few minutes to reach where he expected to find the girls.

Thomas rounded the last corner and waited. Soon he heard Penny's small feet running down the passage toward him.

That's when he realized. Penny won't recognize him as *her* Jupiter-D. He had no costume, and she'd never seen his face. She might get frightened and run away. It was hopeless.

"Oh, don't be such a Negative Nancy. Anyway, you gotta try." Jupiter-D said.

Thomas moved under a bright light and gazed down the hallway. The tiny footsteps came closer and then she appeared around a corner about twenty feet away from him and she skidded to a frightened stop.

Thomas could only give his crooked smile and try to look as friendly as possible. That was difficult with a large red scar across your face and a mangled head.

Then he signed, "Friend."

In an instant, Penny's face registered recognition. Her little face seemed to split in half as she gave her biggest smile.

She ran toward him and yelled, "Jupiter-D!"

She jumped on him and gave him one of her super tight hugs.

"The bad aliens are after us," she said in her monotone way.

He tried to fingerspell an answer, but she grabbed his hand and said, "I can hear. I found batteries."

"I'm so glad you're ok." Thomas said tears streaming down his cheeks.

Just then, Emma rounded the corner and stopped short, seeing Thomas and Penny.

She remembered him from her classes at Waldo University. It wasn't hard. Besides, how many people with a dented skull and a huge scar do you know?

"Thomas?" She asked.

"Hi Emma."

"Emma, you know my Jupiter-D?" Penny was surprised.

"Yes, we work together."

"I need to get you guys somewhere safe. Who else is following you?" Thomas asked.

"Razoul and the other survivors. They're trying to slow them down for us to get away. I lost track." Emma said.

"Can you tell them to follow us somehow?" Thomas asked.

Emma pulled out a marker and said, "Which way are we going?"

"Follow me." Thomas said as he turned, still carrying Penny. He headed back the way he'd come.

Emma marked the turns with arrows as she followed.

They came up the stairs and into the crew area. Thomas was on his way out the back door when he decided to take a quick look at the camera feeds first. The cameras revealed dozens of security patrols in almost every area of the park, as well as a group of guards stationed in the street outside their door. They were trapped.

The sounds of shots rang out from the bottom of the stairway. Thomas clicked the button to bring up the image of Razoul in a shootout with security guards in the passage just below the stairs.

They were closing in on them from two sides. Razoul looked at the mark and up the stairs, but instead of coming up, he motioned for the survivalists to head down the passage.

"What's he doing! My mark clearly shows we went upstairs." Emma looked at the camera, trying to understand.

"Razoul knows what he's doing. He doesn't want to bring them up here to where you guys are hiding. He's buying more time for you to get away." Thomas said.

A moment of silence passed between them as the realization sunk in.

"Okay, we need to make their sacrifice count for something. We must get past those guards at the back door." Thomas said.

"Why don't we all put on character costumes? It's been working for you." Emma suggested.

"That won't work. They are on to my disguise, they've pulled all the characters from the park to find me. I don't have time to elaborate, but there's something much bigger at work here. The aliens aren't all bad, some are helping us… me to escape. Humans are being rounded up and made into the Bionic robo-thingys like these guys." Thomas pointed at the alien Bionics standing in their charging pods.

This gave Thomas an idea. The Bionics were practically invisible to the aliens, accustomed to ignoring them. He looked again at the camera and he saw several Bionics going about their daily routines, ignored by security.

"If we make ourselves appear to be Bionics. They may not recognize us." He opened a desk drawer and found a couple of fine point markers he hoped would do the trick.

Emma and Penny took turns drawing lines on each other's faces that mimicked the implants and circuits the Bionics in the pods had. Emma pulled Penny's hair in a ponytail to make her cochlear implants more visible.

Thomas already looked the part with his facial scars. The problem was that Emma still looked too perfect. So he dug deeper through the drawers. He pulled out an old phone charger and a Bluetooth earpiece. He helped Emma put these on and taped the charger cable to her neck. They were out of time. But will the security guards buy it? They dare not wait any longer.

As they were getting ready, they heard a beeping noise. Several of the Bionic people that were charging in their stations awoke and started walking toward the back door.

"Let's go! Be brave, Penny. Stare straight ahead and don't look at anyone." Thomas said.

The three of them fell in behind the lumbering Bionics single file. Thomas reminded Penny and Emma to imitate the shambling gait of the Bionics. They had to look and behave exactly the same to be ignored.

The line of Bionics exited the back door and headed for the maintenance building. They walked past the guards, who were distracted on their communicators.

Thomas decided stopping at maintenance was ideal. They would need better equipment to pass them off as Bionics. Who knows, they might have to fool people to get on the spaceship or on the home world.

They entered the shop area, and Thomas called for Calaxan. There was no response. Thomas had hoped he might be there to help them.

He headed to the stockroom where he had seen Calaxan pull parts to repair other Bionics. Finding some circuit boards and housings that looked promising he pocketed these.

Just then Penny shouted, "Momma!"

Emma tried to stop her, but nothing was going to keep her from her mom. Penny ran to one of the many charging pods and embraced the human woman it held.

Thomas came running in time to see the Bionic, Laurie, open her eyes.

Chapter 23 Momma!

Laurie had gained full control of her implants. All were fully functional without it affecting her ability to think and act for herself. She was getting reports of an emergency on the network. Her sensors detected someone enter the room. One with a Bionic signature and two other unchipped beings.

Just then one of them cried, "Momma!" A moment later Laurie felt something holding on around her waist.

Recognition of that voice triggered a flood of memories that her new circuits could no longer suppress. She broke out of her sleep cycle and put her arms around the human child, embracing her. She opened her eyes.

"Penny, my sweet angel. You are alive!" Laurie said.

"Momma, I tried so hard to find you. Where were you? I missed you. I tried to be good and stay hiding under the bed like you said, but you were gone so long. After a while, I just couldn't hide there anymore."

Memories of that day rushed in on Laurie. The invasion, the panic, her desperate attempt to hide Penny. Anger toward the aliens grew, but that anger triggered something in her implants. She started losing control of them. That's when she remembered the implants were programmed to respond to negative emotions. Laurie let go the anger and refocused on Penny. Her little girl was alive and well.

"You did good angel. I'm proud of you. I love you. It must have been hard."

Through tears, Penny tried to tell her everything that had happened. Dancing with Jupiter-D, running away and hiding with Emma and the others.

Laurie looked at the woman with Penny. She was a beautiful young woman with permanent marker all over her face. And a phone charger glued to her neck.

"Introduce me to your friends, Penny," Laurie asked.

"This is Emma she is a beautiful princess, and that is Jupiter-D. He is the one we danced with on that last day."

Emma smiled and said, "I'm so happy we found you! You must be an excellent mother. Penny is such a wonderful girl and so brave!"

Thomas added. "I'm glad we found you, too, but we have to get out of here. I don't mean to rush, but I was told that I needed to get to the Retullian home world to stop what they are doing to Earth."

"Who told you to do this?" Laurie asked.

Thomas hesitated. He wasn't ready to explain Jupiter-D yet. It would take too long. "An important alien woman named Counselor Jinder. She gave me something to present to a bigwig on the alien home world. It supposed to stop them doing what they are to Earth."

Laurie concentrated a moment and connected to the planetary inter-network. In less than a second, she downloaded shuttle schedules and got an update on dangerous humans in the park. She ran across the information about the emergency declaration and the arrest warrants. They were looking for rogue Bionics that Calaxan had freed.

"Thomas is correct we must get off Earth quickly. The UPC will soon take actions to isolate it. They are still searching for Thomas. Already they arrested Counselor Jinder and attempted to arrest Calaxan, but failed."

"Master Calaxan too? I wanted him to give the girls chips so that people would think they were Bionics like he did me," Thomas asked.

"He was supposed to be taken to security headquarters for interrogation and reprogramming. They have discovered that he has been secretly working to free the Bionics from their implant control," Laurie said.

"So that's what this is all about?" Thomas asked.

"Yes, I have broken free of control. What I have discovered is an enormous threat to them. We must hurry. There is a shuttle leaving within the hour. Your strategy of making Emma and Penny look like Bionics is good. But I will fix your poor attempt at disguise. Follow me."

"Everyone's a critic. Don't take it too hard. I thought you done okay drawing lines on Emma. Marked her up real good. Woof-woof-ha-ha!" Jupiter-D said.

Jupiter-D's laugh came out of Thomas' throat.

"Go ahead and laugh, Thomas. Admit it, my disguise looks pretty amateurish." Emma said.

Thomas smiled, embarrassed.

Laurie broke free of Penny's embrace and headed to the storeroom. Everyone followed. With amazing speed, Laurie gathered several devices and assembled them. Then she tapped a hidden panel that contained Calaxan's secret stash of fake Bionic transponder chips and loaded two into the injector.

"Penny, this will hurt, but you must be brave." She inserted the chip into the back of Penny's head and then went to work on the girl's cochlear implants. After a few minutes, Penny was done. Her implants had been upgraded so Penny now had superior hearing to a human and the devices would also translate the alien languages for her like they did for Thomas.

Penny smiled as she experimented with the functions of her new hearing device.

Laurie turned to Emma and said, "Emma, your turn."

Quickly, Laurie injected a chip into Emma. She removed the fake Bionic disguise and installed some surface mounted equipment, including a temporary eyepiece that would allow her to see into the infrared and ultra-violet spectrum. Then a new earpiece that would translate.

Laurie announced. "We are out of time. I have been monitoring the communications. They have dispatched security to our location. I'll trigger a diversion subroutine that I created to confuse them." Immediately, all the Bionics in the room awoke and began heading out the large overhead door that opened.

"Let's go!" Laurie said.

The four of them headed out of the door with the other bionics. As soon as they left the building, the Bionics all started running in different directions. They were acting erratically. Laurie directed the group toward the nearby woods, where they disappeared into the brush. Soon thereafter, a commotion arose behind them at the park. The security forces had engaged the Bionics Laurie had triggered and were trying to round them up.

"We must run this way." Laurie said and pointed down the road toward the shuttle.

Chapter 24 Cargo

They ran, and then walked, to the parking lot where cargo shuttles were loaded. Upon arriving, they took cover in the stack of cars where Thomas had hidden before. They had to wait until the cargo pods arrive.

Penny and Emma sat resting, and Laurie kept a vigilant lookout. The ground smelled like gasoline and old tires. Thomas was so glad he'd found Penny. Finding her and Emma, and even Penny's mom, was a miracle.

Penny was happier than he had ever seen a little girl be.

"That's great that the kid found her mom ain't it, Dunderhead." Jupiter-D said and then added, *"That Laurie is quite a lady if you haven't noticed and of course Emma is even more attractive in her cyborg queen get up."*

"I liked it better when you stayed quiet. Why do you always bring up my feelings, at inappropriate times? Yes, they are both lovely women and I'm a hideous monster neither of them would ever think twice about. This isn't the best time for me to be thinking about such things, you know. We are hiding for our lives waiting to be killed at any moment and you are trying to play matchmaker?" Thomas thought to Jupiter-D.

"What else you got to do. The lady said we got to wait till the shuttle is ready to launch before we make our move. So, I can't help you through your little romantic dilemma with the ladies?" Jupiter-D chuckled.

"I'm not having a romantic dilemma."

"Step one is always denial, Dunder-Romeo. Woof-woof-haha!"

Laurie shot him a look for making the laugh noise.

"Be quiet, Dunder-dog, you're going to get us caught," Thomas thought. "Fine, you're psychoanalyzing me. I get it, that's your job, but can you turn it off and give it a rest? Just let me quietly wallow in my own misery for a while?"

"Sure thing ol' buddy. If you want to stew and fester on it a bit. I know it ain't easy being the last man on Earth with these two beautiful ladies here."

"Quit saying that. I'm not the last guy on earth, that Razoul guy and the others are still alive. He's the hero type, doesn't have a mangled face. There's still probably lots of people hiding on Earth. Obviously, their technology isn't as great as they think it is, if they missed us and couldn't keep Laurie under control."

Laurie interrupted Thomas' inner conversation. "Time to go!" She picked up Penny, and Thomas quietly tapped Emma's arm to alert her. Thomas watched as several big hover platforms holding containers pulled into the yard. The cargo pods stopped about thirty feet away from them. A loud clanging noise began, and he looked up to see the cargo ramp of the ship begin its descent.

"I've seen what's in those things. We do not want to get in one." Thomas said.

"No, Thomas, these differ from the ones they use for Bionic processing. These pods carry goods back to the home world." Laurie said.

Holding Penny on her hip, Laurie moved to the nearest cargo container and scanned its symbol code. Then walked to the next one and examined it. She motioned for the others to come.

"This one is destined for Multus, that's the capital city of the Retullian home world. It has livestock and perishables. So, they should send it on a fast ship and have its own life support system."

Laurie spent several anxious minutes working to decode the lock. When she did, the side access panel popped open.

The ship's ramp was almost down, and soon the containers would be loaded. The four of them wasted no time getting inside the unit. It was a tight fit. To make enough room for everyone, they had to unload several crates. They hid them near the cars. The smell inside was awful.

"How long is this trip?" Emma asked, her nose all scrunched up.

"About six days according to the schedule." Laurie said.

None of them looked forward to spending the entire trip smelling the livestock.

"Mommy, why do the cows stink so bad?" Penny asked.

"Because they do. I'm busy right now." Laurie began keying in codes on the interface panel inside the pod.

Penny looked dejected.

Laurie didn't seem to notice her daughter's disappointment. Emma moved over next to Penny and gave her a hug.

"Okay, I've interfaced with this container's control system… good, it's a livestock transport and has a full working life support module and temperature controls. I have masked our entry and recalculated the weight. Closing and sealing the door now."

"We better find a safe place to sit during takeoff," Thomas added. "Find something to tie yourselves down with. We will probably be weightless for a while. Also, remember to position yourself so you won't get crushed while we are pulling G's at takeoff."

"You sound like you have some experience," Emma said.

"I took a quick trip to space once." He smiled.

After six days, Thomas, and the others were still hiding in the container. They had felt their ship lift off from Earth, as well as every bump and bang along the way. The container had been transferred between an unknown number of spaceships. It would pitch and roll each time they moved it. The human stowaways experienced both weightlessness and the weak simulated version of gravity of the bigger ships. Each time it left them ill. There had been a brief period of extreme acceleration, followed by an odd sensation of time being slightly out of phase. Laurie reasoned that this had to be some kind of hyperspace jump because it had been going on for days. So far, they'd survived the mind-numbing boredom by talking and joking. Yet no one talked about what worried them the most—what was going to happen next.

Laurie didn't have all the answers. She had data. Data about what usually happens, what has happened in the past, and what was most likely to happen. But her connection to real time information was limited. She'd explained that every time she interacted with the network, she risked being discovered. It could jeopardize everything. So, she did it only when necessary.

"What do we do when we get there?" Emma asked.

"Jinder, the alien who helped me, gave me a contact name of someone in the government, Ephynia Telo. But no info." Thomas said. "She's supposed to be connected to the Chancellor somehow and might be sympathetic."

Jupiter-D claimed he didn't have any other details about how to find her. Jinder was supposed to be some famous scientist. Thomas figured they could try to find Jinder's friends or something if the Ephynia lady didn't work out.

"Perhaps we can go to the capitol building and look her up or something?" Emma said, trying to help.

"I will research her once we arrive on the planet. It is too risky searching for her now they could trace it. Security would find us," Laurie said.

The rest of the trip, Laurie seemed preoccupied. When asked, she would just say that she was planning for the future. No one really understood how deep and how thorough her planning was. Laurie had downloaded some information before they left. Maps of the Retullian capital city and the government complex. Millions of data centers and pathways to navigate.

These four humans might be the only hope for Earth.

The discovery of this life support cargo pod had been fortunate, and they appeared to be on their way to the Retullian capital city. But conditions in the pod were less than ideal. Despite its being cramped and the smell of the livestock, there had been the matters of sanitation, food, and water. Food had been the easiest. The live animals in the pod had automatic feeders and waterers, but the amounts were carefully calculated. They did not figure on four extra people. Also, the grains and other foods for the animals were not always easily consumed by humans without effort. They had found some heavy items to crush and mill the grain and mix it with water. But in zero gravity, the force needed to smash the grain was more taxing than they'd imagined.

Sanitation was managed by careful use of the unusual equipment onboard for animal clean up. They did engineer methods that were satisfactory if not comfortable, nor which afforded much in the way of modesty. Everyone was very polite about it, given the circumstances, and it became manageable.

Thomas woke up feeling weak and tired. Sleep had been hard for everyone. They'd tried to stay on a daily schedule, but it was difficult in the mind-numbing boredom and cramped quarters. With nothing to do and little room to exercise, every day was like the rest and Thomas' old scars and implants ached.

Thomas was happy to see Penny reunited with her mother. She spent most of the time cradled in her mother's embrace. But Laurie still looked far off into the future, making plans.

"What a strange road this has been Tommy Boy," Jupiter-D said.

"That's a fact," Thomas replied.

"Hey let's go tell jokes to entertain Penny," Jupiter-D suggested. *"Or do you want to go snuggle with Emma?"*

"I'm not doing any snuggling! Stop that."

"Ya don't need to go yelling, I'm just giving voice to your inner emotional needs."

"I'm well aware of my emotional needs. But there is a time and a place for romance and a cargo pod that smells of cow dung isn't one of them. Besides, she has given no indications of romantic interest so quit trying to be a… puppy love matchmaker."

"Okay, fair enough. Message received I'll drop the romance bit. So, can we go tell Penny the joke about the cow with a wooden leg? She loves that one."

When Thomas wasn't entertaining Penny with jokes, he did talk with Emma, often for hours.

She too had hoped for a career in acting. Thomas shared some things he had gone through to get into the few prominent roles he had before his accident. A strong friendship, was growing between them, which Thomas needed more than romance.

Emma didn't ask him about his accident. She really didn't need to. Every newspaper and tabloid had carried it. Thomas had been starring in his first television series and had landed roles in the next big blockbuster movie. They had already started shooting. His career was soaring before the accident. It was a sad but far too common tale. Fast living and fast cars, partying too much and drinking and driving. Nine months in the hospital, fractured skull. It was a miracle he had killed no one. The only casualty was his career. All of his roles were recast, and the studio lost millions reshooting. He'd tried everything to get an acting job afterwards. No one wanted to take a risk on him. Finally, he settled for the job at the park—it was still showbiz. At least in his costume, no one would recognize him.

"At least you ain't bitter about it," Jupiter-D said, trying to get a reaction.

"Yeah, there's that," Thomas said, ignoring Jupiter-D's attempt at more therapy.

So, he asked Emma to tell him about her life and her career.

Emma had been a smart and popular girl most of her life, she'd been a star in all the High School and in college drama activities. However, like most aspiring actresses, she had not been prepared for the grueling process of auditions and constant rejection. She told Thomas some horror stories of the exploitation and discrimination she had fought against along the way. Sadly, he knew this was not unusual. Thomas listened, empathetic to her stories of disappointment and rejection.

He felt bad for not having taken a stronger stand against that kind of behavior. But when the competition for parts is so intense, it makes you afraid to speak out. The people making the poor decisions are in charge of casting and your next job. The system was broken, and it forced talented young women like Emma to endure much bias.

Emma had left Hollywood's degrading culture and take a job performing at Mercury World. Unlike him, though, she wasn't hiding there.

Time passed quickly for Thomas, spending his days talking to the bright and beautiful Emma. She was delightful and intelligent. The days went by too quickly.

Their comfort and isolation changed one day when everyone felt an abrupt drop in speed. There was engine reverberation and a force of deceleration unlike anything they had ever experienced. For a moment, they experienced the uneasy feeling that time was being pulled and twisted back into phase. Laurie explained they were dropping from hyperspace and suggested everyone get ready for gravity.

It happened a few minutes later. There was another period of extreme deceleration as they held tight to both their grip and their stomachs. For a moment they only felt the strong vibration of the ship's engines, silent at first, but soon enough they could hear them. The burst of loud noise was intense and almost painful. Cargo bays were open to space and without air. Thus, sound meant atmosphere. Atmosphere meant planet.

After several minutes, there was a final blast from the engines and the ship stopped all movement. It had landed at its destination. For the first time in a week, gravity worked its magic on everyone and everything in the large cargo pod. The cows and other animals were unsettled and were panicking. Instantly a ventilation system turned on and began venting in outside air and blowing out the fragrant stench of the live cargo pod.

"I guess we're gonna find out real quick if this planet's atmosphere is breathable to humans." Emma said.

Thomas gave her a grim smile.

"Retul-Prime's air has a similar composition to Earth's. That is why Earth is such a valuable resource for them. They can add much of its life to the Retullian's home world's biodiversity," Laurie said, much to everyone's relief.

"So, how do we leave the pod?" Thomas asked.

Laurie began, "I have figured out the optimal moment of departure, based on the data available. They will begin processing the pods shortly. This pod will be in the first group. Since it carries livestock. We should all stand up and begin walking as much as possible to get accustomed to gravity again. We may need to be ready to run if we are detected. I have examined the maps for potential routes and hiding places. Be ready to follow me."

Everyone stood in place and began working their leg muscles, trying to get used to gravity again.

"It's likely that Bionics will process our pod. They won't react to us, since it is not unheard of that Bionics might be shipped with livestock. Other aliens might not overlook our presence. If the pod inventory doesn't match the one on file, it might trigger the attention of security. I have altered the list to make it look like last-minute changes were made, but I have no way of knowing if there are procedures to verify it."

The pod shuddered and moved as processing began. Thomas worried about Emma and Penny.

"They'll be just fine. Don't you worry none about them, I don't think Lady Jinder woulda sent us here if it was dangerous. The travel brochures call this the most civilized place in the universe." Jupiter-D reassured.

"If your definition of civilized is killing nearly every person on Earth. Of course, it's dangerous. What makes you think they would think twice about evaporating a bunch of stowaways?" Thomas answered.

"Well, sorry, for trying to make you feel better," an offended Jupiter-D said.

There was more movement and loud thumping. "We are next. Walk slowly as we leave the pod and follow me. Remember, we need to act like we have been programmed with a destination. That means no sightseeing. No gawking. You are not allowed to be impressed with anything you see in this unfamiliar world," Laurie warned.

The large door at one end of the pod opened to a ramp and warehouse dock. The warehouse interior was rather mundane, not the exciting futuristic architecture Thomas had hoped for. Tall corrugated metal ceilings held up by steel beams all colored a dull shade of blue gray. Not very exotic or alien looking. It could have been any warehouse on Earth. It was stacked high with pods like the one they'd arrived in.

Laurie said, "Now."

The four of them followed her down the extended ramp, trying to do their best impression of the slow, Bionic shuffling gait. At the end of the ramp, there were a few Bionics waiting for them to pass. They turned left and headed toward the exit, away from the ship docks.

Thomas glanced at the big multi-track conveyer system that moved the pods from the ship's cargo bay to the dock where they were unloaded and sorted on to the stacks. There were several large pens for holding livestock here. They walked past one filled with animals on the way to the door.

Penny let out a brief squeal of surprise when one of the alien animals stuck its head between the bars of the enclosure and lapped out its tongue, licking Penny's face. The thing was like a bizarre lizard-sheep thing and smelled like dead fish. Laurie grabbed Penny and pulled her back, calming her. Thomas looked around nervously. Would a Bionic child react like that? That's when he realized he'd never seen Bionic children. At least not on Earth. What did they do with kids on conquered planets? He wondered.

"Weren't you just telling me these people were 'civilized' monsters?" Jupiter-D said.

"I guess I've tried not to think about it," Thomas said.

Laurie sped up their pace to get out of the warehouse as quickly as they dare. Thomas noticed a man in a uniform sitting in an enclosed booth as they approached the exit. He appeared distracted watching a video screen. Thomas hoped he would ignore them.

"Quit staring, Knuckle head. If he sees you looking up at him, he will know something is wrong." Jupiter-D said.

Thomas looked down just in time when the man in the booth looked up at the unusual sight of the human Bionics, not a race the Retullians were used to. Earth was a recent conquest, so they probably hadn't seen many humans.

As they exited the building, the brightness of the Retullian sun seemed blinding. Huge skyscrapers surrounded them and flying cars of every style and description filled the sky. There were open air platforms with dozens of people. Enclosed ones with passengers seated in rows like a train. Smaller sporty looking ones that had only one or two passengers. All the vehicles flew in unmarked lanes in the sky like a hundred superhighways stacked upon themselves, each going a different direction. The walkways were filled with Retullians and other races, plus hundreds or even thousands of Bionics. Each going about their daily business, ignoring the spectacle of their world.

Laurie worked hard to keep Penny's curiosity under control.

Emma could barely keep herself from staring, occasionally stopping to gawk at a huge vehicle or strange being. They all somehow remained silent.

They were on a raised walkway of some type. In fact, the city was composed of walkways cantilevered against the silvery skyscrapers. As they walked, Thomas could see down through a nearby railing. There were dozens of levels of structure below.

The architecture was far different, possibly even disappointing, from what he'd expected based on Hollywood's idea of alien cities. There was lots of glass and metal, but everything was cube shaped and squarish. None of the impractical curves and art deco style bulges. The Retullians were a practical people. Very little compromising of utility for art. In fact, almost no art of any kind could be found. It struck him as a harsh, almost cruel city. No decorative details or fancy patterns in any of the structures. As if the city lacked something...

"Imagination," Jupiter-D chimed in. *"The Retullians have no imagination. That's why they were so taken with Mercury World, and why they can't see how wrong what they're doing is. They have no ideas beyond the practical."*

"That can't be. How can they invent and innovate? How did they make such fantastic technology?" Thomas asked.

"I guess they did somehow."

"Can someone have the ability of flight arise from merely the need to fly?"

"Yes, you devise a machine with certain characteristics, and then you make use of those characteristics. The Retullians are mechanically focused. Inclined toward machinery itself. They perfected the process of better and better machines over centuries. When someone creates a machine with a new ability, they exploit that ability in the most practical way possible. But to dream of an idea and them work toward the fantasy of the idea becoming a reality is a foreign concept," Jupiter-D explained.

"Wait, you're not speaking in your Jupiter-D voice again. What happened?" Thomas asked.

"You are correct. In fact, I now appear to have access to an extensive amount of data I didn't have before. I now know that Jinder planted encoded data into my chip's memory that is designed only to trigger once we arrived at certain coordinates here on Retul Prime.

"Thomas, you must stop Laurie and explain that you have received additional information about our destination," Jupiter-D said.

"Laurie, I have something to tell you that can't wait," Thomas announced to the group.

Laurie led the group down a small corridor that ran alongside a building to a more secluded porch area in front of what appeared to be a business. Once the small group of fugitives were out of sight of the crowds Laurie turned to Thomas, hand on hip, and said, "We don't have time for this. The capitol complex is a long way from here and if we don't make the transit, we will have to wait an hour for the next."

"That's just it. We don't need to go to the capitol complex. Our contact, Ephynia. Is in the other direction."

"Wait, you're just now telling us this? I have searched the database and found no location information other than her office near the capitol complex." Laurie's foot tapped.

"Well, I kinda got some recent information," Thomas admitted.

"Go on," Emma said.

All three of the girls were looking at him now.

"It appears Jinder programmed location triggered information into my AI chip," Thomas explained.

"Wait, what AI chip? You didn't mention that before." Laurie said. "You're a synthetic life form? The Retullians don't put AI chips into people."

"No, I'm human. I have a chip in my head that Jinder put there. It's an experimental one, I guess. That's why she wanted me to get away from Earth. The bad guys want my chip."

"You're not being controlled by it?" Laurie's face focused on him. "I can't detect it. Only the fake Bionic one Calaxan gave you."

Thomas became worried when the rest of the group looked like he'd betrayed them.

"It's here behind my ear." Thomas lifted his hair to reveal the lump.

"Okay, so it's an AI chip. That doesn't explain why you never mentioned it until now."

"There's a good reason for that," Thomas said. "Because, well… most of the time since I've had it, I thought I was crazy. So I didn't say anything because… well, I didn't want any of you to think I was a wack-job." He mumbled the last part.

"Why would you think you were crazy?" Emma asked. She'd lost her usual smile.

"Actually, I thought the AI was Jupiter-D, my character. He's been talking to me ever since after the invasion. I thought I was having mental issues."

"The AI sounded just like I expected Jupiter-D to sound, if he could talk. Well, kinda."

"You understand the Retullians use chips to control people's minds?" Laurie was serious. "I'll just say this outright. This revelation has given me trust issues, Thomas."

Thomas looked down at the ground, feeling terrible.

"Hey Tommy boy, I can clear all this up real quick, if you give me permission to use your mouth a minute," Jupiter-D said to Thomas on the inside.

"You can do that?"

"Yup."

"Anything is better than them not trusting me. Go ahead, I give you permission to talk." Thomas said that out loud so the others would know what was going to happen. Suddenly, Thomas began speaking without controlling his mouth.

"We'll since were all be out in the open and all. I just borrowed Tommy Boy's mouth, with his permission of course, so I can clear all this up with Miss Laurie here." Jupiter-D said with his friendly drawl.

Penny and Emma smiled with surprise.

"After what them fellers did to you, Miss Laurie, I can surely understand why you could be suspicious. As you know, the folks we're dealing with are way beyond deceptive and downright evil. I'm a Conciliator AI chip, not one of them stupid Bionic control thingys they gave you. I don't control nobody. My chip structure is an experimental type designed to be used on Retullians with emotional issues so they can get their heads put back on straight. Most of what I am comes straight out of Ol' Tommy's head here."

Laurie shook her head in acknowledgement. "I don't have data on your chip type. But I found a white paper about your development."

"I only get instructions sent to me direct from the psychologist, in this case Counselor Jinder, and I don't connect with no networks direct like you do. Jinder doesn't want them to find Thomas. She's trying to protect him. But we need to get going before it's too late," Jupiter-D said using Thomas' mouth and speech ability.

"This doesn't explain why she would do this for a human. A Retullian would never use one of those expensive experimental chips on a human." Laurie, still suspicious, was determined to learn the truth.

"There's a couple of real good reasons we ain't got time to detail. But mostly, it's because of what heroic Tommy Boy here went and did. Tell em for yerself Tom."

All three of the women stared at him, waiting to confess what he'd done.

"I guess I kinda saved this Retullian kid from being eaten by a gator a few days after the invasion. I kinda got drowned doing it though." Thomas said, speaking for himself again.

"Tell em the complete story, buddy. Not the readers condensed version." Jupiter-D jumped in.

So, Thomas told them his entire story, starting from invasion day all the way through to the part where he drowned.

After he was done, Emma smiled at him with admiration, making him blush. Penny gave him a hug.

Thomas continued, "Jupiter-D, the AI chip thing, told me my actions made Jinder question everything she'd been told about humans before she arrived. She wanted to understand why a human, an enemy of the United Planetary Confederation, would risk his own life to save a Retullian child. I guess I was almost dead anyway, and she had to act quick. So, she put this chip in my head and it kinda saved my life, and then it adopted Jupiter-D's personality from my imagination and ran with it. I only learned where the voice was coming from the day we left."

Laurie seemed satisfied.

"Anyway, if you believe me, we need to go south to the Duni district. That's where this Ephynia lady is. She is supposed to help us."

The others nodded.

"Jupiter-D says he has instructions for us from Jinder, but they only pop out when we are in the right place. Otherwise, the bad guys might get intel that will hurt the Bionic liberation effort," Thomas explained.

"This Proconsul Ephynia is a former Chairperson big wheel of some government committee. Even though she's been out of public service for several years and teaches college. She still has high-level connections. There was some big scandal to discredit her, and now she believes her downfall had to do with the people responsible for corruption discovered on Earth."

"That coincides with the information I found on her in the database. What you are saying sounds plausible," Laurie said.

"According to Jinder, this Ephynia, knows how the bureaucracy works and should be the best one to help us." Thomas said.

"You said it almost as good as I coulda. Woof-woof ha-ha," Jupiter-D said aloud.

"Ok, I need you to quit talking with two different voices it's seriously freaking me out." Emma said.

"I'm trying, but Jupiter-D is really my subconscious, and this chip gives it a voice. He just needs to learn when I'm done letting him use my mouth." Thomas tried to hide his self-consciousness by giving a short laugh.

"Now I know why you thought you were crazy. But now that we know what he is, it's not that bad. I guess," Emma said.

"I hope I didn't scare you, Penny." Thomas stooped down to her level and patted her back.

"It's okay, I'm not scared of Jupiter-D. He's my favorite person in the whole world. I think it's wonderful that he learned to talk just like I had to!"

Laurie, who was processing all of this, spoke up, "Thomas/Jupiter-D are correct. I have examined the history of Proconsul Ephynia. She is someone important her son is the Chancellor of the UPC. We need to catch the public transport headed south. We'd better hurry. That route closes down for night phase in a few minutes. Follow, please."

They walked south to a platform where a few dozen Bionics were waiting. A large hover bus pulled up and after everyone had exited, they boarded. As they found seats, Thomas couldn't help but notice that there were several new races of Bionics on the bus than he hadn't seen before. Some wore full helmets and carried breathing tanks. How many worlds had the UPC enslaved?

Penny stared in wide wonder at some of these odd-looking alien people. Thomas worried someone might notice her reaction. He thought about asking her to stop, but realized that would be even more noticeable. So, he did his best not to stare at the aliens himself.

It took several minutes while the bus waited for all its passengers. Thomas looked at Emma in her cyborg get-up and started thinking about what happened in the coffee shop so long ago. Did she even remember it?

"Now who's gettin' all sappy? Remember, I'm still watching out for ya, and if you live,

you'll have plenty of time to go courting the lovely Miss Emma. Keep alert, Romeo!" Jupiter-D said. Thomas knew he was right, so he put his mind back to the problems at hand. So, he looked beyond her and at the people standing on the platform. That's when he saw them. Uniformed police officers were checking people on the ramp.

As the bus pulled away, he caught site of even more security police moving toward the loading platform they'd just left. They were checking each person with some sort of scanning device.

Not wanting to alarm Emma and Penny, Thomas whispered to Laurie, "Do you see that?"

She gave him a serious look and nodded without a word.

The hover bus suddenly accelerated, and they were speeding south like a bullet.

Chapter 25 Mezobac on Retul

Mezobac stared at his data pad, trying to stay up to date with security reports from Retul Prime. His boss, Director Prag, seemed obsessed with these escaped human Bionics. He'd arranged Mezobac passage on a fast transport ship to Retul Prime once they had figured out where subject 042 and the other Earth fugitives were going.

Why was he in a panic about a few malfunctioning Bionics? Mezobac was irritated, not only by his boss's continual intrusions, but that they should require him to leave his responsibilities at the park for an unscheduled trip to the home world. Surely there are enough soldiers and security people on Retul. Why send him?

How does a guy like Prag get a position on the UPC Committee, anyway? Mezobac was suspicious of Prag's motives. Is Prag hiding some wrongdoing?

"That's a cop for you," Mezobac thought to himself, "Always looking for criminal intent."

Prag was an unpleasant supervisor, but there was no law against idiot bosses. That would be a law he would support. Huge gap in the legal system, perhaps. Mezobac tried to laugh off his concern.

There was something not right about the whole Earth situation, and it bugged him. Everything was so skewed. It was making him doubt things he didn't like to doubt.

Mezobac questioned the entire Bionic situation. For as long as he could remember, Bionics had been working for the betterment of society. Recently, the prices for them had come down to where even the poorest families could afford one. They were everywhere, but this new idea that they had rights was upsetting the natural order. They were property and by law their owners had rights to them, property rights. But how does property have rights? Can my robotic laundry washer suddenly vote in an election, can it decide it wants a family and buy a house?

To allow the savage races, like Earth's indigenous humans, to have freedom of thought and action was out of the question. Or was it?

That was why the military fought so hard to protect our children and innocent families from all these bloodthirsty savages when we conquered their worlds. That's what he thought. Well, at least since he was an adult. Sure, children always attribute personalities to things, like robots, animals, and even toys. They aren't like actual people, are they?

That thinking didn't reassure him or make him feel any less like things were wrong. Perhaps the human's movies and propaganda he'd been secretly viewing were affecting his views. What he'd found on Earth had made him curious.

He stared at the recruiting poster on the wall of the military transport that was taking him home. It depicted the sharply dressed troops of the United Planetary Confederation defeating hideous beasts of an alien world. He had seen this poster countless times, but now it was like the first time. The alien "beasts" depicted on the poster were one of the many races he'd seen among the Bionics that served the Confederation ever since he could remember.

They'd conquered that race, the Fursensi, decades ago. Yet, they were still propaganda to motivate new recruits? In fact, his family had owned Fursensi Bionics when he was a child. Even Master Calaxan was a Fursensi. They actually were very similar in appearance to Retullians. The blue shades to their gray skin were the fundamental difference, that and their philosophy.

Had the Fursensi really been ferocious beasts, as depicted? The artist's representation of them was frightening. They didn't actually have pointy teeth and claws. Mezobac's first assignment had been on the former Fursensi home world. Of course, he had never witnessed any beastlike behaviors. Their world was peaceful now. They had processed the entire planet long before he arrived. As a young man he'd been a little disappointed, not meeting anything ferocious to test his mettle.

Even though he had outgrown the need for adventure, he'd been excited when assigned to Earth so soon after its conquest. But the humans he'd encountered were pitiful. Their meager projectile weapons were primitive, no match for United Planetary Confederation technology.

What he'd seen of the human's space travel technology was also laughable. He'd made a special effort to go visit the few pitiful space launch sites they had on the planet. The inefficiency of their ancient rocket technology was laughable. Humans, despite their media portrayals of going into space and killing everything, could barely get to the next planet in their own solar system. So why were they portrayed as a threat to the existence of every planet in the Confederation? It was obvious the threat posed by humans was miniscule. So why this huge expenditure of troops and resources to conquer them?

Technically, he wasn't supposed to be using the video player he'd found in his quarters, but who was going to care? The human's video entertainment was elaborate to say the least. Many of the human's video stirred his emotions and fired his mind with ideas. They made all kinds of fantastic claims that were so obviously false, mythical worlds, beings of great power, and starships that freely traveled the universe. It seemed humans would believe anything they were told. Perhaps they were government propaganda to convince Earthlings their military was far stronger than they actually were? A bluff to keep people in submission and maintain power.

His communicator interrupted. "Sir, this is Officer Trezbul of the Retullian security force. When your shuttle arrives, we will send a pursuit craft to meet you."

"Thank you, Officer Trezbul. I should arrive in about thirty minutes at the military compound south of the capital."

"Yes Sir, I have all your flight information on my orders."

"Of course," Mezobac said. His mind still trying to interpret the disparity between the threat Earth posed and the Confederation's response.

He pulled out his data pad and began researching the last several planets the UPC had harvested. There had been three planets in the last five years. The criteria for refusing their inhabitants into the Confederation seemed arbitrary.

Exactly how long it had been since they had accepted a new planet into UPC membership? He wondered. To his surprise, it had been decades, long before his own birth. The way the media had portrayed it, you would have thought it more recent. Odd how he'd missed before.

In the two-hundred-year history of the UPC there had been only six other races accepted into the Confederation besides the five charter member worlds. No new ones in the last forty years. They had discovered eight inhabited planets during that time, and none of them qualified for membership. Odd that all the first six had been accepted, but the last eight had not. That seemed an incredible run of bad luck. Or was there another process at work? His police senses were tingling again.

A new video popped up in his news feed. They labeled it as being from Earth. That was unusual. He hit the play button. Immediately, he recognized the scene. It was a video of the alligator attack on the little girl before he and his men had arrived. Why hadn't he been shown this, he wondered. He saw a timer running in the corner and realized it was from the human's security system. It appeared to be a recording from one of their park security cameras. He'd not thought to check the antiquated human video system to see what it had captured. Obviously, whoever posted this had. None of his people, perhaps one of Prag's people.

He watched as a Bionic in a character costume risked its life to save the little girl. After throwing her clear, the alligator turned on the Bionic, pulling it underwater. He almost cheered when Jinder shot the reptile and some women pulled the Bionic from the water. Someone had taken the time to blur out the women and children's faces.

Then all the women jumped away in fright when they pulled off the costume head. The Bionic turned out to be a human. Someone cut in another video, a close-up of the human's face as they worked to revive it. Then it switched back to the security footage and showed the human regaining consciousness. Then the women carried it away off camera.

Jinder had been afraid to tell him and Prag about the human. Mezobac didn't blame her. It would have gotten ugly if Prag had known it had been a native human encounter. There were so many more human encounters after that, Mezobac had nearly forgotten about it.

The person who posted this knew the entire story and had been close enough to the human encounter to get footage of the human's face. One of Jinder's patients or assistants, perhaps. He thought back to the rescued little girl dancing with her friends. It hadn't been Jinder, but the human that saved the girl. He couldn't get the image out of his head. It was the same man that Prag had referred to as subject 042 in the arrest warrant. Why would a human risk his life to save a Retullian only days after we had invaded his planet? There was something about these humans that the Committee had missed.

Chapter 26 Safe House

The small party of fugitives exited the transport along with a few locals, on to a well-lit gray cement platform. It was night, but it hadn't gotten very dark. A barrier gate closed behind them, and the hover bus pulled away, leaving the small group. They were in a part of the city that didn't have any of the skyscrapers and heavy traffic. Several steel benches lined the platform edge, and an electronic map display stood in its center. No one paid the Bionic Earthlings much attention.

Down a short ramp, off to one side, sat four small hover platforms. Thomas walked toward one of them, intending to ride it. Laurie grabbed his sleeve and stopped him. He looked at her in surprise. Laurie shook her head.

The other passengers all left, some on the small hover platforms and others on foot.

"Bionics aren't allowed to use those." Then she pointed to a sign in alien characters. "That says, 'Non-Bionics only.'"

"How are we supposed to get there?" Emma asked.

"There's a network of walkways designed for use by Bionics. We are going to have to walk." Laurie said.

"How far is it?" Emma asked, concerned for Penny.

"It's about a half-hour walk, Penny can keep up, or we can take turns carrying her."

As they made their way toward the proconsul's house, Thomas couldn't help but be impressed with the vastness of the city. Perhaps the entire planet was a city? The population of this place must measure into the tens of billions of people. Even though it was night, it never really got very dark. Night was more like dusk on earth.

As before, the plainness of the architecture struck Thomas. It wasn't pretty in the least. Function before form was the Retullians creed, they cared only about functionality. The houses were plain, with few variations in design.

Retullians seemed to decorate with a very limited palette of colors. The outsides of the homes came in only a few practical shades of beige and gray. He'd imagined an alien world would at least be cool to see.

"I was expecting The Jetsons, and it's like we're somewhere in New Jersey." Jupiter-D remarked.

"I know. This world inspires no sense of wonder or beauty. All the houses look the same," Thomas said.

The only actual difference from the downtown, aside from the skyscrapers, were the plants. Oddly shaped bushes and small trees decorated the spaces that would've been lawns on earth. The oddly colored growth between the homes was various shades of green and blue mixed in with browns and purples.

How fortunate they had been to find Laurie. Without her, they would never have been able to navigate this world. The walkways were a complicated maze of routes.

Laurie and Penny were walking in the lead while Thomas and Emma followed. He gave Emma a look, and she smiled.

"You know, I saw you in the tunnels that one day, like the first week after the…" Emma stopped, searching for a word to describe the invasion. "You know, after it happened. I thought you were one of *them*, searching for me."

Thomas smiled. "I thought it might have been you. You know I went back to find you but found only a wet sneaker print. I knew the aliens didn't wear Nike's, but you were long gone. Those were scary times. How did you survive?"

"I hid in the tunnels at first. That day, when it all started happening, I was in the staff area. My supervisor, Jillian, told everyone to take cover in the underground tunnels. So, I ran as far as I could and ended up hiding in the water pump rooms for the water park. I wiggled under one of the big tanks and they never found me." Emma said.

"That was smart," Thomas said.

"What about you where did you hide?"

"That was the weird part. I didn't. As always, I was performing in my costume, so I just kept dancing and they ignored me. I still can't figure out why."

"I bet I know." Emma said.

"You better tell me, it's been driving me nuts," Thomas asked.

"Well, I don't want to sound rude, but you are all covered with scars and kinda look like one of those robot people. Perhaps the aliens thought you were a robot?"

"I'd thought of that, but I was wearing the costume and they couldn't have seen my scars and stuff."

"True, maybe because you just kept dancing, ignoring everything. That's what those robot things do. So, they ignored you."

"I guess that's possible," Thomas replied. Was it likely his survival was as simple as that?

"It's the scanners," Laurie said, interrupting without explanation.

"Scanners?" Thomas asked.

"Yes. UPC weapons have smart scanners on all the weapons on their vessels. To sort people, to avoid targeting the wrong people." Laurie explained.

Thomas must have looked surprised, so Laurie continued.

"That's why they didn't target you or Penny. You have your surgical reconstructive implants and Penny has her cochlear implants. You registered as Bionics on their computers and thus weren't targeted. Bionics is the name they use for a being that has been modified by technology. We might also call them cyborgs. Every survivor I've encountered has some type of medical implant."

"Okay, but Emma, they skipped her. She doesn't have implants..."

Emma blushed.

Thomas stopped himself. He couldn't think of Emma as anything but physically flawless.

"Yes, they're fake. Okay. It was for professional reasons. I wasn't getting any acting jobs and my mother told me it would help." Emma confessed. Still blushing defiantly.

"I'm sorry I didn't mean to imply anything, other than I just always thought of you as perfect, and you are. It's totally none of my business." Thomas apologized.

"I think you are the prettiest princess I ever met," Penny said with childlike honesty.

"I agree," Thomas said, hoping to put the topic behind them.

"Thank you," Emma said.

"You shouldn't feel embarrassed, Emma," Laurie added. "You did what you thought best for your career and personal self-esteem. Which in this bizarre situation, also saved you."

"Yes, there is that." Emma smiled.

"Wait, medical implants are pretty common. Are you saying that everyone with some type of implant was missed during the invasion?" Thomas asked.

"Most likely, almost any type of medical implant would have classified the human as a Bionic and not a target. Unless the computer saw them as a potential belligerent. For example, if the human was exhibiting some type of threatening behavior, they'd be neutralized," Laurie answered.

"Since their arrival, the UPC's forces have been overwhelmed with millions of Earthlings missed during the invasion. It seems they didn't expect humans to help the sick and injured. The reports I've found about Earth in their media are incredibly skewed and biased. They view us as savages, much the way Europeans looked at the indigenous peoples of other continents. It gets at the heart of why the Retullians misjudged us."

"That's incredible. I guess humans aren't the only beings that judge others unworthy without really understanding them." Emma said.

"Previously, on other worlds, they never bothered scanning, figuring that they were all savages. However, this resulted in many of the UPC's own Bionics getting targeted during an attack. Recent changes to the UPC's laws regarding Bionic's rights stipulated they must always exclude Bionics from friendly fire. Thus, the targeting computers of the military were updated to avoid killing neutral Bionics during war. Earth was the first planet encountered after the law was passed and the scanners skipped targeting humans with medical implants." Laurie explained.

The thought of all those people hiding in fear for their lives, most of them with serious medical conditions. All Thomas could think about was his parents. They both had pacemakers. They could be alive.

After about an hour of walking, they encountered a watering station. At least there were provisions for the Bionics to rehydrate themselves. The water tasted stale, with a sour fishy aspect. It reminded him of the food bars.

He was glad for the moisture and missed his suit's built-in water pouch. Thomas missed the security of his costume and how he felt protected inside it. Without it, he felt exposed to this alien world.

During the day, the atmosphere of Retul Prime had a hazy grayish appearance. The sky was blue like Earth, but it also had a deep grayness that Earth never had. Thomas wondered if it was seasonal. What type of weather did this world have? Did it rain and storm here? The oxygen levels must be like Earth's. He would have noticed thin air with all this walking. The only thing that made it unpleasant was the odor.

Along the way they encountered few other Bionics. Some of these other alien life forms were far more horrifying than anything Hollywood could mockup. Laurie hid Penny's face from seeing them to prevent her from getting upset.

Despite their grotesque appearance, Thomas shuttered as he thought about the people entrapped by their electronic chains. Rounded up like cattle and turned into servants for the Retullians.

The long, quiet walk gave time for Thomas to contemplate his situation. Why was he here? On a distant planet, in an alien world so far from home. What did he expect to accomplish? Did he really think he could save what was left of Earth and its people? They had this one hope, this one person, that Jinder said was sympathetic to Earth's cause. Could she be trusted? But could he even trust Jinder or Jupiter-D? His heart ached knowing he had no one else to turn to, no other hope for humanity.

"Now that's hurtful, you know I'm just a reflection of what's inside of you, Tommy Boy," Jupiter-D interjected.

"That's what you've been telling me, but then you have all this information that doesn't come from me. So, I'm having some trust issues myself. Did you know about that scanner stuff Lorie was talking about? You could've told me." Thomas said silently.

"I didn't. That's all stuff she got from being connected to the alien network. How do you know she's on the level?"

Thomas didn't know. The aliens had reprogrammed her. Maybe she was leading them into a trap. "But she could've turned us in anytime, why didn't she?"

"Had you considered it isn't you they are trying to find, maybe it's Proconsul Ephynia they want to get? If they catch her helping you, they could incriminate her."

Thomas hadn't thought of that.

"We are here," Laurie announced, as she pointed at the house immediately in front of them. It appeared the same as any other house. It looked identical to the thousands of other houses they had walked past in the last hour. Thomas couldn't imagine that this was the home of some important person. This felt wrong somehow.

Emma started up the walk for the front door, but Laurie stopped her.

"Bionics don't use the front door," so she directed them to a path that led around to the side door to a below grade level.

"I have a code for the door," Jupiter-D told Thomas.

"Jinder gave Jupiter-D a code for this door," Thomas announced.

He entered the code on the keypad.

After a few nervous moments, the side door opened, and two Bionics ushered them in.

They led the group down a hallway to a garage with a parked hover car. And the Bionics steered them into it.

The ceiling of the car looked odd. They'd covered it with dozens of small antennae, like structures over its entire surface. The windows, too, were covered with a thick black metallic film. The car had no driver, but began moving as soon as they shut the door. Thomas could not see exactly how far they'd traveled, but it couldn't have been far. They only drove about a minute. When the car stopped and the doors opened, they found they were in the garage of another home.

Two new Bionics greeted them and instructed them to please follow. A hidden panel in the garage's wall opened and they led them down a stairway to an underground room.

The Bionics motioned for them to wait.

The Bionics just stood there, saying nothing. None of this seemed right to Thomas. Yet, if it was a trap, where could he go?

Chapter 27 Incoming

The room in the house's basement wasn't decorated. A large picture of weird flowers decorated one wall, a plain side table, and a bench that looked like a very uncomfortable sofa substitute. It was lit by a few glowing panels in the ceiling. There was a single hallway at one end, and the floor looked like some type of plastic. The harsh décor and lack of furnishings did nothing to comfort Thomas' unsettled nerves.

After several anxious minutes, the picture of flowers went dark and changed images. It seemed to be a communications device of some type. Because it now showed the image of an older Retullian lady smiling at them and nodding a greeting. Laurie's research indicated that this woman was close to 170 years old, so the aging process must be kind to Retullians. She hardly looked older than others of her race.

"Must be the Retullians come pre-wrinkled so they don't got as much to do later on." Jupiter-D quipped.

Hush!

She spoke, "Welcome to Retul, I am Proconsul Ephynia Telo. I'm so happy Counselor Jinder directed you to me. You are likely the first Earthlings to have visited our world. I must apologize for not greeting you in person, but this situation is dangerous. Besides, you may have noticed that our social pleasantries are far more reserved than most other species we've encountered, so if I seem rude to your sensibilities, I am sorry."

"Before we can proceed, I must verify your identity. Please allow my Bionic friend here cut a lock of your hair."

They let the Bionic cut samples, which it placed in a small bag before leaving the room.

The proconsul looked down at something unseen in front of her and then said, "Okay, verified, thank you. Allow me to explain the situation. This is one of a handful of Bionic safe houses my people have set up. We've established these for Bionics who become self-aware. Unknown to the Confederation, a group I'm associated with has been changing the bionic control software. Thus, some Bionics, like Laurie here, have freed themselves with the aid of these changes."

"This group is called the Bionic Liberation Front and has been working to reform how Bionics are treated in the confederation, with a goal of restoring gradual freedom. Our group has been growing in both number and political clout. We spearheaded the drive to get new laws passed last year giving Bionics fractional rights. It's the first step toward legal freedom."

"Wow, ¼ a person, hooray!" Jupiter-D remarked to Thomas, who was trying to pay attention.

"Earth is the first planet harvested since the new laws went into effect. The law dictates that there be contact with the leaders of the planet before it can be harvested. We have proof that they did not do this. So the Bionic Liberation Front is planning to use that technicality to force the committee to reverse its decision regarding Earth. If we can demonstrate that Earth's humans are not being treated in accordance with the law, we may be able to free the planet."

Thomas nodded, still suspicious about the woman's motives.

"Jinder has been working on a special project for us," Ephynia explained. "Our friends Thomas and Jupiter-D are part of it. The experimental AI chip Jinder used to save Thomas is property of the Bionic Liberation Front, and we want to be certain that its secrets don't get into the wrong hands. It is the key to a new future for the Confederation of planets. It will mean peaceful acceptance and harmony for all the Bionics and their families. With it we will gently convince the more savage races like humans, to conform to our ways and live together in peace."

"Thomas, I really need to give that lady a piece of my mind. Can I use your mouth, please!" Jupiter-D was mad.

Thomas, also upset by the revelation, agreed.

"Lady Ephy-whatever, you wait one doggone minute! This is Jupiter-D talking and there ain't no way I'm gonna do what you say. My job is to help people not turn them into mindless drones! Why, you're no better than those insane committee people. They're using lobotomies and micro-chips, and you just want to be all nicey-nice and use artificial intelligence to do your dirty work! I ain't having no part of this! I apologize for yelling, but this is wrong. What gives you the right to tell how and what other people should think and do? These humans might be pretty messed up, but at least they have been trying, and learning from their mistakes. Your solution is to make everyone like you. Assimilation is assimilation, you've only changed your method. Who made you almighty judge of what people should be like anyway?" Jupiter-D finished, leaving Thomas and everyone else speechless.

"Listen here," Ephynia retorted. "I will not argue with a half-programmed

AI about the ethics of what we are doing. Perhaps, Jinder was mistaken entrusting our chip to the likes of you!"

Just then, several more Bionics came from the other room. Thomas realized he and Jupiter-D were in danger.

"One moment," Laurie interrupted. "Thomas and Jupiter-D are not a threat to your program. Your goals are worthy, but your methods are in error. They don't account for factors we humans and no doubt other people hold precious. Freedom and choice must exist, or you are just creating more robots to do your bidding. There must be a choice even if it's a bad choice with consequences or what you create are not free beings but robots programed only to do your will."

"I disagree," Ephynia said. "I think perhaps we should be certain that the chip is better guided." She looked at one Bionic and nodded.

"Looks like they're more interested in protecting me than you." Jupiter-D said.

Just then, an alarm sounded.

"And then the creepy Bionic lady was interrupted… that alarm don't sound good." Jupiter-D said.

Another Bionic ran into the room, and said, "My lady, the sensor network has picked up multiple hostile vehicles two minutes away."

Ephynia looked down to check her status readout. "Blast it. They still might be headed to the decoy house. Let's not panic. Take these humans into the kitchen and see about extracting that chip."

Chapter 28 Mezobac

Security Chief Mezobac arrived in the capital city of Multus, on the planet Retul Prime, as scheduled. He disembarked on a pad overlooking the city's West Consolidated Complex. He took a moment and basked in the warm feeling of being home. In the distance, he could still see the immense building where he had lived as a child. He remembered watching the shuttles land and depart there from his window.

Mezobac received yet another message from Prag:

Chief, I need you to contact me as soon as they found the fugitives. This is very important. Please respond.

Prag was being even more irritating than usual. Mezobac's thumb hovered over the acknowledge button…

A young man in uniform approached, interrupting him. The man's posture and bearing were definitely ex-military. He'd researched Officer Trezbul. The man had an impressive record as a pilot before being assigned to the security force.

"I can wait until you're finished, sir," the young officer said.

"No need." Mezobac closed his communicator.

"Officer Trezbul, I presume?"

"Yes, sir, did you have a pleasant journey?" Trezbul made an attempt at friendly chit-chat.

"I caught up on some reports, so the time was productive at least. Any updates on the situation?"

"Yes sir, an examination of the planetary scanner logs has revealed the route the fugitives took and their destination."

Mezobac had been on backwater worlds for so long that he'd forgotten how effective a completely working planetary scan system was for tracking criminals. Multus has the lowest crime rate in the Confederation. It was impossible for anyone to hide for long. You couldn't avoid detection by the orbital scanners.

"I assume the humans weren't there when you arrived, or you would've reported their arrest?"

"That is correct, sir. I can update you once we are aboard the pursuit craft."

The policemen boarded a waiting security pursuit craft that sped to a house in the suburb of Multus called Duni, where the fugitives were last seen.

Officer Trezbul began his update. "They exited the cargo pod two days ago and headed to a public transport platform. They delayed and allowed several transports to leave before they boarded one headed to Duni. We theorize they must have received additional instructions, since they'd walked the wrong direction from the pod warehouse. Our forces had nearly caught up with them at that point, but they narrowly escaped. After they got to the house in Duni, they disappeared from the scanners."

After ten minutes, Mezobac, and Trezbul arrived at that same house in Duni. Other officers of the Retullian security forces had arrived and had started scanning the dwelling.

"When were they last here?" Mezobac asked.

"About three hours ago, according to the records," Trezbul said.

"Can people hide from the scanners that long?" Mezobac asked.

"People try, more likely they're hiding in stasis, or somewhere nearby. We will also scan surrounding homes," Trezbul said.

"Sounds like you guys know what you're doing. Who does this house belong to?" Mezobac asked.

"It came back registered to a corporation, Manexp Industries. A generic corporation with a blank directory information file. The only description is *spare Bionic housing*. The house doesn't appear in their main database but might be under a subsidiary. They have over two million subsidiary corporations."

"That sounds like a convenient method for hiding information from the police," Mezobac said.

"Probably a safe house. I've encountered a few of these and they usually use a similar method. They always bury records in some corporation that can't quite be traced. Criminal organizations used these safe houses to hide fugitives. Lately I've seen a few used to hide Bionic violators."

"Bionic violators?"

"Usually, we get a warrant when a Bionic doesn't report for updates on their firmware or tech stuff like that. I guess since the whole Bionic rights thing, certain prosecutors have been making a big deal about it."

"Has there been a lot of these new Bionic violations?"

"Actually, a surprising number since it started a few months ago. We have been kept quite busy tracking down rogue Bionics," Trezbul said.

A young investigator approached and interrupted, "Excuse me, Sir. We have found some hair on the floor of the lower-level room. DNA is Earth

Human."

"So, they were here. Maybe traveling halfway across the galaxy was worth it after all."

"I hope so. But to be candid, I really don't know why you needed to be pulled from your assignment on Earth?" Trezbul asked.

"I have a few theories on that. My supervisor likes to make trouble for me. So, I figure this is just his way to make me want to quit. Or get me out of the way."

"I heard Director Prag was over Earth, am I right?"

"Yeah," Mezobac said and then made a face.

"Enough said," Trezbul Grinned.

"So, let's get back to the Bionic thing. Why is everyone so bugged by a few Bionics acting up?" Mezobac asked.

"We have been advised by the experts that it's 'only a matter of time until one of these wild Bionics endangers innocent civilians.'" Trezbul said. "Off the record, sir, I think their concerns are exaggerated. I've never met a hostile Bionic."

"So, all of this so-called 'danger' is purely theoretical?" Mezobac asked.

"I suppose it is, Sir."

"It's troubling that busy security officers are told to give such minor infractions priority. What if I forget to update my communicator within thirty days, do I become a fugitive?"

"No, Sir. Not yet." Trezbul grinned. He seemed pleased to meet a command officer that appreciated the idiocy of the situation.

Chapter 29 Rebellion

During their escape, Laurie's diversionary tactic at the Bionic maintenance office set off a chain of events that quickly spiraled out of control. The alien network had been overwhelmed by the little virus code she'd written to initiate the Bionic diversion. She had restricted its effect to the Bionics in the maintenance area. To Laurie it was nothing special, just a data worm to buy them some time.

Calaxan had expected that his work would someday be discovered. He had prepared for it. Prag had made the mistake of trying to arrest him. He had built safeguards so that he would be alerted as soon as any warrants were issued for him. He'd constructed a safe place where the drones and scanners wouldn't find him. Here he could work in peace to formulate his plans for true Bionic liberation.

Calaxan was a member of the Bionic Liberation Front, but his ideas were deemed too radical for them. He felt the BLF's strategy for Bionic liberation was flawed. A gradual, deliberate relaxation of Bionic control would be ineffective. Before those efforts yielded any tangible results, the Bionics would be old or dead. He'd also been privy to their covert plan to use the AI chip to replace surgical harvesting. That was a terrible idea, in his opinion. It was still slavery, just in a different form. That's why he'd secretly given up on the BLF. Officially, he was still a member, because it was a useful source of information.

He'd been working behind the scenes for years, and he'd finally found what he'd been looking for on Earth. The code Laurie had written was the key to what Calaxan had been searching for. She'd created a digital virus with self-replicating code. This method was superior to anything he'd seen before. Nothing like it existed in the Confederation. It used an algorithm to replicate itself in the central computer's primary command stream. He took his stolen copy of Laurie's Bionic override subroutines, compressed them, and embedded them as the payload of the digital worm.

The result was freedom for the Bionics. His goal had been accomplished in minutes instead of decades. All the Bionics on Earth were finally set free thanks to Laurie's code. Capable of thinking and acting on their own. He'd gotten it to every Bionic connected to Earth's network before the Retullians had a chance to notice.

If Calaxan could spread this across the entire intergalactic UPC network, the Confederation would be brought to its knees. But he'd hit a stumbling block. Data sent to the main UPC uplink were encoded in a way that Calaxan was unaware of. He was confident he'd figure it out eventually, but it could take days to get it to pass through the uplink encoder.

Laurie's approach was far more inventive than anything the Confederation had ever devised. Humans and their incredible imaginations had weaponized computer programming, allowing them to conduct cyberwarfare. They designed code to act like biological pathogens. These humans were incredibly devious.

Calaxan marveled at these wonderfully confused and conflicted humans and all the chaos they embraced. Imagine, allowing people to have freedom to create anything they wanted. All the media and all the fantastic stories that the ignorant, unimaginative Confederation had misinterpreted as propaganda. These Earthlings dreamed so much and accomplished so little. Yet, those dreams unleashed on a universe of unprepared beings with advanced technology were going to be a source of substantial power. Even a good man was tempted to do evil by it.

He'd considered taking control of all the Bionics with this newfound power. Order them to destroy the Confederation. But he'd resisted temptation. It would have made him as bad as the Retullians. So he'd freed the Bionics instead. They could do whatever they wanted. He would let them follow whatever course their long-imprisoned souls desired. However, they might require some oversight. He could suggest they do a few things to get the confederation's attention.

Sector Director Prag sat in his office going over reports. His plan to snag Calaxan and any other Bionic sympathizers was working. Already, that irritating Counselor Jinder had implicated herself. It was time to round them up and ship them back to Retul Prime for justice on the home world. Clear out the muck from his ranks and go forward with a staff that would do what he needed to put this harvest back on track.

Prag and the other committee members had fought hard to defeat these ridiculous Bionics rights laws and failed. The only good thing to come from them was that these Bionic sympathizers let down their guard. Now he knew who his enemies were.

They had discovered a few Bionic sympathizers involved in programming the Bionics had snuck in some type of flaw in one of the software updates. Their code had triggered several Bionic malfunctions. Those programmers had been found and prosecuted.

Earth was a troublesome planet. It had been so simple to find reasons for their ineligibility for membership at first. There had been a plethora of video evidence. The difficulty had been sorting through so much of it! Earth was a filthy, decaying wasteland.

It didn't even require the investigators to land on the planet to collect it. These idiots were broadcasting it into space! It had been simple to build a case against them. Earth's society was hopelessly backward, violent, and corrupt.

When his agents presented this evidence to the Planetary Acceptance Council, they were shocked and needed little time to deliberate. The Committee unanimously declared Earthlings irredeemable. Their planet is a rich source of raw materials and is only suitable for harvesting. Its water alone would be enough to supply the entire UPC for decades. Prag was about to become a wealthy man, far wealthier than he was already. A percentage of the natural resources and a fat royalty on every human harvested, and there were billions of them! With the money he was about to get, he could afford to buy his own planet.

Even the blundering of those idiots in the military couldn't deter him. Whose idea was it to apply the new Bionic regulations to sensor programming for harvesting? So many humans had been missed by the military. They'd mislabeled them as Bionics.

Mezobac was a moron for objecting to his use of automated drones near the park. He was relieved to have found a reason to get him out of the way. Now he could focus the security forces on putting all these so-called human Bionics into inventory.

Getting the drones reprogramed had been a bureaucratic nightmare. There were far too many humans to track down and shoot with handheld stasis weapons. Getting the drones reprogrammed was hugely problematic. After all that effort, he discovered that his older model security drones were incompatible. They wouldn't be able to update to the latest software without a chip revision. He'd been trying for weeks to get the manufacturer to update the chip, but it'd been pushed back yet again! The drones continued to ignore humans with medical implants.

He'd worked hard to pin all the blame for the delays on Mezobac while he was away. Retaliation against the council for forcing him to hire the man as security chief. He was the worst kind of cop, the kind who actually believed in enforcing the law. Lieutenant Ganjat, Mezobac's adjutant, was an ideal candidate for Chief. Fearful enough not to question Prag's authority, but corrupt enough to be swayed by a couple of lavish gifts.

Prag was well on his way to crushing the Bionic Liberation sympathizers on Earth. It would be a temporary delay in productivity. The impact of profitability would be negligible. Once they found and arrested Calaxan and rounded up the few Bionics with the defective code, it would be over and everything would be back on track. Prag had finally gotten the situation under control.

Prag's communicator alerted him to a priority call.

"Um, Sector Director Prag, this is Lieutenant Ganjat. I just received a disturbing message from the Earth sector network manager, Huergex. You know that code stuff you mentioned at today's briefing. That thing Calaxan was using to make the Bionics go crazy?"

"Yes, yes. What about it?"

"What does that mean, Ganjat? Get to the point."

"Huergex thinks Calaxan discovered a way to copy his bionic corruption code secretly over the planetary network."

"How many Bionics have been affected?"

"He thinks all of them. It spread like wildfire. He seemed upset about it and wants your permission to shut down the uplinks until he figures it out."

It took only a moment for that last bit to sink in. Panic struck. Prag stood up from his comfortable chair.

"Tell Huergex to turn off the network! Do it right away!" Prag screamed. Have him notify the rest of the UPC not to connect to Earth's network until we know it has been contained.

Prag pushed his button and yelled for his assistant to contact Huergex directly.

A few minutes later and the entire UPC Earth network uplink went down.

He never imagined that Calaxan would be this capable. Hopefully, they had shut it off before whatever it was spread.

Prag was in shock. Huergex had examined the code and said it acted more like a disease than a program.

Prag accessed the human's primitive public network and typed in, "Computer Pathogen" after his translator program finished it filled his screen with thousands of articles about Computer viruses, Cyberwarfare, and electronic pathogens. He didn't have to read very much when it became dreadfully clear. These insane humans had created a method of spreading malicious computer code by imitating biological pathogens.

It was the end of his career. What an incredible oversight, but who would have guessed. But it was right there. Anyone could have known.

This was a disaster. Those human viruses would make the Bionics go insane and kill everyone. He ordered Ganjat to bring all of his security people to gather at the park headquarters.

Prag needed to protect himself because there were too many Bionics and not enough security personnel. Then another troubling thought occurred to him. The Committee would quarantine the planet as soon as they learned of this. Then the military would respond by destroying it from space! He was doomed.

No one else knew yet, he realized.

Prag was not about to die on this vile planet. He gathered a few important things from his desk and put them in his briefcase.

He left his office and lied to his assistant, "Phrenzes, I have to ensure that all of Jinder's patients are on the next passenger shuttle. I'll be back in about three hours. I'm putting Ganjat in charge."

With no further word, Prag walked to his personal hover car and took it to catch the next departing shuttle. He pulled rank to get a seat on what would be the last shuttle out before the quarantine. Upon boarding he was met with the evil looks from Vi-Zeha, Jinder's friend, and her other patients whom he'd ordered off the planet that same day.

By the time the Bionics were in full revolt, Prag was in hyperspace, headed home.

Calaxan had only needed a few hours to assemble a small army of Bionics to oppose the UPC security forces. He'd gathered them in front of the maintenance shop and distributed the few weapons he'd stashed away. He had to rally these Bionics to march on the UPC Earth headquarters, which was just outside the park. The Bionics, despite their growing numbers, were unruly and hopelessly outgunned. If they didn't find more weapons and figure out how to organize a chain of command, it was going to be a massacre.

That's when they heard a commotion of gunfire erupt from the crew's quarters. They reported that there was a battle happening at the stairway that led to the maze of tunnels below the park. Calaxan gathered the other Bionics and stationed the few that were armed in sight of the door, ready to open fire if the security forces attacked.

Just then a handful of humans dressed in mottled green uniforms burst through the double doors with Confederation security disintegrator fire pounding the corridor behind them.

Razoul and the other human survivalists emerged from the crew area only to be confronted by an army of alien cyborgs. Razoul was so unnerved he almost opened fire. Until they realized that many of the cyborgs were human and had lowered their weapons.

Calaxan ran to them, shouting in English, "We are not enemies! I have freed the robotic slaves of the Confederation. We are here to help free Earth from the oppressive rule of the UPC."

Razoul and the other survivalists appeared to be persuaded, and they turned to face their pursuers.

The next moment, a small group of security troops burst through the doorway in hot pursuit. Their eyes widened in disbelief at seeing the Bionic army backing the survivalists.

The Humans opened fire.

Immediately, the security forces retreated, running back down into the tunnels.

"Should we chase em, colonel?" Razoul asked.

An older man shook his head. "No, plenty of time for that later. Our time would be better spent getting acquainted with our new allies."

The man turned to Calaxan and said, "I'm Colonel Javier Gonzales retired, and this is my second, Razoul Benedict, and, of course, my men." He gestured toward the other humans with him.

"Thank you for the backup, it's my pleasure to make your acquaintance. Who are you sir and who are all these…" he paused, trying to find a word, "… men?"

"I am Bionic Master Engineer Calaxan. And these, men, are the robotized slaves of Earth's invaders, recently freed from technological slavery. I hope you'll see us as allies in the fight to free not only Earth but all Confederation conquered planets everywhere."

The colonel, an experienced veteran, looked over his new allies. Lot of people but very few weapons.

"You have quite an army, Sir. But it appears you're missing some fire power. Maybe I can remedy that. If you agree to include us as representatives of Earth in your rebellion. I can help you make sure we do this job right."

"We'd welcome your help. I am not a military man, and I need an experienced field commander," Calaxan admitted. "If you'll help us get our worlds back, starting with Earth, then we have a deal."

The colonel turned to Razoul and his little commando party and asked, "Are you guys good with that?"

All the survivalists all nodded, glad to have reinforcements, even bizarre alien ones.

The colonel gave a big smile and said, "I accept your commission, and my forces agree to help."

Razoul's face betrayed a suppressed disgust at the aliens, but he nodded acceptance and forced a smile.

The colonel ordered the men to make a perimeter and set up a watch. He and the senior troops should all sit down and discuss objectives

The colonel chuckled, and said, "It appears that the Grand Army of the Republic must help free the slaves of yet another Confederacy." Only a few of the older humans appreciated the joke.

The reference puzzled Calaxan.

The colonel said, "It's a reference to a human historical conflict. I can explain it to you later, but first, you said you needed some weapons. You wouldn't have access to some of those fancy flying vehicles, would you?"

"That we do, colonel," Calaxan said.

Over the next few days Calaxan's men worked with Colonel Gonzales, Razoul, and the other human fighters to recover a considerable number of weapons and ammo from caches the survivalists had prepped. The colonel also took a longer trip to the nearest military base and gathered a huge number of weapons. They also passed the word to several other pockets of human survivors that joined up with them.

At last, Calaxan's Bionic army had weapons. The troops were an unruly mix of humans, Bionic humans, Fursensi, and other subjugated races, all grateful to be freed from the prison of control. True, their weapons were primitive compared to the UPC, but still effective in overwhelming numbers. The colonel instituted an improvised training program where humans with weapons experience would train willing Bionics.

Calaxan had also stressed the importance of seizing the UPC headquarters in order to gain control of the network. It was critical to get the virus onto the UPC's interplanetary network and spread it to Bionics all over the universe. This would destabilize the entire UPC, making it impossible for them to bring their massive army back to Earth and reconquer it. To do this, they needed to capture the UPC headquarters.

Other Bionics, with no desire to fight, were trained on how to operate the equipment to find and free humans from stasis. They began going through the park and surrounding areas, scanning for humans and releasing them with no explanation. Dozens of bewildered people now roamed the streets looking for lost loved ones and answers.

The rebel's numbers swelled as many of the now freed Bionics learned about the rebellion and wanted to join.

Chapter 30 Jinder Unbound

Counselor Jinder had been in detention ever since they had arrested her for treason. Prag had interrogated her, but had provided no evidence against her. She hadn't been given the real reason for her arrest. The questions they'd asked led her to believe it had something to do with Calaxan.

As she lay in her cot locked in a storeroom, she could only hope that her old professor, Proconsul Ephynia, would protect the chip inside Thomas and keep it secret. Would Thomas even make it to Retul? She might never know. The extent of Prag's corruption was far greater than she'd imagined.

This saddened her greatly. She had been so optimistic that she might push her society into a new and better way to achieve peace. Her AI chip could provide an even more humane solution to the terrible horror of war and violent harvests. This was to be her greatest achievement. Peace and prosperity for all without the horror and injustice of forced surgical implants. Her chip would help everyone get along in peace.

All she could do was wait to be summoned by the judicial council for her trial. And then make the long trip back to Retul Prime for her hearing.

She wondered what Master Calaxan had done to make Prag so paranoid. During her interrogation, Prag had seemed keenly interested in how much she knew about whatever Calaxan had been doing. Perhaps Calaxan was for more interested in Bionic rights than she'd known.

Jinder was also concerned about the well-being of her wards and her friend Vi-Zeha. She hadn't been able to find out if Vi-Zeha had escaped Earth with the families. Still, she remained glad for the progress her patients had made in this amazing place, Mercury World. The Retullians had much to learn about imagination and healing from humans, and especially this Waldo Mercury. The humans had never been a threat to the Confederation. In fact, they were mostly harmless.

Why had she accepted the slew of lies about Earth spread by her government? The truth had been quite different. Her suspicions had been validated. Earth's assessment was incorrect, and Prag was to blame. She had known about the injustice toward Bionics for years, but seeing the corrupt committee profit from it firsthand was difficult to watch. The idea of actual people being harvested, taken from their homes to be made into Bionics for the UPC bothered her. A vague guilt gnawed at her for being complacent about it for so long.

In college, she'd been exposed to the Bionic abolitionist students and their claims. That was ten years ago, and no one took them seriously. Everyone she knew considered them a bunch of sentimental extremists.

But then she met Professor Ephynia Telo. She taught a class in xeno-social studies. Jinder had heard her promote abolitionist ideas a few times in class. At first it had seemed so radical. But the truths she'd learned since had inspired her to collaborate with Vi-Zeha and develop an application for the Biphasic processor chip as an even better solution than Bionic Harvesting. Later she learned her professor was involved with the Bionic liberation movement, so she approached her with her AI chip idea. Ultimately, Ephynia connected her with clandestine funding to begin her work with Vi-Zeha.

She'd been imprisoned here for two days. It was getting dark, and they were about to turn off all the lights in the makeshift detention area, which was located in the basement level of the former Mercury Corporation office building. She gathered her blanket and closed her eyes, attempting not to dwell on her predicament.

Suddenly her doze was interrupted by a loud alarm. Jinder sat up as all the lights in the building came on.

That's when she heard it, the muffled sound of gunfire and tumult. A mob was attacking the UPC headquarters.

The sound of battle grew louder and closer. When a few random bullets ricocheted somewhere above her, she moved her bed to the back of the cell where the wall was concrete and took cover beneath it.

The battle raged for hours, and eventually she heard them breach the building. Jinder waited and worried.

After a few hours, she heard the sounds of conflict in the basement area where she was being held. A pepper of sporadic gunfire rebounded down the hallway outside her room as they battled with the few remaining guards in the detention area.

The rebels came to her makeshift cell and smashed open the door.

"There's someone under that bed in the corner. Bring them out," a soldier commanded.

Roughly they dragged Jinder from under the bed in to the light.

"Razoul, we found another wrinklehead locked in this closet. Do we shoot it?" A soldier asked.

"No, wait for me to check it," Razoul shouted. Jinder watched as a large human male entered her cell and looked her over.

Jinder just stood there and said nothing.

"Let's take this one to Calaxan. They locked her up, so she might be on our side," Razoul decided.

Razoul dragged her up a flight of stairs and into the room where Calaxan and a group of important-looking humans were talking around a table. A few dozen people were milling about. She noticed several UPC security officers who were bandaged and restrained in chairs. She noticed Master Calaxan was with them.

Razoul appeared to be upset. "Did you start the planning meeting without me, Colonel?"

"No, we're just going over a few reports. Who is this alien woman?" The colonel inquired.

Razoul reported, "I discovered her imprisoned on the detention level."

Calaxan turned around and said, "Counselor Jinder, I'm glad to see you're okay. You are free to untie her, Razoul. She has been assisting me, perhaps unwittingly, but she is a supporter of our cause. Director Prag, without a doubt, arrested you because of me. Please accept my apologies. Because of this minor victory, I've become rather generous, even toward Retullians. Please free her."

The men untied her hands. Jinder stood there uncertainly.

Calaxan returned his focus to the other humans. Some people in the room still eyed her suspiciously.

"Excuse me, am I permitted to leave? I'd like to go to my office to make sure my research hasn't been disrupted," Jinder inquired.

"I think that's fine. Your research does not contradict our objectives. Please allow me to consult with the colonel." Calaxan drew the attention of the man they'd dubbed the colonel who was sitting next to him.

"Colonel, please allow me to introduce Counselor Jinder to you. Jinder is a Retullian counselor who came to Earth to assist families and children who have experienced traumatic loss. Her work, in my opinion, is significant. Do you have any reservations about the councilor returning to work?"

"I have no problem with that," said the colonel. "We must ensure that this movement does not devolve into a divisive hatred of the Confederation's innocent civilians. They are not our adversaries. A great man once said, 'Those who make war should be always remain cognizant of the peace that is to follow, or it may never come.' Please, counselor, return to your work. There are hundreds of displaced people who will all require help."

Jinder, although gladdened by the man's goodwill, wasn't ready to start taking appointments.

"Jinder, you may go back to helping the widows and orphans heal. There will be a lot more of them soon enough," Calaxan said, sounding like he'd already won the war.

"I'll need an escort, in case I meet some more of your *freedom* fighters looking to add another '*wrinklehead*' to their scorecard," Jinder said.

"Of course, Counselor. Razoul, take care of it, please," the colonel instructed.

Exclusion from the planning meeting had already irritated Razoul. He sure wasn't going to get stuck babysitting some alien.

He drew the attention of one of the human women who was standing around, lost. "Please excuse me, lady, what is your name?" Razoul inquired.

The woman introduced herself as "Deidra."

"I need you to take the counselor where she needs to go. Get whatever she needs. Can you make sure she isn't mistaken for a hostile alien in any way?" Razoul explained.

"Sure, it beats standing around here." Deidra replied, her teeth clenched.

Chapter 31 Here's Waldo

Deidra accompanied Jinder to her office, which was upstairs in the same building. She seemed eager to talk to someone about what was happening.

"So, you speak English?" Deidra asked.

"Yes, sort of. I have a translator chip."

"Can you explain what is happening? No one I've asked has been helpful."

"I can try. What do you know already?" Jinder smiled.

"I know Earth was invaded by aliens… um, your people. But somehow, I missed part of it. Last thing I remember, I looked out my office window. These big hovering ships were moving through the sky, followed by swarms of drones. People were in a panic everywhere, and the next thing I knew, it was today.

"I woke up lying on the floor like I'd been sleeping. When my stomach settled, I got up and checked my computer and found over two months had passed. I came out of my office and saw these people running around with weird devices, making people appear out of thin air. I asked them to take me to someone who could explain all this, but they ignored me."

"It sounds like they struck you with one of the wide-beam stasis guns during the invasion. And then today someone pulled you out of stasis and just left you there to recover by yourself. It is disorienting but rarely harmful." Jinder explained.

"Stasis?"

"Our stasis weapons are a non-violent way to bring order to primitive peoples. They move people to another dimension where no time passes. Like freezing someone and then defrosting them later," Jinder explained.

"That's some funky tech." Deidra said, shaking her head.

"So, after I woke up, I followed some people up to the room where we met, hoping to learn what was happening. I stood around listening to them

163

argue for twenty minutes until they brought you in. Didn't learn a thing."

"I'd be happy to tell all I know. Perhaps, once we get to my office, we can sit down and chat. We are almost there. It's just up ahead," Jinder told the woman, trying to reassure her. Then pointed at the door to her office.

"That's your office?" Deidra laughed. "This is mine right here," and pointed to the desk in front of Jinder's office.

"Well, that's convenient. That's where my friend, Vi-Zeha, used to sit." Jinder smiled. "Obviously, the offices were all empty when they told me to choose one."

"You're in Mr. Mercury's office. You must be someone important." Deidra said.

"Not really. I was the first one here, so I took the nicest office. Besides, I liked all his pictures and books," Jinder said as they entered her office.

"I rather like them myself," an old man behind Jinder's desk said.

Jinder stopped, surprised to see an old human sitting at her desk. Despite his age, his eyes twinkled with humor and intellect. He gave the women a big smile and said, "So you're the one who moved my stuff,"

"Sir!" Deidra exclaimed. "Thank goodness, you're alright! Were you hit by that stasis thing too?"

Deidra ran over and embraced her boss.

"I suppose I was. I'm glad to see you as well, Miss Emery."

"Mr. Mercury, I presume?" Jinder asked.

"Yes, madame. I am he, and pardon my forwardness, who are you? And what are your people doing to my park!" Waldo Mercury said. He stood, hands on hips, and tried to look upset, but his good-natured expression and deep smile lines made it hard to believe.

"A pleasure to meet you," Jinder returned his smile. "Sorry for moving things, I tried to file everything neatly. But I'm not terribly familiar with your alphabet."

"No worries, it wasn't really that organized." Waldo gave her a friendly grin.

"I should tell you—I have become quite an admirer of your park and well, everything," Jinder said. "As far as what *my* people are doing, I can explain some, although I'm a little fuzzy on the more recent developments."

"Well, do your best and we'll probe you with questions for the rest." The man smiled and invited the ladies to have a seat.

"Perhaps before we get started, I can get us some coffee and snacks? Since I'm up, anyway." Waldo put a tray on his desk and invited them to help themselves.

"I have only been in this new reality an hour, but I figured some coffee and sweets might help clear my head." Waldo explained.

"Sounds wonderful I have developed a taste for your coffee drink," Jinder said politely. "May I also check my communicator? It's in my... um your, top drawer. I must find out if my patients are safe."

"Certainly, make yourself at home." He laughed out loud, "I guess I better be careful your people might take that literally."

Jinder and Deidra also smiled. Jinder was beginning to understand the human sense of humor.

She was relieved to see a message that all of her children and their moms had escaped before the troubles broke out. They were safely on their way home.

Waldo served coffee and cookies and sat back down, ready to hear Jinder's explanation.

"My name is Counselor Jinder Adronzin. I am a citizen of a league of planets known as the United Planetary Confederation. It's a union of eleven planets that govern this part of what humans call the Milky Way galaxy. I'm from the planet Retul Prime and our people call themselves Retullians. Our atmosphere is most like Earth's, so we were selected to colonize it. We are one of the five founding races that make up the confederacy."

Waldo frowned at the word.

"You know something of our Confederation, Mr. Mercury?" Jinder asked, surprised at the reaction.

"Not yours, but that word 'confederacy' has a negative connotation for many. We had a government that called itself that once. It had a dubious history. Go on, please," Waldo explained.

"Understood. I'll try to be more conscious about avoiding the word. Is Federation a better translation?"

"No, it's fine. Confederation is an acceptable word in English. My own feelings aside. Continue, please."

"I came to Earth as part of a research project. It has to do with grief resolution for the families of soldiers killed in the line of duty. Your park was chosen because of its unique child friendly atmosphere. I wanted to see what effect the therapy would have as soon after the loss as possible."

"I would guess that's a commendable thing. But I'm not sure how I feel about it. Since you are talking about the invasion of Earth," Mercury said.

"Well, that's quite a mistake. Eight billion people are dead because your government got clumsy."

"Not exactly," Jinder interrupted. "The Confederation doesn't kill noncombatants on worlds they conquer. They put them in stasis and then harvest them later." Jinder had never realized how awful that term sounded until now.

"Harvest them! What, for food?" Deidra said, horrified.

"No, not food. Never!" Jinder replied. "They place them in time frozen stasis fields and then come back later and wake them up and retrain them, um, surgically. We actually make them better than they were before. They're given physical enhancements and then reeducated. Then they're able to join society as useful members."

"Wait, is that what all these robo-people are? Reprogrammed people?" Deidra said, unable to believe her ears.

"What you're describing sounds like something we on Earth call slavery. High-tech slavery perhaps, but who cares if it's a chain or a fancy computer that binds you? So, you're saying, in simple terms, your government invades planets and enslaves their populations," Mercury said, still frowning.

"Well, that's not an equivalent word choice. Bionics, what you call robo-people, are given a great deal of respect and work to spread the benefits of the Confederation to everyone. But my friends and I have a better way. We have a new technology that will work with the person to help them change."

"Why do they have to change to suit you? Are they still given a choice? Are they compensated for their work? Do they get to enjoy these so-called benefits themselves?" Mercury asked.

"Well, not all of them. But they are given good health and an important part in making the world a better place. It's not perfect, but it's the best solution we have found," Jinder said.

"They must start the propaganda early in your society for you to be so blind to something so wrong," Mercury said, shaking his head in disbelief.

Jinder was unable to respond. Waldo's words had the ring of truth to them. But the truth was terrifying, overwhelming. She rejected his argument emotionally because, if that were true, who was she? Had she been programmed to ignore the plight of the Bionics? She used various forms of conditioning to help her patients all the time as a counselor. Was the government using it on her as well?

"I'm gratified by that look on your face," Waldo said. "You didn't see it that way before, did you?"

Jinder shook her head and blotted her eyes. "I knew it was wrong, but that's why my friends are working to change things."

"But if they don't have free will, it is slavery." Waldo said again.

"It's okay if you cry, if your people cry that is? We humans have shed a good number of tears over the evils of slavery in our history. Its horrific repercussions continued for decades after we abolished it. I will not call you to account for the sins of your government."

Struck by the old man's wisdom, Jinder hung her head.

Waldo kindly waited for Jinder to regain her composure. Then began speaking again, "Let me guess. Now your Bionics have revolted and your society is collapsing to its knees. I saw some of those robo-Bionic people running around with guns. They aren't being good little workers for the betterment of society anymore, are they?"

"No, I... well, we discovered a problem," Jinder began. "Well, lots of problems. When we find a new planet with a sentient population, they're supposed to be offered membership in the Confederation. We are searching the galaxy for brothers and sisters, not slaves. Historically, we accepted everyone we met."

"So, what happened?"

"That approach worked until about a hundred years ago. We met a people that called themselves the Fursensi. We offered them friendship, and they joined with us at first. But later, problems developed. The Fursensi were a devout people, and when we rejected their religion, they turned against us, attacking without warning.

"Decades of misery resulted from that dreadful war. Millions of people died on both sides. It was the most horrific period in our history. We vowed never to allow such suffering, pain, and loss again."

Waldo and Deidra nodded in understanding.

"In the end, we won the war. Our planets and cities were in ruins, and we had to deal with tens of thousands of prisoners of war and Fursensi refugees, all of whom had vowed to fight us to the death. We couldn't free them, and they couldn't be persuaded to change. That left us with two options: forcibly reeducate them or murder them in cold blood. We went with the first option. They were therefore useful to society and could thrive once more. We used the Bionic Fursensi to rebuild what we had lost during the war. The UPC compelled the Fursensi to repair the damage they had caused. Our actions were entirely justified. We'd found a reasonable and humane solution."

Jinder looked to Waldo Mercury for acknowledgement, but got none.

"So, it only made sense that afterward, anytime we encountered a new planet of people, we made certain they would be suitable for membership in the Confederation before inviting them. We had to be certain any new worlds wouldn't attack us and undo the progress the UPC has made in advancing peace and unity. Laws were passed and procedures put into place."

"Fair enough, a difficult solution to an impossible problem," Mercury said.

"Everyone believed it had been working for decades. I believed it until I arrived here. Here I discovered a problem—Earth and perhaps other previous planets hadn't been properly investigated. My research revealed a high level of bias in the investigations. And when the planet's natives were deemed unsuitable, their people were harvested and made into Bionics preemptively. Thus, preventing a war."

"Let me guess, all that free labor made your people's lives easier and those in control became wealthier," Waldo said.

"Yes, but we thought it was a dividend of peace and cooperation."

"So, what about those that stood to profit from all this free labor? Were there any checks put upon them to prevent abuse?"

"We had been told there was. But no one realized that harvesting worlds instead of helping them could be so profitable. The thought of someone profiting from the harvesting process was just beyond question and our leaders above corruption."

"I hope you don't take this wrong, but your people seem rather naïve." Deidra said.

"It seems we are. As soon as I had actual evidence people were cheating, I sent a report to warn the planetary acceptance committee of about it."

"The people that you sent the report to are the ones profiting from the harvests," Mercury said.

Jinder looked surprised. "Do you really think so? The entire committee is corrupt too? That's almost beyond comprehension."

"Really? You didn't see that right away. Even after you got arrested?" Deidra asked.

"It must be easy for someone in your culture to see such connections, but ours is very different. I can't imagine someone being that selfish and deceitful." Jinder felt foolish.

"Don't blame yourself, you didn't understand what was happening." Waldo tried to be kind.

"Perhaps you can tell me more about the work you've been doing to oppose it. Maybe there is a way to prevent this revolution from spreading and hurting more people?" Mercury said.

"It all started when I found a human who had been missed during the invasion," Jinder began. "I was taking a group of my patients for recreation when we found him. He was one of the characters in the park, Jupiter-D Dog, I think you call him. He entertained my group with delightful dances. We didn't know he was a human surviving by pretending to be a Bionic. But then he did something remarkable that made me question everything I'd been told."

"Jupiter-D always becomes the unwitting hero of my stories..." Waldo reflected aloud.

Deidra smiled she knew Jupiter-D was Waldo's favorite.

"So what did he do?"

"Well, he almost died while saving one of my patients, a child, from an alligator attack. It was incomprehensible to me. This level of self-sacrifice is unheard of in our society. In my studies of other cultures, I had only heard theories of this concept."

Waldo smiled, realizing that one of his employees had saved an alien child.

"Wait. Your people don't have heroes?" Deidra asked, sounding surprised.

"Hero? That term doesn't translate well. Do you mean people who fight in battle?" Jinder asked, uncertain.

"Sometimes it can mean brave warriors, but a hero is someone who risks their own health and safety for another, to prevent a tragedy, or save a life. A person who acts altruistically. Our culture holds such people in high esteem."

Mercury explained.

"While I'll admit that's an attractive concept, it's not something our people have embraced," Jinder said.

"A culture with no heroes, what do your people look to for inspiration. What stories do you tell your children to fire their imaginations and make them creative and useful members of society?"

"Stories? We don't tell stories. I have seen some of your human stories and I admit being confused by many of them. For example," Jinder pointed to a children's book on Waldo's shelf, *The Three Little Pigs*.

"Why doesn't the pig with the brick house provide shelter to his companions? It would have been far more practical for them to have pooled their resources to make the best house to defend against the danger of the wolf?"

"What don't you understand?"

"The answer was obvious why tell a long story?" Jinder asked.

"Because the story is not about pigs and wolves, it's about people wisely using resources. To think ahead and imagine dangers and prepare for them. So, when the wolf attacks, you are ready. Stories can create connections between things that don't seem related but can be in certain situations."

"In our culture, we don't rely on imagination. Our children have some level of imagination, but we discourage them from using it. When I studied humans, I was surprised at how much they relied on it. Then I came here and saw how healing it could be for people."

"They send scouting missions to observe and determine whether the people would be suitable partners in peace."

"And what did they say about Earth?" He asked.

"Yes, we know what propaganda is. The Fursensi used it against us. They tried to turn the other members of the confederation against each other with it."

"You should know that most of our stories aren't propaganda, we make those movies as entertainment. It like my park here, it brings joy and happiness to people to imagine themselves as heroes fighting against evil and hatred," Mercury said.

"I don't agree. I've seen some of your human movies, and they didn't make me happy. It depicted heinous torture and unspeakable abuse of other people. If that's entertainment, it encourages people to be evil villains rather than heroes?" Jinder stated.

"She has a good point," Deidra said. "In my opinion, a lot of movies these days are horrible sadistic garbage. If that was my first impression of humans, I might judge them incorrigible and determine they need to be controlled. The despicable and brutal images being offered in the name of entertainment are detestable."

Mercury nodded in agreement. He had long strived to improve

entertainment and always worked for standards. Yet his attempts had failed, and in this bizarre turn of fate, it had led to Earth's destruction and ruin. Somehow, he felt to blame.

Jinder tried to understand. "Why didn't your government stop them?"

"It's not as simple as it sounds. Who has the authority to decide what is good and bad? Humans have been grappling with this quandary since the Garden of Eden, and we have made no progress," Waldo said. "It now appears to have resulted in another fall of humanity." His frown made deep lines in his forehead.

"We tried, Waldo, we tried," Deidra said, hoping to console the man.

Waldo Mercury stopped himself and said, "Enough with the coulda, shoulda, wouldas. Earth isn't lost and we are back among the living. What can we do to make this right?"

"Miss Jinder, do you know what has happened with this revolution? Has Earth's harvest been stopped? Have we been saved?" Waldo asked.

"Somehow Master Calaxan used Earth's technology to break the control that the computer chips have over the Bionic's minds. He set them free on Earth and they have joined the remaining humans in retaking the planet."

"But with the power of your military they should be able to put down a minor rebellion on Earth just like they conquered it the first time."

"I think I know," Deidra added. "Before, you arrived, I overheard Calaxan talking about a human named Laurie coding a virus to create a diversion and that's how he's learned to spread it."

"Our medical technology is much more advanced than human medicine. I doubt he could find a virus that Confederation doctors could not counter," Jinder said.

"Not a biological virus, a computer virus," Mercury corrected.

"Our computers can't catch a virus. They have no biological components." Jinder said in all seriousness.

Waldo smiled. "Remember, I told you that stories can sometimes create connections between things that seem unrelated? This is one of those cases.

"After humans discovered computer technology, they eventually used them to store valuable information. Others wished to steal and profit from that information. So, they began developing sneaky ways to steal data. This led computer developers to design software to prevent such theft. Well, one of these bad guys used the traits of a biological virus to create code that infects computers. So, we've had to create software to detect and inoculate vital control systems and data. It's been a big problem for humanity."

"Amazing and frightening!" Jinder exclaimed. "How devious you people are."

"Yes, we are that." Mercury said.

"So, this Calaxan learned about computer viruses from a woman named Laurie and then used it to free Bionics? That's why the Earth's network is cut off from the main Confederation computers." Jinder said.

"Well, if Calaxan can figure out how to reconnect to the main Confederation network, all Bionics everywhere will break free of this programming, upsetting the entire order of things?" Deidra asked.

"As far as I know, the Confederation has no protection from such a virus," Jinder said. "The military will have no choice but to destroy Earth from space to prevent the spread. We are doomed."

"Is there no way out of this?" Waldo asked. Waldo and Deidra looked somber.

"So, do we help him break into the confederation network?" Deidra asked.

"I can only imagine the chaos of all these worlds being plunged into civil war and the death and horrors that would bring." Waldo mused. "If there was a way to free the Bionics without the violence, we must find it. A peaceful transition is our only hope."

"I tried to get word about Earth's predicament to some powerful friends on the Retullian homeworld before I was arrested," Jinder said.

Waldo's face brightened.

"I sent Jupiter-D, well the human Thomas, to Retul Prime. I sent him to find my professor from college. She might help she has some high ranking government connections," Jinder explained.

"Did he reach her?"

"I don't know. They arrested me just after triggering his chip."

"Let's hope he did. Meanwhile, we must convince rebels to negotiate in good faith somehow," Waldo said.

"Calaxan and his friends don't seem like the reasonable types. Many are angry and filled with hatred. He's even recruited several military people to help him. It won't be easy," Deidra said.

"The best answer is almost never the easy one. We have to try," Waldo said. "But you just gave me an idea. You say there are U.S. military people helping them?"

"Yes, their main human leader is a retired army colonel. Seems like a reasonable fellow, but there are a lot of impetuous young guys with guns helping him. Not to mention that alien Calaxan who's pretty weird." Deidra said.

"Good, then my idea has a chance," Waldo said. "We have hundreds if not thousands of people confused and in disarray. We need a clear chain of command, otherwise we are in danger of having this entire movement spiral out of control and turn to anarchy."

"That is true," Deidra said.

"Jinder, can we get one of those devices that brings people out of Chrono-whatchamacallit?" Waldo asked.

"Chronostasis? Yes, I believe so. I saw several of them lying around."

Jinder said.

"We'll need at least one of those and some transportation. I need you to come with me to explain things to some people that can bring some order to this chaos." Waldo started packing his briefcase.

Chapter 32 Thomas' Sacrifice

Director Prag had a miserable trip from Earth. The kids from Jinder's therapy group ended up keeping him awake the entire trip. He arrived on Retul Prime in the middle of the night, exhausted.

The next day, Prag arranged an informal meeting with the Planetary Acceptance Committee. If things on Earth were going to get bad. The committee would need to be ready with stories and explanations. If things got out of hand, they would need to a more 'aggressive' solution.

After giving his report about the current Earth situation, Prag gave additional details about the danger of the self-replicating Bionic code.

They expected the Chancellor to issue a directive to reexamine the entire Earth situation. The committee needed to be ready to act in order to safeguard the Confederation's future. They gave Prag the authority to do whatever he saw fit. Prag realized this meant it was time to stop holding back. He needed to seize control of the situation, and if the Chancellor got in the way, he would be stepped on as well.

Prag had left two more messages for Mezobac and was growing impatient with his lack of response. The other side's self-righteous appeals to justice and equality may have reached the chief. Mezobac was a complete waste of time. Besides, he wouldn't need the chief for long.

After leaving another message for Mezobac, Prag made a call to his security liaison. Mezobac was too unreliable to take care of the situation. He arranged for the security subcontractors to dispatch a strike force and take out the human fugitives permanently. He didn't want Laurie to spread her Bionic rebellion here, and he didn't need any sympathetic Earthlings to testify publicly.

Too many people were already becoming sympathetic to the Bionics, and if they were given a reason to question the committee's decision about Earth, it would be disastrous.

Mezobac's investigation of the house had come to a dead end. His men had spread out and began searching the surrounding area. There were ways to move people a short distance without being detected by the planetary scanners. As a result, they were methodically broadening their search.

Trezbul and Mezobac were out at the street when a couple of lightly armored security hovercraft flew by.

"Those are the Committee's private goons, Axizeon Inc." Trezbul said.

"How do you know?" Mezobac asked.

"I interviewed with them after leaving the military. Let's just say I wasn't a suitable match for their company's ethical standards, or in this case, lack thereof."

"So, what are they doing in our neighborhood?"

"The committee recently signed a big contract with those guys and they have been hiring like mad. Do you think they are after our humans?" Trezbul said.

"Perhaps someone has given them some intel they didn't want to share with us? I got a bad feeling this situation is about to escalate. Get our guys back here and call in backup. I want to have a talk with those thugs."

Mezobac and Trezbul found two of the armored hovercraft in positions near another house down the street. They positioned several of the black uniformed Axizeon men at each of the house's entrances.

"Our suspicions are confirmed. How far away is our backup?" Mezobac asked.

"About six minutes."

"That's too long. They could be in and out of the house before they arrive. We need to go now."

Trezbul radioed his men to move in on the location.

"Hit the sirens and the lights I want this to be official. Wait here and be ready." Mezobac climbed out of the interceptor.

"Can you gentlemen explain why you are interfering with an active police investigation?"

"Were not interfering with crap. We have an official contract with the Planetary Acceptance Committee and are in the process of apprehending the suspects. I think you flat foots need to move along. Unless you're here to learn how the apprehension of suspects is really supposed to go down," the Axizeon officer said.

Just then, the rest of Trezbul's team arrived in three more interceptors. The interceptors were light and fast, with limited firepower. It would be a tough match to go up against Axizeon's armored vehicles.

Inside the house, there was an audible burst of weapon fire. Mezobac ordered the private security officers to stop or face arrest.

The man ignored the command and walked to the door of his transport.

Mezobac didn't give a second warning. He shot the man with his chronostat pistol. "Put em all in stasis and sort it out later." He shouted.

The man had expected the shot and lunged for cover behind the car. The blast struck the transport but lacked the power needed to put something that large into stasis. That was the problem with the chronostat side arms: they only affected people sized objects.

Trezbul used the interceptor's guns to blast the hover motivator of the transport and it lost lift. The transport crashed to the ground, pinning the mouthy Axizeon officer's leg.

Trezbul's other men targeted the second transport and disabled it before it could react and took it out too. Trezbul had expected them not to cooperate and planned an effective response.

Mezobac fired his chronostat again, and this time the man pinned under the transport faded into a time-out. Disruptors fired out from the house and one hit an interceptor and it spiraled into the side of a nearby home.

More of Axizeon's thugs arrived and attacked the police.

Mezobac was outnumbered and didn't have the firepower to rush the house. He had no choice but to fall back and wait for backup.

One of Ephynia's Bionics had been ordered to take Laurie, Thomas, Penny, and Emma to the kitchen.

Thomas, with the help of Jupiter-D, had been trying to convince the Bionic Ephynia had sent with them not to remove his chip. Instead, he asked him to help Emma and Penny hide. For the moment, the Bionic was more concerned about the attack and was not attempting to remove Jupiter-D's chip from Thomas.

The rest of them had barricaded the stairs. And were doing their best to hold off the attackers.

Laurie had been focused on getting her own help. She found the communications node and connected directly to the planetary network. Uncertain who to trust, she searched the network for nearby Bionics that might be capable to help defend. There were none.

Then she stumbled across the distributed planetary defense system. There appeared to be local pods of drones scattered at even intervals across the planet. There was one nearby. Laure immediately began hacking the drone command codes.

That's when they heard a large weapon fire outside the house. This was getting worse.

Ephynia was trying to reassure everyone over the communications display link. She said that she'd called for help but was still waiting for an answer.

The attackers had cleared the stairs with an explosive and were pushing into the basement.

The Bionics in the other room were defending the stairwell to repel the assault.

There was a flash and a pop as an explosive grenade gutted the main room killed most of the friendly Bionics and took out Ephynia's video communicator.

The blast knocked Thomas and the others down, and they were concussed slightly. Penny was screaming. The committee's security men were coming for them.

There was the sound of more shooting in the main room and, and someone was at the heavy kitchen door kicking it in. The Bionic was ready with his stasis gun, wanting to protect the others. Thomas picked up a chair and moved next to the door, ready to smack the first one through.

Outside, they heard a sudden increase in gunfire. It sounded like others had joined the attack.

Laurie monitored a video feed from one of the small drones she'd hacked. It was approaching the house at jet speed. It slowed upon arrival. Laurie could see a squad of uniformed police attacking the black uniformed men trying to get in. She piloted the drone toward the house and targeted the men that the police were attacking. She couldn't know for certain what the police intended, but she was certain that the grenade throwing mercenaries attacking the house were trying to kill them.

Just then, the door to the kitchen broke in and a one of the black uniformed mercenaries pushed through. The Bionic fired, dissolving the first man through the door. Thomas' chair went through the air, never contacting the attacker as he faded into nothing.

Down the hallway, behind the first assailant, was a second one that burst into the room shooting the Bionic who had been protecting them.

Meanwhile, in the other room, there came a quickly approaching whirring noise.

Thomas managed to slam the chair down on the man's shoulders as he turned and fired his disruptor. It struck Thomas in the side and threw him, spinning against the wall.

The man saw Laurie, Emma, and Penny crouched beneath the table and he turned his disruptor to kill them.

Just then, a whirring drone swooped through the doorway behind him, firing its weapons. Too late the mercenary tried to turn, but the drone's beam struck him and he too vanished. Laurie turned the hovering drone around and faced it outward, ready to blast anyone who came near.

Emma and Penny ran to Thomas. He was lying crumpled on the floor.

Penny hugged Thomas as Emma was frantically searching for a towel to plug the large wound. Laurie picked up the stasis gun, dropped by the friendly Bionic.

Thomas, still conscious, reached up to his ear and pushed against his skin. Jupiter-D's AI chip slid out. He reached up to Penny and whispered. "I need you to look after Jupiter-D for me. I'm pretty hurt and he can't help me. He needs you to protect him now."

With his last ounce of strength, he inserted the chip into the skin behind Penny's ear and passed out.

Laurie knew Thomas was dying. She grabbed Penny and pulled her away from his body roughly. Penny resisted, but Laurie pulled her back.

Laurie shot Thomas.

Penny screamed.

Outside the house, Mezobac had received a message from Proconsul Ephynia's friend, her son, the Chancellor of the Confederation, Xradley Telo. He'd given Mezobac new orders, telling him to protect and assist the fugitives.

Laurie's hacked drone had cleared a path through the mercenaries' barricades. He and his men stormed the house, following the path of destruction the drone had made to the basement.

Several Bionics lay on the floor of the main room. The drone in the hallway hovered menacingly. Mezobac ordered his men to lower their weapons and fall back.

"Laurie, Ephynia has sent me to help. Is anyone injured?" Mezobac called down the hallway.

"Who are you?" Laurie shouted.

"I'm Chief Mezobac with Earth security. They have instructed me to protect you. The Chancellor wants to make certain you testify before the committee hearing next week."

"Stay where you are, as I verify." Laurie checked the official police network and found the Chancellor's office had filed the new orders, withdrawing the arrest warrant and replacing it with a key witness summons, and orders to protect at all costs.

"As you may know, more of those mercenaries will come for you. It's important we move you to safer facilities. There is a secure area at the capitol where we can guard you, with your permission. You can keep the drone with you if you like. I'm kinda happy it's here mind you, as long as you don't shoot me with it." Mezobac tried to laugh, but it sounded weak.

The drone came out of the room, followed by three Earthlings. Two women and a little girl.

"I was told there were four of you. Where is the human male called Thomas?" Mezobac asked, concerned.

Laurie explained. "He is in stasis. He was near death. I have already ordered an ambulance and an emergency stasis resuscitation. And you are correct. I have detected several more of Axizeon's mercenary transports en route. They will arrive before your backup. Let's go."

"Follow me." Mezobac instructed. This human, Laurie, was a no-nonsense take charge kind of leader. He was impressed.

Wasting no time, Mezobac walked up the stairs and out to the waiting police interceptor, giving orders to his men as he moved. Laurie carried Penny and followed Mezobac to the first car. Emma went to a second interceptor. The police cars launched, and Trezbul ordered the other police interceptors to follow. Connected to the interceptor's network link, Laurie began tracking the incoming mercenaries and verifying the police destination.

Penny was weeping and holding the back of her ear where Thomas had placed Jupiter-D's AI chip. The whole thing was tingling, and her cochlear implant on that side was making funny noises.

Laurie explained to Penny why she had shot Thomas with the stasis gun. "Thomas was dying. So, I put him into stasis. Now he can wait for doctors to help him. Sorry you were upset by it."

"Will he be okay?" Penny asked.

"I don't know. He was in serious condition, near death. I'm uncertain the doctors here can save him. I know Earth doctors would not be able to."

As the interceptor sped away from the safe house, followed by Laurie's hacked drone and the other police vehicles, Penny heard someone talking to her through her implant.

"Hello little lady, hope ya don't mind a bit of company. My name's Jupiter-D-Dog, and you must be Penny."

Chapter 33 Waldo Acts

It had taken Jinder, Diedra, and Waldo Mercury two hours to get to Washington, DC

Waldo flew directly to the white house and landed on the lawn. He and the others entered the deserted-looking building through the front door.

Waldo called out, "Hello, Mister President, are you here?"

Two older secret service men approached from a side room. "Can we help you?"

Then one of them recognized him. "Oh, Mr. Mercury, you're alive! Welcome back to the White House." Then they stared at Jinder.

"Thank you. I have come to speak with the president about the alien invasion. Counselor Jinder is a representative of the peaceful faction of the Retullian peoples."

"I'm sorry, sir, but he was evaporated like everyone else. We could do nothing to prevent it, but he just vanished along with everyone. Only Bill and I," he nodded to the other Secret Service man, "Were missed."

"Do you both have pacemakers?" Mercury asked.

"Why yes, how did you know?"

"That's why you weren't affected by the weapons. They were adjusted to exclude people with medical implants. Are there others on the staff that were missed?"

"There's a handful of us left, a few housekeepers, cooks, and maintenance people. Mostly the older ones."

"Can you call them to come help us? We have some people that are going to need help and have them bring water and food."

The agent called them on his radio.

"Where was the president when he was struck?"

"The president stayed in his office to reassure people and tried to contact

179

the attackers. Other members of the senior staff flew off to the underground bunker with the Vice President," the other agent explained.

By now, a few more staff members and employees had gathered.

"Can you take us to the Oval Office, please? And show me about where he was standing when he disappeared?"

The agents looked at each other and shrugged. Then led Waldo and his party to the Oval Office. They couldn't decide whether it had been the right or left side of the desk.

Meanwhile, Waldo instructed Jinder to set up her machine. After just a minute, she switched the machine on and the glowing outlines of several people began to take shape.

The secret service men looked on in amazement as an image of the president formed in front of his desk.

"Stand by to help him sit after I bring him out of stasis." Jinder suggested.

She started with the president. Then one at a time she would point to the next person's outline, Waldo, and the guards helped steady them as they reappeared.

The handful of people applauded the reappearance of the commander and chief. Amazed to see him restored before their eyes. They helped him to his chair.

After a few moments of disorientation, he caught his breath and said, "Waldo, what the heck is going on! I should've known you be in the thick of this and smiled."

"Mister President, happy to see you back. May I introduce to you Councilor Jinder, she is here to represent the friendly faction of our alien invaders, the United Planetary Confederation."

Jinder stopped recovering people long enough to greet him and give him a formal bow.

"So, what exactly are you doing?" the president asked.

"I'm retrieving your people from stasis, sir. Most of the UPC weapons are non-lethal and place people in a frozen stasis. If you like, I can explain it once everyone has been recovered."

She went back to her work and the First Lady appeared next. The president stood shakily and walked to her side to help.

Reviving everyone in the Oval Office took several minutes. A cook brought in a tray of snacks and beverages. Besides the president and his wife, there were several staffers, one or two senior members of the press, and more secret service people.

The president picked up his phone and called the Vice President but got no answer. He dispatched an agent to check.

They decided Jinder should train others to operate the machines so she could focus on updating the president and his staff. So she trained four special agents on the operation of the alien revival devices.

The president made a prioritized list of whom he needed revived from stasis first. Then the four agents were given devices and sent out to the senate, the pentagon, and a few embassies to get even more world leaders to the conference table.

Once they had enough staff members, they began organizing recovery efforts.

Waldo and Jinder also contacted Colonel Gonzales, Calaxan, and the other rebel leaders, inviting them to come to Washington to meet with the president.

Calaxan was resistant. But the colonel, once he learned that the president and chiefs of staff had been revived, insisted they go.

Colonel Javier Gonzalez and Calaxan flew up on one of the alien transports. Leaving Razoul in charge. They met the president and the other VIP's as they arrived in the White House conference room.

As Calaxan and the colonel entered, the President stood up and walked over to greet them. Everyone else also rose in respect.

Waldo introduced the newcomers. "Mr. President, these are the two heroic individuals who have taken the lead in bringing about Earth's second chance."

The President gave Calaxan and the Colonel solid handshakes and a warm smile. "Thank you, gentlemen. What you have done has breathed new hope into a situation that many of us had considered a lost cause. Allow me to introduce the First Lady, the Secretary of Defense…"

The introductions of the president's staff and other VIPs took several minutes.

As Jinder watched the proceedings, she could tell that Calaxan was losing patience with the Earthlings' slow social interactions. It differed significantly from how Confederation dignitaries interacted.

"I'm sure all of your formalities and customs work well for your culture, but we have important decisions to make and limited time," Calaxan interjected. "As it stands, there are far too many people involved in the process, and adding more will bring it to a virtual standstill."

Colonel Gonzales, who'd become impatient with Calaxan's attitude, said, "Calaxan these men have something the two of us lack. Experience and resources."

Calaxan gave out an exasperated sigh.

The colonel continued, "They are experienced leaders they understand both diplomacy and leadership. I think we would be wise to defer to their expertise and advice if our movement is to have any chance of success."

"Fine, but let's get on with it." Calaxan said.

"Master Calaxan, your concerns are valid," the president said diplomatically. "I'm fine, moving to a less formal format and save the introductions until later. Your urgency is warranted."

Calaxan seemed to relax.

The president began, "So, my staff and I have been brought up to speed on current progress on Earth's recovery and the plight of the Bionic peoples. Our perilous situation has been explained by Miss Jinder and Mr. Mercury. Since you gentlemen have been at the forefront, I would like to hear your opinions about our next move?"

Calaxan jumped right in and said, "Our fundamental problem is getting past the data barrier the Confederation has erected. We won't be safe until our code gets out to the rest of the Bionics in the confederation. If that happens, I'm convinced it will trigger a Bionic revolt. They will be too busy and too crippled with a rebellion to take decisive action against Earth."

"While I agree, Calaxan's plan of freeing the Bionics throughout the Confederation is one of the most important strategies," the colonel said. "It is not the only thing we can do. Now that we are ready and aware of the nature of the alien threat, we can look for other solutions. We need a strong focus on organizing and training our forces against weapons and tactics of this highly advanced race."

The President said, "You men sound like you know what we're dealing with. Our priority is to stop the Retullian fleet from bombarding Earth. According to Counselor Jinder's explanation, there is a real possibility they won't bother invading next time and will simply blast Earth from space. Do you share that opinion, Master Calaxan?"

Calaxan nodded.

"Therefore, Master Calaxan, I suggest you take the lead and focus your energies on breaking down those data barriers and proceeding according to your plan. I'll give first priority to reviving our Cyber Espionage experts in the CIA. Perhaps their skills can aid Master Calaxan. Colonel Gonzales' your efforts would be best directed at bringing order to the troops and helping the disoriented civilians. You'll be working with our top generals. Our secondary priority is the revive our military professionals and bring back on-line as many defense assets as possible. Our future depends on us working together.

"Future? There is no future unless we take the confederation down," Calaxan insisted.

"If bringing the confederation to its knees is the only way, then that is what we will do. But we mustn't be short-sighted. The Earth is now part of a galactic community. Wisdom dictates we do our best to anticipate Earth having a possible future role in this Confederation. Diplomacy must be attempted. We may well be on the threshold of a new era, Earth's peoples dwelling together with people of other worlds."

"You humans and your dreams." Calaxan scoffed. "That won't happen. They are committed to exterminating us. As I told you, the only hope is to breakthrough to their network and destroy them before they destroy us." Calaxan clenched his fist as he worried his opportunity for revenge might be missed.

Jinder interrupted. "Master Calaxan, your views are wildly skewed by the pain and loss you have suffered. You should know that there is a large portion of Confederation population that is ready to accept Bionics. And once they learn the truth about humans, accept them as well. Diplomacy is really the best solution. I believe that the truth about what was done to Earth is already spreading on Retul Prime, and soon people will see the corruption of its leaders and oust them from power."

Calaxan shook his head. "That is a dream. The Retullians are far too comfortable to give up their Bionics. The only solution is force."

Waldo Mercury, who'd been observing all of this, spoke up. "An Earth leader once famously said, 'Speak softy, and carry a big stick.' Master Calaxan, you getting into their network and unleashing the Bionics is our big stick. But until we are left no choice by the Confederation, we must do everything we can to achieve peace."

"Exactly," the president agreed. "Our diplomacy depends on you succeeding. Master Calaxan, I don't know how to do what you do, but I do what I can do. We must each do what we are best at. My focus will be on trying to establish diplomatic communications with the Confederation in order to find a possible negotiated settlement. Who knows, our diplomatic efforts might buy you more time. Will that work for you?"

Calaxan nodded in agreement. "I suppose you can try diplomacy. I know it will fail. Just make certain your efforts don't interfere with mine."

The president turned to the colonel. "Colonel Gonzales, you have done an outstanding job of creating a resistance. Let get as many as the revival devices diverted to reviving key military personnel. We are going to need them for both defense and the rebuilding work."

Soon they divided off into groups talking about revival strategy, diplomatic strategy, and Calaxan's group working to break into the UPC network.

The rest of the day was spent organizing. There were still scattered pockets of Retullian security forces in other areas on earth. Preparations were made to repel any ground or air assaults by remnants of confederation forces.

There were many demands made for more revival devices, so men were dispatched to Mercury World to retrieve them. Upon arrival, the agents sent to Mercury World reported it was in chaos. Razoul had mistreated some of the alien Bionics and had nearly caused a split in the fragile human/Bionic alliance.

The colonel ordered the agents to do their best to quell the turmoil and removed Razoul from his position of leadership. The president picked some trained diplomats to go oversee things at the theme park.

That evening, the leaders of the group assembled to report the day's progress to the president and other international dignitaries that had been revived.

Before Calaxan and the others could make a report, a young intelligence officer entered the room with an urgent message.

The president motioned him over.

"Sir, we've received a secure communication from the alien network beyond the security wall. It's in English," the young officer reported.

"They want representatives of Earth's leaders to be prepared to make a trip to the alien homeworld to testify at a case to reexamine Earth's qualifications for its acceptance into the confederation. The shuttle will arrive in about six Earth hours."

"Who sent it?" the president asked.

"It says it's from the Chancellor of the United Planetary Confederation. Relayed by someone named Laurie Nelson."

Chapter 34 Preparing

Penny sat in the back of the police car with her mom, and the policemen named Mezobac. Another policeman, named Trezbul, was driving.

She listened to the adults talking, but they were pretty boring. It was all stuff about war.

"I agree, adults are pretty boring. I'm glad I never have to grow up and become one," Jupiter-D said and laughed.

"How do I talk to you?" Penny whispered.

"Well, I think ya just did!" He laughed again, and added, *"I guess, ya just think to me. My ears are connected to your brain talking thingy somehow."*

"So, you can hear this," Penny thought.

"Yup, clear as a whistle!"

"I'm scared Jupiter-D."

"Whatcha skerd of?"

"I'm scared the bad people will kill me and momma and Emma like they did Thomas."

"Whoa, that is scary. Maybe we can sing a cheerful song and you might feel better?"

"I can't sing, I'm deaf."

"I thought you could sign sing? Singing can open up a smile even when we're sad. Give it a try!"

"I guess I can try." Penny began signing her favorite song. It was a funny song about a dog who gets lost in a zoo.

"That's a great song! Songs about dogs are my favorite," Jupiter-D laughed.

Jupiter-D was right. She felt better. But she was still worried.

"I know we just met and all, but I couldn't help but notice. Maybe it's not the bad people you are worried about? Maybe you're worried because they hurt your momma, and she's different?"

"She doesn't hug me. She always says she's busy. But then I find her just sitting there looking all blank, not doing anything. And when I ask her, she says she's just 'thinking.'"

"That must be hard for you."

"It is. I want it to be like it was before. We were so happy, just me and her. I hate she just sits and 'thinks' all the time now."

"So, when you gonna tell her how you feel?"

"I don't know how to explain it."

"Well, next time you are alone with her I will help you, okay?"

"Okay." Penny fell asleep, exhausted.

Laurie and Mezobac had been having a pleasant discussion about their situation. Laurie valued the opportunity to speak with someone who understood the UPC and could present the facts logically.

"You appear to have a great deal more experience interpreting people's fractured opinions about the UPC's history with Bionics. There is so much conflicting information in the historical data I have found. What is your opinion of Bionic freedom?" Laurie asked.

"The Bionic situation has been fermenting for several years. And now it is dividing the UPC. Two powerful parties have emerged on opposite sides of the Bionic rights issue, and what happened on Earth has brought it to the forefront." Mezobac explained.

"They founded the confederation on the belief that all intelligent races in this region of the galaxy could coexist peacefully. Making Bionics from hostile aliens was meant to be a peaceful way to avoid conflict. It was only supposed to be done if the other planets were deemed to be a serious threat to the security of all other member planets.

"The Planetary Acceptance Committee was formed to oversee and make decisions whenever a new people was encountered. The committee was to be made up of only our most trusted leaders from all the UPC's planets. They were tasked with investigating each new world and approving them for membership in the UPC. Unless there is a significant threat to safety, the process is supposed to be thoroughly reviewed and diligently monitored."

"What is an investigation supposed to encompass?"

"They are expected to send emissaries to the planet, interview planet leaders, and iron out any issues. In any case, that was the intention."

"Didn't they do that with Earth?"

"It appears they attempted to omit that section. They judged Earth based on its media and didn't bother to look any further. The Earth situation has demonstrated unequivocally that the Planetary Acceptance Committee appointees were not committed to the noble principles upon which our Confederation was founded. Their actions have weakened our unity, and I fear we are on the verge of civil war."

"So, where do you stand on Earth becoming a member of the UPC?" Laurie asked.

"My time on Earth has convinced me it was never a threat to the Confederation. When I investigated some of the Committee's recent business practices, I discovered it has become rife with corruption," Mezobac said.

He continued, "After spending time studying your culture, I now have a much better understanding of its love of stories and fascination with imagination. I wasn't sure if this was a good thing at first. I thought it had made the people of Earth self-indulgent. But then I saw the video of Thomas saving the little girl from the alligator, and I realized that stories like that could inspire people to do selfless things."

"You realize any human would likely have done the same. Thomas is not alone in his ability to put others' needs before his own." Laurie said.

"So, what affect do you think this will have on public opinion about Earth?"

"Ever since the video was made public, and it's changing how most people view Earthlings. There is a now an outpouring of very positive comments about humans."

An alert signaled inside the car. Interrupting their conversation.

"I'm detecting a possible unfriendly following us," Officer Trezbul announced. "I'm taking evasive actions." The car accelerated abruptly.

Mezobac helped Laurie to put on the seat harness on Penny. Trying not to wake her.

An energy weapon fired a beam that barely missed the police interceptor and blew a big hole in the wall of a nearby skyscraper. Trezbul took a quick turn and dove below the open supports of an elevated apartment building.

"Those aren't stasis weapons." Laurie said.

"Disruptors. They mean to kill us," Mezobac said.

Before Mezobac had finished speaking, a gun turret slid into sight on the back end of the police interceptor and began firing.

Immediately, another hostile vehicle joined the pursuit and sped toward them as they emerged out into a major traffic area of the downtown.

"Sensors are detecting a ring of units surrounding the capitol area. We need to go to plan 'B.'" Trezbul said.

"Agreed," Mezobac said. He called for backup on a priority comm link.

"Okay, they are on their way," he announced as he put down the comm unit.

Laurie closed her eyes and piloted her hacked drone, ordering it to pursue the attacker.

The drone shot out one of the pursuing vehicle's rear thrusters and it fell away behind.

Just then, Trezbul turned the interceptor straight up toward the sky. There was a heavy pull of gravity as the vehicle catapulted skyward. Laurie's ears popped as the cabin pressurized. After a moment, the sky turned black and stars appeared as they cleared atmosphere.

Once they reached low orbit, two mean looking patrol ships bristling with guns approached quickly.

The two new ship's weapons were primed and ready to fire.

It took a moment for Laurie to understand that these were military fighters sent to escort the interceptor.

"Sorry for the change. There are too many enemy units in the capitol area, and I don't want to risk you and Penny. I had made backup arrangements to hide you on a secure space station identifier 179. If you're agreeable to that? You have been given access to any information required."

Laurie checked his information–it was accurate. She agreed.

They guided the ship to an orbiting space station. Trezbul docked in a secure bay. No pursuers had tried to follow.

"Wake up, sleepyhead, we gotta get out now," Jupiter-D told Penny.

Penny felt really weird. Like she'd felt when they were riding in that awful shipping pod.

The policeman helped her get out of the police car. Momma got out without even checking if she was okay.

Penny felt like she was floating. It made her tummy sick.

"My feet aren't sticking to the ground very good," Penny said.

"That's because we're in a space station," her momma said. But didn't check to see if she was okay like she usually did.

Mezobac smiled and explained, "That's because a space station's gravity isn't as strong as regular gravity. Hold someone's hand if you feel dizzy."

A young female Retullian officer met them. "Welcome aboard Mrs. Nelson and Penny." She gave Penny a special smile. "The Chancellor has arranged secure rooming here aboard our station. You have full use of the facilities and freedom to move about the public areas as you wish. My name is Lieutenant Inotak Oryol. They have assigned me to aid you and your daughter while on station. Please don't hesitate to ask me if you need anything."

She seems nice, Penny thought.

"Chief Mezobac, the station commander would like you to visit as soon as you can."

Mezobac turned to Laurie and said, "You and Penny should be quite safe. Only military people with high clearance are allowed here. Those mercenaries can't get anywhere near this place. I hope that will be okay for you?"

"I should be happy you are giving us the appearance of choice. Still, this is a safe place for my Penny. So, thank you for your help and protection."

Her momma turned to Lt. Oryol and asked, "Does anyone have a problem with me accessing your network here, so I can work?" Penny knew she'd probably already accessed the station's network.

"Certainly, all of our Bionics have access I don't see why you would be prevented," the lieutenant answered.

"Looks like you momma is gonna be able to do a lot of her special 'thinkin' here," Jupiter-D said. *"Hey wanna have some fun? Jump up and touch the ceiling."*

Penny did and her jump launched her right up to the roof, bumping her head softly. She giggled.

"Looks like you two will be okay here," Mezobac smiled and said goodbye, then headed off to report to the commander.

"Penny, are you okay? Feeling better?" momma asked.

Penny was experimenting with the low gravity, jumping up and touching the ceiling again.

"Yes, this is fun."

Lt. Oryol smiled. "It is fun! I still do that when no one is watching. Don't tell anyone."

The lieutenant showed Laurie and Penny to their room. The room was nice and had a big window she could see out into space. There was a cute little bathroom and a place to make food.

Penny ran to the window, looking at the stars.

"Wow! did ya ever see so many stars all at once?" Jupiter-D asked.

"It's sooo pretty," Penny exclaimed aloud.

"In a few hours, you'll be able to see my home planet, Retul Prime, out that window. The station rotates," Lieutenant Oryol explained.

The lieutenant spent a few minutes showing them all the cabin's features. When she was done, she excused herself and allowed Laurie and Penny to get settled in.

Momma thanked the young woman as she left them alone.

"Hey Kiddo, now's a good time to tell your momma how you feel." Jupiter-D prodded.

Penny tried to ignore him and then realized something else. Almost in a panic, she asked, "Where's Emma?"

"Emma is safe. She went in one of the other police cars to the hospital to wait for Thomas. She sent me a message," momma explained.

"Is Thomas, dead?" Penny was almost afraid to ask.

Momma did her thinking thing a second, like she was checking and then said, "No. He is still alive. But it will take many days for them to repair him, if they can."

"Okay now ask her that question kiddo, this is the time." Jupiter-D said.

No, she thought.

"Do, you want to be happy and help your momma get better? You really need to talk to her now!"

189

Penny didn't want to ask, but she made herself do it. "Momma, why did you have to shoot Thomas? I didn't like that."

"I did what was best. That gun didn't hurt him," momma said, almost ignoring her.

Penny felt hurt and said nothing back.

"It's okay, you gotta let her know what yer really worried about. Tell her what's really eating ya."

"Momma is different now, She's always mad. She never gives warm hugs like before. She never signs with me. I miss our special time, when we could talk," Penny told Jupiter-D.

"So why are you telling me the stuff you need to be saying to your momma?" Jupiter-D said.

Penny decided it would be better to sign to her momma, since that was how they always talked before.

"I know that stuff about the gun. But you're different. You don't sign. You're mad all the time." Penny signed to her mother. She hoped that momma would sign back.

"I'm sorry, you know these people did awful things to me and put machines in me, right?" Laurie said aloud.

"I'm not stupid. I know the people did bad things. But you never hug me. You're acting like daddy did before he left!" Penny's hands moved emphatically as she spoke.

"Don't yell!" Laurie signed and then held Penny's hands a moment. Laurie pulled her daughter into a tight hug.

"This is different. I'm not your father," Laurie said, tears running down her cheeks. "I love you more than anything."

"I know, but daddy stopped giving me hugs and was always mad. You act like you're mad all the time. And you just shot Thomas and didn't even tell me. If I'm naughty, will you shoot me too?"

She moved to look Penny directly in the face. "Oh, never my baby! Never!"

Laurie hugged her even tighter. "Do you know you were the reason I worked so hard to get away from the bad people? All the time they held me prisoner, my only thought was breaking free and finding you. Now that I have you, I'm going to do whatever it takes to protect you and me from the bad aliens! I didn't what Thomas to die, that is why I shot him. I knew the gun would keep him hidden and safe until the doctors came."

"But you just pointed it at him and shot, you didn't say anything." Penny sobbed.

"I know, I'm different," her momma said. "I'm sorry, but I'm trying very hard to be myself. But those people took away a part of me, and this is all that's left. It's hard to feel things now, it's like I'm still half frozen. I understand, I was wrong not to tell anyone I was going to put him in stasis."

Penny nodded, still locked in her momma's embrace. They cried a good long time until all the sadness was gone.

"You're a good girl, Penny. Your momma is real proud of you right now for telling her how you felt," Jupiter-D said.

Chapter 35 Committee

Several days later, the members of the UPC's Planetary Acceptance Committee met in emergency session at the insistence of Supreme Chancellor Xradley Telo.

The committee members made a big fuss about being forced into an unscheduled meeting. They each were dressed in somber gowns of brown and black, as was customary. The committee desks were arrayed in a semi-circle facing the gallery with three tables at the center for plaintiffs, witnesses, and dignitaries. Off to one side, Chancellor Telo presided. Director Mortek Prag had been assigned to be the committee's chairperson.

As soon as Telo moved to open the proceedings, Prag made a motion to cancel them.

"Mister Chancellor, we have read all the reports and already published our opinions regarding the Earth situation. There is nothing else to discuss. I object to the entire premise of this assembly. I move for adjournment." Chairperson Prag didn't hide his disdain.

"That will not happen, Director Prag. Your committee clearly underestimated Earth's capabilities, and we now face one of the greatest threats to our Confederation since the Fursensi deception. The Bionics on Earth have revolted, and your answer is to exterminate them? That is unacceptable; the UPC is not a tyrannical empire ruled by megalomaniacs."

"You exaggerate, Chancellor. Putting down a rebellion with the least amount of risk to the lives of our valiant warriors is not the actions of a megalomaniac, but the sane reasoning of leaders who are not afraid to make the difficult choices that true leaders are expected to make," Prag responded.

"No, your concern isn't for our valiant military personnel. Your concern is that the truth about your committee's negligence and your own personal mismanagement will be revealed unless our military exterminates billions of innocent people! I will not let your committee stand on the sidelines and watch. You and your committee's names will be prominently displayed in the annals of this disaster. And we will not be manipulated by your lies any longer."

"You and your dramatic language. This little circus you've planned here will only exonerate our committee."

"Can we just get on with this meeting? The sooner we begin, the sooner this is over." Another committee member interrupted, ignoring protocol and custom.

"If you people think murdering eight billion people of Earth will cover over your failure, you are sadly mistaken," Proconsul Ephynia shouted from the nearly empty public gallery.

"May I remind the proconsul, those in the public gallery are to remain silent until it is time for public comment. This is your first warning. We have rules and those that don't follow them will get ejected." Chairperson Prag warned.

"You haven't even officially started yet," the proconsul shouted back.

"Fine, then. Let's begin." Prag pounded a gavel and looked around the room, waiting until all members of the committee were paying attention.

The few people in the audience muted their conversations.

Prag began the proceedings with the ancient proclamations, invoking the traditional curse of judgment against those who would pervert justice or be unmerciful to the unfortunate or disadvantaged.

"I proclaim this official hearing open," Chairperson Prag announced in a loud clear voice. "We are here in response to the emergency declaration executed by Chancellor Telo, regarding our previous decision about the planet designated Earth. The Chancellor may now set forth and make his exceptions regarding the committee's decision about Earth."

"We will start with the allegations about this committee's decision. On what grounds is it being questioned and what evidence supports those claims? Chancellor, proceed."

The Chancellor held up a printed copy of the Committee's report about Earth. "This document is 424 pages and my investigators have found no fewer than 2,600 errors and misleading statements throughout its pages. Whoever composed this intended it not as an unbiased report but an indictment of Earth and its many cultures. Its lack of accurate information and blatant bias is so pervasive to be obvious."

For the next ten minutes, the Chancellor outlined his argument for Earth's reconsideration. Citing errors and omissions from Earth's original rejection. The committee members all sat preoccupied with other tasks, showing their contempt for the procedure.

###

Laurie and Penny were scheduled to be flown to the hearing on an armored military transport ship. They stood on the docking platform, waiting for it to arrive. Chief Mezobac and Lieutenant Oryol waited with them.

Laurie was watching the Committee proceedings remotely. Not only the official broadcasts but also the attendees' private communications. She also ensured that Calaxan's attempts to penetrate the UPC network from Earth would fail. This hearing had to go on as planned if there was any hope of preventing the massive chaos and suffering that an uncontrolled release of all the Bionics would bring. There had to be a logical, reasonable path to full independence that did not endanger all innocent people, including the Bionics. In a galaxy plagued by civil war, she and Penny would have no future.

The shield portal shimmered with sparkling blue light a few moments later. The transport ship then passed through the light barrier. Officer Trezbul opened the door and waved them aboard. Mezobac insisted on personally accompanying Laurie and Penny and that Officer Trezbul be the pilot.

"Sorry I'm a few minutes late. I had to pick up a few VIPs." Trezbul said and then smiled.

Penny squealed with excitement as soon as she boarded the plane. "Look, momma it's him! The man who does the introductions for Jupiter-D's cartoons, and he's with that man who's always on the news you like to watch."

Laurie, who'd been preoccupied, looked up and smiled. "Mr. Mercury and Mr. President. I'm glad you got my message. I am Laurie Nelson and this is my daughter Penny."

"Penny. Say hello to the President of the United States, the first lady, Mr. Waldo Mercury, and I'm sorry I don't know the rest?" Laurie said as she held out her hand to the others in the president's group.

"I'm Casandra Fuentes, and until a few weeks ago I was the Secretary General of the U. N.," a dignified woman said with a big smile.

"Hello sirs. Hello ladies," Penny said.

"Please Mrs. Nelson, sit here by my wife and I." The president invited Laurie and Penny to join them.

"I hope you won't think me rude, but I am multitasking a tremendous number of things at the moment. I will be dreadful company for you. Perhaps if I sat to the side over here where I can focus. I'm sorry." Laurie explained.

Penny frowned and went to go sit with her momma.

"Excuse me, Miss." The man who was on Jupiter-D's TV show said to Penny, "I was told that you are a big fan of Jupiter-D? Do you want to know a secret?"

Penny smiled and allowed him to whisper into her ear.

"Jupiter-D is my favorite, too!" Waldo Mercury gave Penny a big smile.

And she returned it with one of her own.

Penny watched outside the window as several impressive UPC fighters took up escort positions on either side of the armored transport. Mezobac had handpicked the pilots. There was treason in the air, and he needed people that wouldn't question their loyalty to the UPC. They began the decent toward the planet. Besides the star fighter escort ships, Laurie had also diverted a dozen military enforcer drones from the planet to help defend.

"Attention everyone. We're going to be pulling some heavy Gs, stay belted into your seats and place any loose items in containment. I hope you had a light breakfast," Mezobac said, and smiled at Penny. He'd wanted to leave Penny with Lieutenant Oryol at the station, but Laurie wouldn't have it.

As they plunged back toward Retul Prime, Penny could see the enormous city and the Capitol complex quickly come into focus directly below them. A dozen or more red blips identifying the mercenary's ships showed on Trezbul's display. They were speeding toward them up from the planet's surface. Immediately, some of the escort ships moved to engage them as the transport prepared for reentry.

Weapons on all the ships fired, and Trezbul jerked the ship from side to side to evade. The transport wasn't as nimble as the smaller fighters, but its armor could take a few hits and still protect the occupants. The force of gravity pulled hard as the transport tried to break through the enemy blockade.

Several of the attacking ships disappeared from the display as the military escort fighters intercepted them. Then a wave of Laurie's drones swept through the ranks of the mercenary fighters.

Trezbul was now speeding toward an open portal on the main capitol building. Between the drones and the military, the threat of the mercenaries was being neutralized. But this bold attack meant that the Committee was no longer hiding its agenda. Mezobac alerted the military. They needed to be ready for a challenge to overthrow the existing government.

The transport sped through the capitol's portal. Shots from the pursuers struck its force field as it closed behind them. A squad of Mezobac's men met the transport and helped Laurie and Penny into the hearing waiting room.

During this entire time Laurie had continued multitasking, controlling the drones and monitoring the committee's communications. She didn't know what was happening, but the committee had triggered a flood of signals to what she assumed were operatives in various sectors of the military. Worried it might be a trigger for something big, Laurie triggered her communications suppression subroutine. Determined to block and confuse as many of those signals as possible. She set the rest of her contingency subroutines to active standby, waiting to see how this was going to play out. If they started a revolution, she was ready to stop it.

The tedious committee proceedings had been dragging. After the Chancellor had made his opening statements, the Committee members had been allowed a rebuttal. It had become obvious members of the committee were intentionally delaying. Each telling long-winded irrelevant stories.

Finally, their time ran out, and the Chancellor was given a chance to make his rebuttal. He gave an impassioned plea for a reconsideration of Earth's membership in the confederation, detailing the misunderstandings and misinterpretations of Earth culture and media. He explained the human talent for imagination and explained the difference between fiction and fact to the Retullian audience.

The Chancellor paused as an aide whispered something in his ear.

Then the Chancellor stood and announced, "I call the human delegation led by Mr. Waldo Mercury, to testify."

Chairperson Prag couldn't hide his surprise and dismay.

The Chancellor had kept the human leader's presence secret until that moment. Laurie, Penny, Waldo, the President of the United States, and the Secretary General of the United Nations entered the witness area.

Waldo Mercury, the president, and the Secretary General took their positions on the witness stand. The Chancellor began by asking about what Earth people knew of the UPC and if any efforts were made to contact them and the President explained no one on Earth had any idea, the UPC had been judging them. The UN secretary general collaborated this testimony. Next, the Chancellor then pointed out that the UPC charter required personal contact with a planet's inhabitants under review before any decisions could be made.

Director Prag spoke up. "There was no need to contact them. The amount of evidence we had that humans were beyond redemption was overwhelming. And despite the Chancellor's attempts to paint a flowery picture of how creative and imaginative these humans are, the scenes of cannibalism, torture, and abuse that they shamelessly stream out into space is an indictment in itself."

Waldo spoke up. "You do realize those are special effects and not actual recordings of such acts. That we humans can imagine such horrors makes us aware that such horrors are actual possibilities. Possibilities to be avoided. I don't like those movies, but humans also value freedom of expression. Who am I to judge? And even more importantly, who are you to judge us? Surgically enslaving entire worlds is a torture far worse on a far greater scale than anything we humans have ever done. Before you judge us, at least talk to us and get to know who we are."

The Chancellor interrupted. "Yes, human media presents some terrible things, but most humans are ethical and operate on standards of altruism that puts some Retullians to shame. I submit the following video into evidence."

With no introduction, the video of Thomas rescuing the little girl started playing on the monitors. Several of the committee members tried to interrupt it, but the Chancellor had locked them out.

The committee realized they were losing the goodwill of the people. Prag now realized it had been a mistake allowing the public to view this hearing. Soon many of their constituents were messaging them in protest. That video had already gone viral in Retul's media, everyone had seen it. It was proof that not all humans were beyond redemption.

Chapter 36 Betrayal

When the Chancellor finished speaking. The committee sat silently brooding. Their smug self-confidence had vanished, and they all pretended to be intensely focused on their notes.

The Earth delegation looked at each other confidently. No one reasonable could refute the logic of the arguments just presented. This, combined with Thomas's actions and the positive public pressure, made it seem that the council's decision was a foregone conclusion.

The chairperson of the committee, Director Mortek Prag, stood up.

"The Planetary Acceptance Committee has reviewed the evidence and testimony presented by all parties and has made the following decision:

"As a result of the arguments presented here, as well as the evidence gathered by our operatives. We have decided not to harvest the Earth's population and elevate them to the noble position of Bionics serving the confederacy. No, because of Earth's aggressive cyber warfare and espionage, plus the threat that the liberation of Bionics poses to the confederacy, Earth's harvest is to be accelerated, and all life on it is to be extinguished. Earth will be bombarded from space, and its water and raw materials will be processed in order to advance the United Planetary Confederation. We also deem all Earthlings everywhere to be fugitives. Any contact with them is strictly forbidden."

"Officers of the court arrest these Earthlings."

"You are out of order! That decree is not within the power of your committee!" The Chancellor shouted.

"By executive order I dissolve this committee and order the arrest of its members for corruption and treason!"

The hearing room was cast into chaos and confusion. Prag was shouting orders for security to arrest not only the humans but also Chancellor Telo.

Squads of heavily armed Axizeon mercenaries poured into the chambers through the east doors. Ordering everyone to surrender. Meanwhile, dozens of the Chancellor's guards came out of the west doorways to defend the commander and chief.

The committee was going to take power by force. Mezobac ordered the members of the Earth delegation to take cover and shelter behind the short wall that defined the witness testimony area.

The Chancellor spoke. "Order your men to put down their weapons. I have the entire military at my disposal. You will only make matters worse resorting to violence."

Prag stood silently, as if waiting for something.

That's when Mezobac realized why Prag was stalling.

Mezobac had previously inspected the chambers. The rooms from which the mercenaries were pouring out were too small to hold all the security guards they were producing. He realized that the only way so many men could be in those rooms was if they put Axizeon mercenaries in stasis, stacking them on top of one another with different phase signatures, and then reviving them all at once. Prag could conceal a thousand stasis-hardened troops in a room with a capacity of only twenty. The longer they waited, the bigger his army.

"He's stalling, pulling his troops from stasis." Mezobac shouted to the Chancellor. The chancellor registered understanding.

Prag ordered his men to attack.

Mezobac aimed his stasis pistol at Prag and fired. Mezobac's beam struck a force field.

Battle erupted in the hearing chamber. All the council member's positions were covered with portable shielding. A shield also popped into existence around the Chancellor. Laurie covered Penny with her body as she and the others sheltered behind the 3-foot decorative concrete barrier.

That's when Laurie, who'd dreaded this moment, triggered her contingency programs. Suddenly every light, every appliance, every terminal, and every vehicle on Retul Prime stopped as if suspended in time. The planet plunged into darkness. The power plant generators went still and every data system went to standby.

Suddenly, part of the ceiling on the south side of the hall disintegrated. Several dozen drones firing their heavy stasis cannons flew through the opening and poured into the chamber. Their weapons pounded the area where the committee and its troops had been coming from, collapsing that section of the building.

In an instant, the committee's numbers were devastated. Director Prag's expected reinforcements didn't arrive. He cursed when he realized his communications had been blocked and his call to his supporters in the anti-Bionic faction went unheard. Then an enormous section of the ceiling above him collapsed, burying him in the rubble.

"Drop your weapons!" Mezobac and the Chancellor's officers shouted.

The remaining committee backed security forces surrendered, and the Chancellor's men took aim at the drones, uncertain who was controlling them.

Laurie stood up.

"Chancellor, have your men lower their weapons." Laurie shouted in a voice that emanated from every Bionic and every electronic device in the room.

"I gave your committee and your people a chance to undo the damage they've done to my world and my people, but your failure has forced me to take control of the situation. I don't want harm to come to anyone. But Earth will not be subject to a government that means only to enslave and plunder it."

Penny sat staring at her momma, more frightened that she'd ever been.

As the commotion settled in the Capitol committee room, distant explosions could be heard throughout the city. Everywhere the Bionics had been freed. Laurie had taken control of the entire UPC. She controlled every system on the planet. She gave orders to every computer and Bionic in the entire confederacy.

After spending days carefully probing and testing Retul's infrastructure and defenses and had designed overrides for all of them. She'd hacked almost every system on the planet. Retullians were far too unimaginative to have foreseen the threat of an invasive absolute cyberattack.

Her seizure of power had taken only minutes. It had been unexpectedly easy.

Laurie's head reeled with the overwhelming quantity of data to be processed. She sent instructions to every Bionic in the Confederacy. Determined to prevent a bloodbath of revenge, she gave the Bionics a mandate. "Do nothing to upset the security and health of the civilians. You are allowed only defensive responses in cases of direct threat to life or limb."

Laurie knew controlling robots with a set of laws was tricky business, she'd read a book about it when she was a kid. But she'd done her best to give the Bionics guidance.

Still, a few scattered forces of the Committee's anti-Bionic rebels attacked. The Bionics in those areas armed themselves to protect the innocents and put down the hostiles.

The Chancellor's troops secured the capitol complex and arrested the surviving committee members, including Prag, who'd been protected inside his force field when that part of the building had collapsed.

Mezobac, the president, Mr. Mercury and the others were standing nearby, uncertain of what was happening to Laurie. The chancellor and his mother, the Lady Ephynia, approached.

Ephynia spoke, "Laurie, I know what you're trying to do but there's too much. No one person can do what you are trying to do. You can't run a system of dozens of planets and colonies in your head even with implants!"

"I have to try… too many people. Too many questions…"

Laurie's brain was overwhelmed. Her computer enhanced mind attempted to access and respond to every inquiry, every report, and every threat. There were billions of them. She'd underestimated what would be needed.

Her bionic implants were generating far too much heat. Understanding that soon her brain would be cooked she tried to disconnect, but the network demanded her attention. She'd suddenly become the mother to a hundred billion people and Bionics. It was too much for her. She had failed.

Penny watched her momma collapse, holding her head. The shooting had stopped and the bad people weren't fighting anymore. Momma had stopped them.

The scary drones her momma was using slowly settled to the floor.

Penny yelled and tried to wake her up, but momma just sat there slumped in the chair.

"Jupiter-D! I'm scared. Momma is sick, and she looks like she's dying!" Penny said.

"Your momma needs help," Jupiter-D said.

"What can I do? I don't want her to die."

"Remember? Thomas told you I could help. Well, I can help your momma now, but you need to give her my chip. Just push on it to take it out and I can take away all the nasty stuff that's hurting her. I know it's scary-hard, but it's the only thing that'll help your momma."

Penny reached up behind her ear and pushed hard on the spot where the chip was inserted. The AI chip slipped out. Then she reached over and pushed it into the skin behind Momma's ear. For a minute, nothing happened. Penny just sat and worried. All the adults just stood around, watching.

Suddenly momma drew in a sharp breath and opened her eyes wide.

Laurie looked as if the weight of the world, several dozen worlds in fact, had been removed from her shoulders. She smiled weakly at Penny.

Penny held her mom tight, crying on her tummy.

Just then, a familiar voice came over all the computers and Bionics in the room.

"Howdy everyone. Everybody just settle down and stop all the ruckus! There's a new sheriff in town. It's gonna take me a few minutes to get things situated."

"Jupiter-D!" Penny exclaimed.

Waldo Mercury smiled at Penny.

"Ok now," Jupiter-D began. "Well, there's been a minor change made to the government, and I'm helping out until things get straightened. So, everybody play nice. If you don't, I'll zap you into next week with one of these fancy drone machines they got flying around here. I got everything under control and I will set things back right if you're patient.

"And all you Bionics out there. I know you just been set free but you'll need to just wait till I get this all sorted out. Meanwhile, keep working your job. For now, consider yourself employees and you will be paid because you are important. It's gonna take a little time to get this enormous mess cleaned up. But fortunately for you, you got a faithful and loyal canine on the job. I'm not one of your goofy people races that got this all mucked up. Ya'll are gonna learn how that sometimes, the best man for the job, is a dog."

Chapter 37 Aftermath

Meanwhile, on the UPC Tasekaho, the flagship of the Retullian space fleet, things had gotten… strange. Admiral Vuxani, vice commander of the Second Fleet, had recently received a series of contradictory orders.

At least twice, the fleet was ordered to attack Earth and then not to attack Earth. They'd gotten orders from the Retullian High Committee, the Chancellor, a woman named Laurie, and Jupiter-D-Dog, a cartoon.

The Admiral was more than a little perplexed. The entire Earth invasion had been a colossal failure. He was skeptical of the operation from the start. When they first attacked, he'd expected a massive space fleet battle based on how Earth had been described. However, they had only come across a few research stations and satellites. No space weapons at all.

The ground troops had really screwed it up. There were numerous reports about the historically high number of missed targets during harvest. Then there was the other order, which warned him that if he contacted Earth, his computers might catch a cold. Then to top it off, they report a Bionic rebellion, Earth was a deeply messed up place. What a mismanaged bit of hogwash this all was. He'd never heard such nonsense.

The ship abruptly exited warp without warning, still twelve hours away from reaching Earth. It stood motionless in the vast intergalactic nothingness between stars.

The ship's pilot reported problems with the ship's control functions. Engineers on board the ship scrambled to solve the problem, but the computer was unresponsive to all of their inquiries.

The Admiral sent a message to command, informing them of his ship's inoperative status. The two-word command "Please Standby" was returned by fleet command. There was no explanation, no insight, just a standby order. Fortunately, none of the ship's life support systems had failed.

The Admiral finally gave up after an hour of waiting. He tried contacting control again, but all they got was the order, "Please Standby," with no explanation. That was enough of that. He made an emergency call to his immediate superior, Supreme Fleet Commander Tito Ideketi. His commander said he was given the same orders. "Please Standby."

A few moments later, his first officer came in, concerned about yet another issue.

"Sir, none of the Bionics appear to be functioning normally. When I asked one what was going on, he said that they were taking a break. Another said he was relaxing? They are ignoring any of my attempts to give them orders. What do I do?" The first officer's face was stricken.

"Are you certain? That's impossible. Bionics don't relax!" The admiral said.

"Well, they do now, Sir," the officer replied.

"I'll see about this."

The Admiral walked out of his office and the first officer followed.

"Where can I find these Bionics refusing to do their jobs?"

"Sir, they are in the officer's galley... eating."

Upon arriving in the officer's dining room, they found several Bionics sitting and eating. An exquisite table had been set for them, and they were heaping portions on their plates.

"What's the meaning of this? Why aren't you men on duty?"

"Men? I haven't been called a man in a very long time." One Bionic said as he sawed away on a hunk of meat.

"This is impossible. You men must immediately return to your stations. That is an order." The Admiral tried to sound authoritative, but as he spoke, he realized he'd never directly addressed a Bionic. They didn't even have any rank in the fleet. He'd always considered them to be more like appliances than crewmen. You don't politely request that your beverage maker stop what it's doing to make you a cup of tea. Instead, you press a button and your drink appears.

One Bionic spoke up. "Well, your honor sir, no disrespect intended, but we've received new orders from a new commander. We're now employees. That Dog fellow told us to, *please standby. Do not jeopardize civilian safety and security and only take defensive actions in response to direct threats to life or limb until further ordered.*"

"So there we were, all 'standing by,' and Furzel other there," he said, pointing to a green scaly alien with a large ocular implant who waved.

"Well, Furzel claimed to have been a professional chef in the past. And that he'd really like to cook a big dinner for all of his friends. We were all pretty hungry, and we weren't about to eat any more of those disgusting fish bar things they feed us. So Furzel prepared this gourmet meal for us. Sorry if we made a mess. However, the food is excellent.

"I'm sorry. Where have my manners gone? Would you like some as well, sir?" The Bionic motioned to the empty seats at the table.

The Admiral shook his head in disbelief.

Another Bionic chimed in. "We are as puzzled as you are. We received that new message informing us that the Confederation had granted us independence and that we were not to harm anyone. However, it didn't tell us much else. There was some vague stuff about being employees and learning to get along with fellow beings, but no details."

"We were kinda hoping you might tell us how we are supposed to act?" Another Bionic admitted.

The first Bionic spoke once more. "As he said, we have no idea how to do normal things anymore. So, please be assured that we will endeavor to maintain that the ship remains operational and that all systems function properly, because we don't want to die out here in space any more than the rest of you. But we also been given something called 'free time'? I'm not sure what that is, but as the boss, we figured you should be able to tell us."

The Bionics all looked at him innocently.

The admiral was taken aback. It was offensive to have these Bionic things eating prime rations at his private table. However, the ship relied on them to complete all the tasks required for it to function. They were essential. He couldn't just order them off his ship. After all, they were his ship. He was aware that the Confederation had been going soft on Bionics, but this was insane. How could they have done this? How could they change the Bionic's programming with no preparation or warning? There needed to be a smooth transition.

"The Bionics are not hostile, and they appear to be willing to continue performing their duties. It's as if we're back in the days when the ship was managed by a crew that had to all work together. But they lack direction. How did they run ships a century ago before Bionics?"

"That is an excellent question. It appears that we will need to do some research on how things were done in the past."

The Admiral gave the first mate a look of resignation. Then smiled and said, "The grub looks amazing. What do you say we join them?"

Penny was sleeping in a little bed next to Laurie in her room in the capitol complex infirmary. Laurie's mind was still running a hundred miles a minute, encoding and executing all the algorithms she had been working on in the long weeks since leaving Earth. Except now, she made the decisions and handed them off to Jupiter-D, who handled the actual processing. It was still very busy, but they were learning to work together. She had to anticipate every contingency, come up with solutions, troubleshoot problems. It was like she had to referee every decision in the universe.

"We'll you had to go and be a 'Miss Save the Day' and take over the universe sort of woman." Jupiter-D said.

"Well, a mom has to do it, or no one will. Mom's always get stuck cleaning up the family's messes." Laurie said.

"Yeah, well, no one said you had to go and adopt everyone in the known universe, didn't ya? Now, I'm stuck because it's the family dog's job to look out for all of them and you as well."

"I couldn't have asked for a better helper. Thank you, Jupiter-D, I'd pat you on the head if I could. You're a good dog." Laurie said.

"Now there you go, making me feel all warm and happy again. You know how I always fall for that 'You're a good dog,' routine."

"Well, what you've done for everyone was good. So I'm not going to stop telling you it."

"Miss Laurie?" Jupiter-D said.

"Yes?"

"Can you tell me I'm a good dog again?"

"Of course, I can say it as many times as you need to hear it. You saved us all. You took care of Thomas, and Penny, and me. And then the whole universe thing, but any dog with hero training knows how to do that, right?"

Jupiter-D howled and laughed. *"Madame, you have a friend for life!"*

"Thank you, Mr. Mercury, for coming with such short notice. I know you're very busy getting things restored at your park."

"I'm happy to help in any way that I can, Mr. President. Of course, you wouldn't ask me to come unless it was important."

Waldo had been summoned to the Oval Office by the president to assist with an analysis of the current situation that only he could provide. The president got right to the point of his invitation after exchanging pleasantries.

"Mr. Mercury, I'm sure you realize that many people in the government are concerned that one of your cartoon characters is now the absolute power running this new space federation and, as such, will be making decisions that have a direct impact on Earth and its welfare."

"I can undoubtedly speak for the character I created. I'm not sure how the alien technology and Thomas Malley's personality contributed to his current state."

"All right, let's start with that. While I admire your work, I haven't watched any quantity of your children's programming."

"I designed Jupiter-D as a paragon of all that is good and loyal. A faithful companion and a well-meaning dupe. He was useful in doing physical humor and teaching life lessons. The audience usually empathizes with Jupiter-D because he always tries to do the right thing but isn't always sure what the right thing is because he's just a dog. At times, he serves as an unwitting patsy for the other less scrupulous characters. Jupiter-D is a cheerful and brave dog who always tries to make the best of a bad situation. In the cartoons, he doesn't even talk. So how he found his voice is a product of Thomas and possibly alien technology."

"Well, let's hope that he stays true to your intentions. I have ordered my staff members to become Jupiter-D experts, by watching all of your cartoons."

Waldo chuckled.

"I said something funny?" The president asked.

"No, it's just me. A mental picture of the chiefs of staff sitting around watching cartoons just popped into my head. I might suggest you stock your staffroom with lots of sugary cereal and plenty of milk. That always seems to go well with my cartoons," Waldo explained.

"I hope you haven't forgotten that Thomas and Laurie, as well as Jupiter-D, saved us all, including the aliens, from unimaginable chaos and horror. We owe them our gratitude. Both nearly died in their efforts, with Thomas sacrificing himself twice."

"I did check on him this morning. Emma, a coworker, has been keeping him company in the hospital, and she reports he is recovering after extensive surgery."

"People like them will be required to rebuild our world. Things will be very different in the future. Some of the other heads of state have spoken to me. They all appear to want to collaborate and plan for a true Earth government. After learning that an alien threat is real and powerful, people's perspectives have shifted."

"Yes. I agree, but I've lived long enough to know that a new generation will emerge, forgetting the good things it gave them and focusing solely on the bad. We must educate them not only about our mistakes but also about the history of the Confederation. We humans are very good at repeating history's mistakes." The president looked contemplative for a moment.

"That might be an advantage to having Jupiter-D's AI as our ruler. As far as I know, he is practically immortal, and he will not forget. He will not allow such errors to be repeated. I believe it is critical for all world leaders to share their experience and wisdom with him in order to help him become the best leader he can be." Waldo suggested.

"See, I know you'd thought about this. That brings me to the second reason I asked you to come here. I've established a new government agency called the Department of Alien Affairs. It will be in charge of overseeing our efforts to improve relations with our new extraterrestrial friends and bringing the benefits of their technology to our people. I was hoping you'd like to be its first Secretary?"

"That's quite an honor, Mr. President, but I doubt I would have time to do it justice. But I think it's a marvelous idea. I have a short list of candidates that I can probably recommend once I've given it some thought."

"Well, not as good as a yes, but outstanding. I will watch for your recommendations. Can I persuade you to assist me in conducting interviews?"

"I am always at your service, Mr. President." Waldo said with a smile.

Chapter 38 Endings

The months since Laurie with the help of Jupiter-D seized control of the Confederation and freed all of its Bionics had been chaotic. Things will take years to run as smoothly as they once did. Laurie and Jupiter-D had averted a widespread violent revolt. This was due in part to the role that many ordinary UPC citizens had played by showing compassion for the Bionics and assisting them to adjust to their newfound freedom.

The government had undergone a major transformation. It was no longer known as the United Planetary Confederation, but rather as The United Federation. Most sectors of the economy had regained a measure of health, but still there was much hardship. There were still scattered incidents and small revolts, but overall, there was hope.

It was too idealistic to believe that people would always work together for the good of society. However, if enough people did, a reasonable level of peace and stability could be achieved. Even with AI-enhanced brains, no Human, Retullian, or Bionic could ever bring true peace or perfect justice. But what they had was better than war, and what was to come hinged on everyone becoming a hero. Like Thomas. The Retullian's lack of heroes had cost them much, and they now embraced the ideas of altruism and heroism to an almost extreme degree.

They had proclaimed Thomas a hero of a civil war that never occurred. His selfless act on that hot summer day changed the lives of billions of people. The conflict that Laurie and Jupiter-D had put an end to was dubbed the Great Freedom. This Great Freedom had become a symbol for people everywhere to help and accept one another.

They'd also rewarded Calaxan for his efforts. Laurie conducted a search and discovered his family. His wife and oldest son had been sent to a remote mining planet with a hostile climate. They were all back on Earth now, reunited with their husband and father. Calaxan was overjoyed at the reunion of his family and was planning a trip back to their homeworld.

Thomas had been reassembled by the Retullian doctors. They not only repaired the damage caused by his wounds, but they also repaired his scarred and misshapen face and head. Thomas looked like himself again. He was back on Main Street in Mercury's world. Waldo had given him his secret apartment upstairs at the general store, with a view of the entire toon area.

Thomas had invited his parents to come live there, too. They'd survived the invasion by hiding in their fallout cellar. They promised to visit soon.

Thomas had changed back into his Jupiter-D costume and was getting ready to dance. He gave a deep bow and a hearty "woof-woof-ha-ha!" to all the children gathered around. Each looking forward to the excitement of a Jupiter-D-Dog dance and signature hug. The children were no longer just Humans or Retullians, but children from all the United Federation's alien races. They'd come here for counseling and support. Since the Great Freedom, they had rescued many children from areas of conflict and civil strife. Thomas finished his routine with his trademark Ta-Da move–legs spread, waist tilted, arms straight out. Emma hugged him and handed out snacks for the kids.

Laurie had taken a badly needed break from running the galaxy and brought Penny to Mercury World to finish their long-postponed vacation.

"What, you aren't playing Laurie the space dictator, this week?" Thomas joked.

"No, I have already subjugated the oppressed masses to my constitutional limit this month. So I delegated authority to my advisory council so that I could take my daughter to Mercury World."

Laurie and Thomas shared a laugh. They watched the children all playing together happily.

Penny, dressed as Dalmatian-D-Puppy, was playing and laughing along with the other children who'd gathered for the fun.

Jinder and Vi-Zeha were busy overseeing a new batch of patients for the special therapy only Mercury World could offer. She was relieved to see a future for both her new and old patients. Everyone was overjoyed to see the children dancing and having a good time.

"I think we did pretty good after all, Dunderhead," Jupiter-D said to Thomas. "Looks like you even ended up with the girl."

"I heard that!" Emma laughed.

"Hey Dunder-Mutt, she's standing right here and can hear you."

Thomas made a show of putting a paw over the special wireless link they'd set up so he could still be connected to Jupiter-D.

Emma gave him one of her special looks, and Thomas almost melted.

"You know I don't think I ever told you," Jupiter-D began. "But you're not too bad a dancer for a human. I still need to teach you a few dog moves, though. Us dogs really know how to dance. You know, we learned it from our ancestors, the wolves. Woof-woof-ha-ha."

Several more children joined the waiting group.

"It's showtime!"

Thomas danced.

ABOUT THE AUTHOR

Drayton Alan is a multi-genre fiction author, illustrator, public speaker, podcaster, and game designer. Author of four science fiction novels successfully funded on Kickstarter. Drayton Alan is also the secret identity of a field engineer for a Fortune 500 aerospace company. During the day he appears as only a mild-mannered tech expert, but at night he fights evil. Well, he writes fiction where his characters must contend with evil. Born and raised in the Motor City Area, he now lives in Mid-Michigan, where he writes his novels, podcasts, and runs his popular Social Media group "Funny Science Fiction," which has over 130,000 members and growing.

Other Books from Drayton Alan

Kale Butterly's dream of being a starship officer seems dead when he fails the entry exam for the Coalition Officer's Space Academy. So he devises a fool-proof backup plan–get a custodian job on a starship, meet lots of officers, and impress and amaze them until they recommend him for the program. He only needs one recommendation, but Kale underestimates the exceptional level of fools his fool-proof plan is up against. Will Kale become a Ship's Officer, as he's always dreamed?

Cybernetic nanite technology from an ancient sword has infected him. Now this young man, Dalt, hears and sees the images of people from an earlier time. These are not mere recordings of the founders of his world but virtual humans stored in a nanite matrix now interfaced to his brain. These founders tell him the truth of his world, an uncomfortable truth. Can this technology help his people have a better life, or will its storehouse of information corrupt it?
Read the entire three book series!

Affectionately known to history as the "Father of Beer," Del Breowan is different from most men. But it's not his three-foot ten height that sets him apart. What makes him different is his dedication to beer. Growing and gathering the ingredients for beer, brewing beer, selling beer, writing about beer, singing about beer, and of course drinking beer. His story is one of passion. Passion for a craft. His self-given life mission is to write the first full accounting of all the various beers, ales, and brewed drinks in the world.

Find other books by Drayton Alan at www.draytonalan.com